DAYS OF WINTER

CASCADE OF LIES
BOOK 1

Cora Flynn

Content Notice

This book is intended for mature audiences, recommended for readers 18+ years only. It features scenes of recreational and addictive drug use, graphic depictions of violence after the fact, and instances of questionable consensual sexual decisions. It contains profanities, sexual innuendo, and detailed sexual scenes. This is a why choose/reverse harem romance novel. The FMC will end up with more than one love interest and will not have to choose between them to find her HEA.

This novel is written in American English by a Canadian author, and the spelling, terminology and grammar have been edited accordingly.

This book has been edited multiple times by multiple people, both personally and professionally, but the imperfection of human beings is a beautiful and inevitable thing. If you notice a typo in any form, please contact me at coraflynnauthor@gmail.com with the subject "Typo Found."

Thank you!

xo
Cora Flynn

Acknowledgments

Thank you, dear reader, for picking up this book from a relative "nobody" author and taking a ride on this adventure with me. I hope you love reading this story as much as I have writing it. And, of course, there is a lot more to come!

No one on this earth can be successful in a vacuum. I most definitely am no exception.

I am so grateful to my husband, used to the random paths and rabbit holes I decide to follow on a whim, and yet he never holds me back from discovering more about who I am and who I want to be. Thankfully, you knew what you were getting into when you married me.

Huge thanks to Rebecca Quinn, fellow reverse harem author and dare I say, my author mentor. You've been so open sharing your knowledge about this industry. It was your experience, insight, and direction that made me actually pull the trigger to publish this story. You're a gem.

To my reading team: Shelby, Amanda, Paula, Brianne, Carrie, and Emily. Wow. Some of you I've known a very long time, and some of you I just met this past year through Facebook groups; yet you all had a significant impact in making this book the best it could be. I am so incredibly grateful for your time, your thoughtful insights and suggestions, and your investment in this story. You guys are the BEST and I'm thrilled you're all joining me for book 2!

To my editor, Lara. You are fantastic at your job. Thank you for making my words shine.

To Artscandare Book Cover Designs. You blew my mind with this cover, and I can't wait for the next one!

And to this fantastic wonderful community. Every single author I have reached out to has willingly shared their knowledge and encouragement. It is the most positive creative environment I have ever known.

To all my book boyfriends, past, present, and future:
Thank you for keeping my fantasies fresh and my panties
damp. I would be lost without you.

To the real hubby who keeps my soul singing, my heart
thumping, and my bed warm at night. No book boyfriend
could ever take your place.

...

Probably.

CHAPTER 1

"**O**h, fuck off, Logan!"

Hillary shoved her metal chair back across the tired linoleum and stalked out of the diner. I flinched at the nails-on-a-chalkboard sound, almost spilling coffee over the mug I was refilling. Logan, to his credit, scowled for a second and then proceeded to dip his greasy French fries in ketchup, nonchalantly munching like Hillary hadn't just bailed out of there like a hurricane.

I looked at my watch. It was barely afternoon and they were already at it. If my count was correct, which I knew it was, that would make this hissy fit the fourth one this month. Now, you may be thinking that having a public blow up with your partner over wedding invitation patterns, not to mention *four* blow ups in a month, to be excessive. Au contraire, my friend. This was the least I'd seen the two of them fight in my four years working at Johnson's Diner.

Hillary was a hothead, who would stop at nothing to get her way, and Logan never bent to her will. At least, I'd never seen it. The couple could be poster children for dysfunctional relationships, yet here they were, planning a wedding, because Daddy Dearest — her daddy, not mine — told her he would foot the bill as long as she was married by twenty-five. Something about a family inheritance requirement or something. You overheard a lot of private conversations as a waitress; the gossip at the diner was just fabulous.

Logan continued to eat while eyeing me up, again. His lean frame loomed over the bar top while he ogled — what was it this time, my boobs? Yeah, probably my boobs. I tried to avoid eye contact with him as much as possible. He was your typical polo-shirt-wearing, slick-backed, dark hair-sporting, trust-fund-baby douche bag. Why he and Hillary continued to frequent this little greasy spoon when there were at least ten other restaurants — fancier restaurants — in town was beyond me. They certainly weren't coming for the quality atmosphere. Johnson's Diner had opened in 1972 and it hadn't received a single aesthetic upgrade since.

I went back to scrubbing the front booth next to the counter, its deep tangerine cracked leather polka-dotted with various food items from years of use. The rectangular fiberglass tables with metal piped edging I was sanitizing were scarred with the evidence of toddlers scraping forks across them, teenagers etching lewd designs, and just plain aging. They were clean, mind you; the owners took incredible care of the place, which was the reason it was still standing. That, and the very loyal following of customers they had cultivated over the years. The food was surprisingly delicious, albeit saturated in trans fats. The kitchen, however, was state of the art. A bad grease fire a few years before my time had taken it out, and Carl had bemoaned that insurance wouldn't reinstall the original fryers from the glorious seventies.

Carl, the cook, loved working here; it was probably the nicest kitchen in all of Cascade Falls. He actually had formal training, so he kept his skills alive serving up diner-inspired food with hipster names like "falafel waffles" and "persimmon pancakes." Tourists loved it, and in an alpine skiing town they paid the bills half of the year. Joe and Eileen Johnson, the owners, gave Carl almost complete freedom to experiment with the menu, on the condition that he never screwed with the greasy items the locals loved — we needed their business too. I couldn't picture Ralph Sutton, Cascade Falls' sheriff and number one customer — think Chief Wiggum from *The Simpsons* but in real, living color — eating persimmon pancakes for the life of me.

"I take it you're paying for this today, Logan?" I asked, busying myself by filling ketchup bottles as he ate at the front counter. I glanced at him out of the corner of my eye, really not wanting to get into it today. He hit on me as many times as he and Hillary fought in a month. So dysfunctional. So creepy.

"Oh, you know how she is, Princess." *Gag.* "She'll be back to pay our tab tomorrow. Joe's fine with it."

He was fine with it, but I hated it. Hillary's money — ahem, Hillary's daddy's money — had a lot of sway around here, and letting Hillary pay for things on credit was pretty typical for most of the stores in town. Not that I had anything against the wealthy. I certainly hadn't grown up poor, but Camden Lane's wealth was next-level rich. He owned much of the land in the mountains — *how can anyone actually own a mountain?* — and aside from a few major ski hills in the area, he practically owned this town. Unfortunately for my sorry ass, it meant that I had to serve Hillary and Logan a lot.

Logan leaned over the counter, helping himself to a freshly filled bottle of ketchup, and smirked at me. He wasn't unattractive; his pale face was smooth and blemish-free. The result of a rigorous and expensive skincare routine, no doubt. His dark brown hair was always impeccably styled, never a strand out of place. He had honey-brown eyes with long lashes, high cheekbones, and a square jaw, and, while he was leaner than my usual taste in men, his clothes were always tastefully chosen. The man exuded money.

The problem with Logan was he had the personality of a pit viper. Smooth and languid, until he attacked with such force you couldn't help but be surprised by how quick you'd been bitten.

We went on a date once when I was 16. I had thought that was the end of it, yet he hadn't stopped subtly — read: not-so-subtly — eyeing me ever since. But of course, in true viper fashion, he never did it when Hillary was around. Since she stormed out of the diner eighty percent of the time, I was just so incredibly lucky to have all of his focused attention. *Gag.*

"What are you doing tonight, Winter? Are you coming out to Après? I'll save you a dance."

He licked ketchup off his fingers in a way I imagined he thought was seductive, but it came across as a sloppy toddler trying to get all of the sticky mess off with their tongue. This guy had zero game.

Après was the local bar, colloquially named for the Swiss custom of "Après les ski", the drinking and socializing after a wicked day on the hill. The upscale rustic establishment had the best drinks in town and was haunted by locals and tourists alike. It was early October, so tourist season was just starting to ramp up, but the locals liked to get out as much as possible before our town was invaded by sweaty ski bums. Yes, I would be going. But not with Logan.

"I'll probably be headed out with Quick, yup. Why, Logan? It's not like Hillary would be caught dead in there. And before you ask, no, I will not go with you."

Shane, or Quick as I affectionately called him, was my best friend and we went to Après almost every weekend. I turned back to the counter, filling the sugar jars next. We were coming into the supper rush soon and Cascade Falls regulars loved their sweetened tea.

"Presumptuous, much? I wasn't asking you out, Win. I'm just making sure that you actually get out of this place once in a while. I don't think Hillary would appreciate that insinuation." He smirked at me again, his eyes darkening. What an ass.

Ding.

The front door bell chimed to indicate a new customer. Thanking the universe for the welcomed distraction, I turned my head to see the devil himself, Shane Quicksilver, strolling into the diner. Yes, strolling.

Shane had a fluidity about him and moved with the grace of a panther. He had deeply tanned skin with captivating gray eyes, high cheekbones, and silky shoulder-length jet-black hair.

We'd known each other since we were five. Our fathers had gone to university together and eventually moved to Cascade Falls to start an engineering firm in the nearest local city, Carlisle.

Shane and I didn't have a choice in being friends; we were brought together too young to be able to make a conscious decision, and we'd been inseparable ever since. Besties. Board bums. He was studying engineering like his father. Unfortunately, I hadn't inherited the "math gene" and was taking a general business degree. I had no idea what I wanted to do with my life, but at the moment, that was fine with me.

Shane looked up from his phone as he walked in and grinned. His perfect teeth lit up his tanned face, a long feather earring dangling from his left ear. Behind him, Blaise, his on-again, off-again boyfriend, slid through the door and let it shut.

Blaise was boy-next-door cute; curly red hair sat in tight waves across his brow, and his bright green eyes gave him a boyish charm. He was incredibly sweet, but the contrast between his docile demeanor and Shane's boisterous, borderline obnoxious personality often brought more conflict to the relationship than fun. Hence the 'on-again, off-again' dynamic.

"Hey, Snowflake!" Shane's voice boomed over the barely occupied diner, and I quickly turned my attention from Lecherous Logan to him.

"Hey, Quick!" I squealed and reached up to give him a big bear hug. Compared to my average frame, Shane was massive, well over six feet, and built like a rugby player. His puberty years had been a sight to be seen. He'd changed radically, from a five-foot-nothing pipsqueak to a giant in the span of six months. His lithe movements were inherited from his father, another gentle giant.

He picked me up and spun me around. We did this every time we saw each other, a corny habit adopted from an old movie we had watched as teenagers. Secretly, I loved it. It was silly, stupid, and eye-roll cringe-worthy. Just perfect. I hadn't seen either of them in two weeks since Shane had started his engineering co-op position at our fathers' firm, Wallace Anderson Quicksilver, WAQ, or as we lovingly referred to it: "Wack."

"Did you get back early today?" I unraveled my arms from around his neck, and grabbed my order pad from the counter. Blaise was interning at a competing firm in Carlisle, so they often carpooled.

It was after two on a Friday afternoon. I hadn't been expecting to see them until well after dinner. I had Fridays off from school, which meant that I was at the diner from nine to five, and sometimes until seven or eight, depending on the supper rush. Saturdays were all day affairs too, but I took Sundays off for homework and leisure.

My parents could have afforded to pay for my schooling, but in grade eleven we came to an agreement; I could pursue whatever I wanted, in my own time, but I would pay for it myself. I knew they would bail me out if I was ever in a hole, but my pride would never allow that to happen. I had received multiple scholarships, and working hard at the diner for three summers and part time through the school year had already paid for three years of education. There was just one more year to get through until — well, I hadn't figured that part out yet.

"I had a bridge inspection on Old Falls Bridge," Shane said as he glanced at the "Carl's Creation" of the day on the board — blueberry jalapeno chicken and waffles — and wrinkled his nose. "Eccles is joining us on the rebuild project, so Blaise got to join me. We finished up early."

He settled on a stool in front of me with Blaise on his right, and he made a coffee-pouring motion. "Coffee?" he asked hopefully. I poured two mugs in quick succession as he continued to browse the menu. This man was always starving, and his order would likely be as large as that of every customer in the place combined.

Logan perked up. I had forgotten he was there for a moment. Eccles Engineering was his father's company. Dad hadn't mentioned anything about a partnership project when we met for dinner the week before. Mom was out of town to promote her newest book, "Your Sexual Shelf Life — How to rejuvenate your bedroom health." As an internationally recognized sex-therapist, she wrote a book every few years on a different sex-related topic. My teenage years were highly embarrassing with a sex-therapist for a mother, but the sex-positive, no-shame environment I grew up in was a far cry from many of my friends.

"That project is going to be the first of its kind in North America," Logan bragged, crumpling his napkin, and getting to his feet. "I'm excited that Dad's finally putting this town on the map."

As much as I hated to admit it, Logan was a clever business man and had received top marks at Harvard for his MBA. Despite making poor choices when it came to brides and eating establishments, he was smart about real estate; what Hillary's father didn't own in town Logan was quickly snapping up, thanks of course to the start-up cash he received from his own daddy-dearest, and he had refurbished many of the old crumbling buildings into gorgeous, chalet-style retail stores and salons. Logan usually could call a sure-thing with accuracy.

I rolled my eyes dramatically and turned to him. "Yes, Logan, because Cascade Falls isn't yet on the map."

No, not *that* Cascade Falls, home to a well-known preparatory academy and world-renowned teenage thief. One of the biggest ski destinations in the US, *our* sleepy town was as well-known as Aspen, and celebrities and superstars could be found in town every winter. We're even featured in a couple of movies. You know that beautiful, picturesque mountain scenery you see above sleepy towns on brochures and postcards? That's Cascade Falls. We were already *on* the map.

Logan smirked at me again and shrugged on his brown leather jacket before heading toward the door. "I'll see you tonight, Princess," he said, winking as he headed outside. *Ugh.*

Shane, having finally decided on the bourbon vanilla French toast, two sides of maple bacon, and an order of sinfully cinnamon and spiced peach flapjacks, looked at me seriously across the counter, his brow furrowed into a deep frown. "He giving you a hard time again?" he asked, his gaze following Logan through the windows to where he was unlocking his Audi in the parking lot.

I sighed, waved my hand airily, and turned back to the counter to finish the sugars. "Logan is just being Logan — an entitled, offensive, asshole. He's just treating me like he treats all pretty and unattainable women in Cascade — like we're meat. I guess Hillary's money isn't enough for him."

Truthfully, Hillary's money — ahem, Hillary's daddy's money — wasn't enough for him. At least, that's how he acted, and everyone knew it. Their marriage was the result of family convenience and old alliances, not any sort of love. I was convinced Hillary actually loved him, or maybe she just loved trying to control him, but it was clear to any single female in Cascade Logan wasn't trying to be faithful. I really hoped he wouldn't be showing up to Après that night. Looking over my shoulder, I raised an eyebrow at Shane. "What's the plan for tonight, anyways?"

He grinned and threw an arm around Blaise, winking conspiratorially. "I was thinking we'd show Blaise a good time this evening. He just got a promotion."

"What!?" I clapped my hands together in surprise. "Congratulations, Blaise, that's great news!"

I came around the counter to give him a big hug. While I didn't expect the two of them to be long-term, I really liked Blaise and I enjoyed having him around. He wasn't originally from Cascade Falls and had met Shane in university, so I didn't know him all that well, but if he was good enough for Shane then he was good enough for me.

Blaise blushed a cotton candy pink, and gingerly removed my hands from around his trim waist. Right, he wasn't a hugger.

"Thanks," he said and smiled, gently pushing away from me as I went back behind the counter. "It was a surprise, but I'm excited about it."

"He's going to have his own division one day," Shane said, a proud gleam in his eye as he eye-fucked his boyfriend.

I laughed, trying to cut through the now building sexual tension with talk of our plans. "Okay then! Après for apps, drinks, and a little dancing?" I wiggled my eyebrows at Shane suggestively.

The man loved dancing, and was easily one of the best on the dance floor whenever we went out. His cat-like reflexes and liquid movements made him a popular partner for men and women alike. He never missed an opportunity to show off, either.

"That's the plan." He reached for his meal as I took it all from under the heat lamps and served it to him, bacon steaming from the deep fryer. Blaise reached over to snag a piece as he sipped his coffee. Not a big eater either, I noticed.

"You're going to have to dress up, though. It's Ladies Night."

Ladies Night simply meant women at the bar got a dollar off drinks and snack foods, but the local ladies used it as an excuse to get all dolled up instead of wearing the plaid jackets and t-shirts usually seen at the bar.

"What!?" I held my hand to my heart in mock horror. "You mean I have to wear something other than boots and skinny jeans?"

My hand hit my forehead like I was about to swoon like a 1950s damsel in distress, and his eyes lit up in amusement. He was wearing a red and black plaid long-sleeve button down with a black Metallica t-shirt underneath, paired with dark jeans and white Adidas on his large feet. Most days, I wore the female equivalent in some fashion or another. I called it 'Lumberjack Chic.'

"Yup. You have two hunky men at your side tonight, so you're going to have to up your game, Snowflake."

Snowflake, his nickname for me since third grade, always warmed up my insides. Not very original, mind you, with the first name "Winter," but it was kitschy and it was our thing. We had a lot of things with a history as long as ours. I think it made Blaise uncomfortable, but he had to know I wasn't a threat. Shane was a part of me, but he wasn't that part of me. I was an only child, and he was the closest thing to a sibling I'd ever had.

"I'll think about it." I grinned brattily, then left the counter to do my rounds of refills and bill collecting. "Pick me up at eight!" I called back to Shane as he finished up his meal and stood up, heading towards the door. He had a tab here too, and I never bothered billing him until the end of the month. He waved a large hand as he and Blaise left, the door chime singing cheerily as they made their way out.

CHAPTER 2

WINTER

Après was busy when we arrived. Friday night was hopping in our small town.

Shane had picked me up in his beat up red pickup truck, the same one he had bought with his own money at seventeen. Old and decrepit then, it wasn't much better now; the cracked black leather seats squeaked when you sat on them and the dusty smell of old motor oil permeated the vehicle, no matter how many air-fresheners were used to try and cover the scent. It didn't smell bad though; to me it smelled like home and comfort.

Blaise was meeting us, but hadn't show up yet, so we cozied ourselves into a center booth and watched some early dancers mosey around the floor, while munching on hot fried pepperoni and tater tots. I sipped my cider, happy to be relaxing in familiar territory.

The oak wood floors shone through years of wear, shiny scuffs all over the deeply grooved treads. Hand carved maple tables held large beer glasses and red plaid table runners, with mini ski-themed centerpieces. Black globe pendants with soft yellow light hung down at various lengths across the beams of the white-painted pine ceiling. The booths had deep red and black vinyl seats, with matching plaid seat cushions. It was a unique mix of rustic lumberjack with high end finishings, and it was elegant and as cozy as a cabin all in one. I loved it here.

"I thought Blaise would be here by now," I mused, snatching the last piece of pepperoni before the hungry bear could take it first. I grinned wickedly as I popped it into my mouth, lips opening to taunt him with the final morsel of deliciousness.

"Asshole," Shane muttered as he took another sip of his beer. Looking at his watch, he took note of the time. "Yeah, he really should be. I'll send him a text."

He grabbed his phone from the end of the table — we had a "no-phones" rule when we were out — and glanced over at me. "Are you on the prowl tonight? You look gorgeous, Snow."

I smiled at the compliment. I did look good tonight. Taking his "upping my game" joke to heart, I had taken my time to get ready this evening. My shoulder length brown hair was swept up in a loose bun, auburn highlights glowing in the tendrils around my face. I had put on some mascara and a sparse ring of eyeliner around my light blue eyes, with a smidgen of gold eyeshadow to make the green flecks around my irises shine.

I forewent any concealer or foundation to allow my natural freckles along my upper cheeks and nose to come out, and I had finished with a neutral pink lipstick. Silver dangly earrings, a silver blouse, tight black skirt and black calf-length boots completed the look. I knew how to look good. I usually didn't put in the effort.

Shane looked dazzling. He had ditched his signature plaid and sneakers for a cream-colored long sleeve dress shirt, black khaki joggers, and black loafers. His hair was in a ponytail too, but he swapped out his feather earring for a small silver hoop. Just a model, he was.

"I don't know. I guess we'll have to see who shows up tonight." I shrugged my shoulders with indifference. I wasn't here tonight for sex, but if sex happened to happen, I wouldn't be sad about it. Après hosted a lot of tourists and university students from nearby towns on Friday nights, and there was always an opportunity for a commitment-free fun evening.

I wasn't a stranger to one-night stands. With Miranda Wallace, sexual freedom enthusiast, as a mother, I never had any hang ups about enjoying physical company and moving on, but it wasn't something I did with any frequency. If the mood hit and the chemistry was there, sure. If all I got out of the evening was an enjoyable night with friends, dancing, and another batch of pepperoni, I'd go home a happy camper.

Shane turned his gaze to the dance floor and the bar at large, looking for a potential suitor. He always did this when we went out, but he seldom chose men I would actually like. To his chagrin, I had taken a few of them home, but they were usually mediocre nights and awkward mornings. I didn't need his suggestions in my life.

"What about him?" Shane discreetly pointed over my shoulder and winked evilly. I turned around to see who the lucky man was, and laughed out loud.

"You asshat." I giggled, as I watched Drew Johnson see us amid the crowd and start to head over to our table.

Drew was Joe's son and helped run the diner; it was likely that he would take over when Joe finally retired. Handsome, he was a few years older than me, with a short, dirty-blonde crew cut, and deep hazel eyes. Over six feet tall, his broad shoulders filled out his black Henley long-sleeve nicely, over dark jeans and black boots. He and Blaise shared the boy-next-door look, but whereas Blaise was gay, Drew was definitely not. I'd had a crush on him for years, but it never went anywhere. Just the friendly banter of loose friendship and a few stolen glances here and there.

Truthfully, if Drew had asked me out, I would have leapt at the opportunity, but our dynamic was more protective older cousin — I refused to think of him like a brother with the thoughts I had of him; cousin was bad enough — and he never did, so we never did. I could have asked him out. I had no hesitation doing that with anyone else. But with Drew, it just felt ... wrong somehow. Crossing an invisible line I didn't know who had put up in the first place.

At first it was Sadie, his long-time girlfriend, stopping any advances, but they broke up over two years ago. I had given up on any potential fun and moved on. Shane didn't hesitate to tease me about Drew any chance he could, though. I had a sneaking suspicion it had more to do with him wanting me to date someone, so that I wasn't the third wheel for he and Blaise any longer.

"Hey, Drew!" I called out over the loud rumblings of the restaurant around us. "Come take a seat." I beckoned him over with two hands and moved closer to Shane to make room. Drew sat down and gave me a soft peck on the cheek. *Woah, that was weird.* He had never done that before. Just how drunk was he?

Shane glanced at his phone and held up the screen. "It's Blaise, I'm going to take this." He scooted out of the booth and made his way to the front door, one finger in his ear to try and hear over the din, leaving Drew and I to our own devices.

I turned to face him, noticing the soft outline of day-old stubble along his jaw, and the small crescent shaped scar on the underside of his left eye. He really was handsome — hotly handsome. Introduce-to-the parents handsome. That was a useless thought; my parents knew Joe and Eileen well and ate at the diner whenever they were nearby. Reintroduce to the parents as my boyfriend handsome? Wow, my imagination was really working on overdrive tonight.

"Hey." I smiled and took another sip of cider, motioning to the almost empty bowl of tater tots. "Help yourself. Do you want to order something?" I grabbed a menu from the other side of the table and handed it to him.

He chuckled. "You can't turn the job off, can you?" he teased. "Those waitress skills just don't quit." He briefly browsed the grease-stained paper menu and waved to the nearest server. "Want anything else? I'm buying."

"Definitely another order of their pepperoni. It's delicious."

Despite how comfortable we were acting, this was the most time I had spent with Drew outside of the diner in years. He had gone to Ryker's for his own business degree and graduated a few years ago, but with all the time he spent helping Joe and Eileen, I never saw him around town unless he was on errands for the diner. Drew seemed to always carry the weight of the world on his shoulders, and I often wondered if the diner was even his dream at all.

I leaned in to hear him better over the incessant noise, and we fell into casual conversation, catching up on family updates and life at the diner. Randy Dykens had skipped out on paying the bill again, his fifth time in as many months. I thought Drew might ban him, but Randy had fallen on hard times, and Drew didn't seem to mind looking the other way for the time being. I softened at Drew's empathy and kindness. He truly was one of the good guys.

"Where is Shane, anyways? Is he coming back?" Drew asked as he raised a hand to order another beer.

The pepperoni had already arrived and was half devoured — mostly by me — and I had forgotten all about Shane until that moment. Guiltily, I reached for my phone still at the end of the table. We had established that rule years ago out of respect for each other's time and space, and it never quit. I appreciated it in a world full of instant notifications and constant distractions. When we went out, it was about us — the world could wait.

Sure enough, he had messaged me twice, then left a voicemail. *Fuck. Sorry Quick.*

Quick LongJohn Silver: *Bad fight with B. Need to cool off. Want to go to the lake?*

Quick LongJohn Silver: *You probably don't have your phone and are waiting for me. Sorry Snow, I'm going to have to bail tonight.*

I plugged a finger in my ear and held up the phone to try and hear the message.

Hey, Snow, thought I might get you with a call. I know how loud it is in there. Long story short, Blaise just ended things. I'm pissed, but I'll be fine. Sorry to bail on you like this. I'll come in for pancakes in the morning. Love you.

I sighed and tugged at my silver arrow ring that encircled my thumb, twisting it around and around until it chafed. This wasn't the first time and I wasn't surprised. As nice as Blaise was, he and Shane just didn't seem compatible. Blaise was quiet, hated the spotlight, felt uncomfortable in social settings, and really hated PDA — the exact opposite Shane in every way.

They kept trying to make something work that didn't seem to exist, and Shane would need some time to cool off. Likely, he was heading to Silvan Lake for a joint and a stargaze. He didn't smoke often, but tonight was a likely candidate. I sent him a short text acknowledging the messages, letting him know Drew and I were fine, and I put my phone away. I wouldn't need it anymore until I called for a cab home.

"Quick had to bail, something about Blaise not being able to come," I said, leaving out the gossip for the sake of his privacy. "Do you mind just hanging out with me tonight?"

Shane and Drew had been good friends once upon a time when they both taught skiing at Spruce Acres as teenagers. While Shane still taught on Saturdays throughout the season, Drew had quit years ago to attend Ryker's, and then spent his free time on the weekends at Johnson's. I wasn't sure if he'd want to stick around if it was just me in the booth tonight, and I wanted to give him a polite out, if not. There were plenty of people I knew here, and I wouldn't mind pulling a chair up to another table to crash someone else's party. It happened to us more often than not; the more, the merrier.

Drew's brows knitted together in a frown and his hazel eyes darkened to a shade of amber. "Of course not, why would I mind that?"

He scooted closer towards me in a very uncharacteristic way, like this was now a date and not two people sitting together, catching up. My stomach turned over in an excitable flip-flop.

Would I get lucky tonight with *Drew*? Now that would be something to write home about. Hallmark movie material at the very least: "Small town girl finally nabs cute diner manager." Although with the thoughts now running through my head, that Hallmark movie would quickly turn into a graphic porno.

His high school football shoulders filled out his shirt like a dream. We had never even hugged before, but I could imagine just how safe a gal could feel between those arms, cuddled up against that sculpted chest. Now that he was closer, I could feel the heat of him and the soft scent of cinnamon and citrus infiltrated my senses. Could men smell delicious? Because he did — like a sexy Christmas candle. *Get it together, Winter.*

"I'm sorry, I — am I reading this right?" Drew dipped his head toward me as he put his beer back on the table, elbow leaning against the hard wood. He looked uncomfortable suddenly, like he was afraid of the answer.

I laughed, the third cider hitting me all of a sudden, warming my belly and shooting a tingling sensation up my arms and legs. I shivered, debating if I should speak my mind tonight. Fuck it.

"If you're wondering if I'm into you, Drew, that should have been obvious by now."

Wow, I guess that boundary was being crossed now, huh? Four years of tiptoeing along the line and I was just now going to plow right through it, pun intended. I took another long sip of my cider. Either I was going to continue enjoying Drew's company after that confession, or I was going to head out to find someone else to take that embarrassing moment off my mind.

He visibly relaxed, long fingers stroking the neck of his glass as he turned his body fully toward me, giving me a long look. His eyes followed the line of my exposed calves, up my thighs, across my hips and up to my chest. I had average boobs, they truly weren't anything special, but this shirt accentuated them where they needed it most. False advertising, sure, but didn't we all have something to hide?

It didn't matter anyways — Drew saw me almost every weekend in the creamsicle-colored diner shirts, and they hid *nothing*, so he knew what I was really packing under there. His gaze landed on my full lips, and he visibly gulped. Until this moment, I didn't think he felt anything toward me other than familial affection, but there was no mistaking his intentions tonight.

His eyes flitted back to mine, trying to read me to see where he should take this — if he should take this anywhere at all. I felt a prickling heat, but I couldn't take my eyes off of his. Was he going to kiss me? Should I kiss him?

"What are you thinking?" I blurted, the tension getting to be too thick in the already hazy air. Much later in the night now, the dance floor in front of us had darkened and the smoke machine — *are those even legal anymore?* — pumped out puffs of steamy swirling vapor at full force. The lights had dimmed and there wasn't much to see outside of our cozy space. The perfect spot to hide.

He leaned in, cinnamon and citrus once again covering me like a blanket, his lips mere inches away. "I'm thinking I've waited too long to kiss you."

Then he did. He closed the small gap between us and pressed his lips to mine, tasting of beer, and pepperoni, and just plain deliciousness.

His lips were soft and tentative — not a chaste kiss, but not aggressive — taking his time as I pressed my body against his. He raised his right hand to cup my cheek in his palm, and a switch was flipped. Immediately, he deepened the kiss and pushed me deeper into the booth cushions.

I gasped, surprised by his quick turnaround, but reached up behind his head to pull him even closer. He was a good kisser, a *really* good kisser. My nipples responded in my flimsy bra, and I was thankful we were covered in a smoky haze for the moment, so Drew couldn't see just how much he was affecting me.

A sizzling sensation licked up my spine. My lips parted and his tongue delved in to explore my mouth. Fuck, I wanted to eat him alive. This was going to escalate quickly, but I didn't care. A soft moan escaped my lips as my hands traveled the length of his chest, down his abs, towards his belt buckle …

"Oh hey, Winterrrrrrr." A devilish voice purred just outside our cozy den of lust. I pulled away from Drew abruptly to see Logan, of all people, interrupting one of the best kisses of my life. *Fucking prick.*

"I told you I would see you here, Princess. I didn't know you and Johnson had a thing, though. Couldn't save yourself for me?" His eyes scanned Drew's as he assessed the situation, his smirk widening into a full-blown smile on his smug face.

"What do you want, Logan?" I spat, furious the moment had been broken by this pompous prick of a princess. He was *engaged*, for fuck's sake, and even if he wasn't, I wouldn't have enough interest in him to fill a pinkie fingernail. Cheating was a hard line for me, so just looking at Logan filled me with disgust. *What. An. Asshole.*

He slid into the booth beside me and slid an arm around my shoulders, breathing into my face. He was drunk – really drunk. It was a wonder he had the ability to walk over to this table. Where was Hillary anyway? She seldom came to Après, but she also wouldn't let Logan out on a Friday night without her.

Why was he crashing my parade, when he could be with his sickeningly rich fianceé?

He grabbed my hands and tried to pull me in tight to his chest. I pushed him away hard, and he laughed obnoxiously, stealing a sip of my drink and knocking the rest of the glass over straight into my lap.

"Fuck! Logan!" I screeched, jumping up from my seat, now saturated in cider.

"Drew, I think our evening has come to an end," I said angrily, pushing him to move out of his side of the booth so I could get past, my skirt dripping sweet cider all over the floor. The moment had been thoroughly ruined. Now I was just tired, not to mention I would have to soak this skirt as soon as I got home.

I had seen Logan this level of drunk a few times at Après, although never toward me, and I had no intentions of sticking around to see him come out in full force. What. An. ASSHOLE.

Drew hastily grabbed his coat from the hook on the corner of the seat and let me out, his hand running nervously through his short hair. I could see he wasn't very pleased with the interruption either, but he held his tongue. Logan could hurt the diner's business if he wanted to, and he would, if given the right motivation. Besides, there was no reason to assume the cider spill wasn't an accident — it wasn't — and causing a scene with Logan Eccles wouldn't do either of us any favors.

I gave Drew a quick peck on the cheek and turned to make my way through the packed tables to the door, needing to call a cab to get my buzzing ass home. Drew grabbed my hand, pulling me back a step.

"To be continued?" he asked, raising a hopeful eyebrow.

"Not tonight." I gave him a small, somewhat forced smile and stepped back toward the door, turning my head. "I'll see you tomorrow."

I glanced back at Logan to see his teeth glowing wickedly in the dark hazy air. He knew he had ruined my night and looked quite proud of himself for it.

I stalked out of the bar and climbed into the waiting cab a few moments later, fuming at the events that had unfolded. I got home to my little apartment, locked the door, and fell into bed, falling asleep to dreams of sweet kisses that turned into antics far sexier.

CHAPTER 3

SHANE

"I'm not coming tonight, Shane."

Blaise Borden, apparent ex-boyfriend, just broke up with me, again. *Fuck*. It was the third time since we had started dating a year ago, and I was getting sick of this shit. I really cared about him, hell, I think I could have even loved him if he had let me. I was done for good this time. No trying to get him back, no trying to get back into his good graces by subduing myself into the man he wanted. Done.

I rubbed a rough palm down my face and flicked the ash off of my joint with the other. The lake was beautiful tonight; the fall moon was almost full, a bright wheel of cheese in the night sky, and the water beneath was a sheet of glass, begging to be broken. It calmed me in a way nothing else could.

I wasn't about to beat myself up for this third breakup. It was over and, of course, Blaise decided to do it over the phone, while I was waiting for him to show up for *his* celebration, instead of in person like a man. Coward.

"Tonight wasn't for me, anyway, Shane. You didn't even ask how I wanted to celebrate, you just went ahead and made plans with Winter and decided to bring me along."

He wasn't wrong, but I could count on one hand the number of times Blaise made the effort to make plans in the time that we had been dating. If it were up to him, we would never leave the house.

Of course, I invited Snowflake. I hadn't seen her in two weeks; that was a lifetime as far as we were concerned. I had always gotten the vibe Blaise wasn't really into my relationship with Winter, but we were a packaged deal — her for me and I for her. That wasn't negotiable.

I took a deep inhale of the sweet, acrid smoke, filling my lungs and releasing them in one slow breath. I was high now, my body floating on a cloud of air, my head filled with soft cotton, a warm tingling through my limbs. I was much higher than the original aim to just take the edge off my anger. I'd have to sleep in my truck tonight or get someone to come pick me up. No. Better idea.

I picked up my phone and dialed a familiar number. "Hey, what are you doing right now?"

Mandy Acker's sultry voice came through the line. "I just got off from work, big guy. What are *you* doing right now?"

"Want to come meet me at the lake? I'd like some company."

Company, aka, sex. Mandy and I had been casually hooking up since the summer after high school. It didn't happen often — probably five or six times a year since we both started college, depending if we were seeing someone. As far as I knew, she wasn't with anyone right now, and thanks to my earlier phone call, I wasn't either. It was the perfect arrangement that worked for both of us.

"Yeah, that sounds fun." She laughed. "I could use a little company myself. Let me get cleaned up and I'll be over in twenty. South entrance?"

I hung up the phone and I sat on the top of the rickety, wooden picnic bench, watching the water pebble in the cool evening air.

I'd need to grab the old blanket out of my truck for Mandy. The October chill was getting brisker by the minute, and a light frost had settled into the short blades of grass beneath my feet. Snow season and ski lessons would be starting in just a few weeks at Spruce Acres. I taught a few snowboarding classes there through the winter.

I used to be good — *really* good. I had been training to go pro when I was seventeen. I had won a few competitions nationally at the US Open and my coach had been pushing hard to get me to the next World X Games, but I hadn't liked the pressure and decided to put my energy toward school instead. I hadn't wanted the attention that came with boarding; I just wanted to board. Instead, I worked hard and got a full scholarship to Oulten Tech for engineering, which made the change worth it.

Despite it being Dad's path, I had wanted engineering to be my path too. Being an Olympian, if I would have even made it that far, would have been a dream come true, but becoming an engineer and building a legacy through my designs and creations? That mattered more to me. I missed the intensity of training and being on the hill every day of the season, though. Giving lessons to giggly little kids and gangly awkward teenagers was rewarding and a hell of a lot of fun. I was looking forward to it.

I glanced at my watch. Mandy would be here any minute. Stubbing my joint on the red peeling painted wood of the picnic table, I got up from the bench and opened the tailgate to grab the dusty camping blanket on hand for emergencies. This wasn't the first time we'd hooked up at the lake.

Truth was, I had never told Winter about this little arrangement. I didn't know why. She wouldn't have been mad; Miranda had given us all well-intended lectures on sexual freedom as teens, much to my own mother's dismay, and I knew she didn't have any hangups about causal encounters.

I had come out as bisexual at sixteen, and while I dated guys more often than girls, she knew I had hooked up with my share of women. She even seemed to like Mandy, although they didn't know each other all that well. Mandy ran in different circles and we had never hung out in high school, other than the odd party of a mutual friend.

I should have told Snow ages ago, but to admit it to her after all this time would make it seem like a bigger deal than it was. So, Mandy would remain my little secret. Besides, it was just sex. It wasn't going anywhere beyond that, so did I really need to bother telling her? No, no, no, I didn't.

Still, a pang of guilt flashed through me.

Mandy pulled into the gravel lot, parking her little silver Prius next to my old Dodge. I grinned at her stepping out. I was almost a full foot taller than Mandy. Busty and curvy, with blonde hair, sea-blue eyes, and a dimpled smile, Mandy was hot in a Betty Cooper sort of way. She had dressed in a casual gray sweater and faded blue jeans. No need to impress, just here for the sex. Easy.

She smiled and walked over to me. I reached out to pull her between my long legs, enveloping her hourglass figure in a warm hug. She giggled softly. "Hey, big guy. Rough night?"

She ran her fingers through my dark hair, undoing the ponytail and ruffling it into waves around my face. These hookups were casual, but we always fell into a familiar routine. It was comfortable and I liked it.

"Blaise." I sighed and pulled her in closer to smell her hair. Freshly washed and smelling like honeysuckles. "For good this time. Help me forget him?"

She leaned and nipped my bottom lip, pulling at my belt buckle. I let her take my mind away to better places. She took me in her hand, then her mouth, and within minutes I was coming apart, Blaise long forgotten.

I woke up to the trill of birdsong and the smell of motor oil. It took me a second to realize I was lying in my truck, windows slightly rolled down and my body uncomfortably molded to the back seat. *Fuck.*

I wiped the sleep from my eyes and ran a finger through my hair. Drool had dried to the left side of my face; I felt disgusting and sore. I didn't mean to get so high last night, but I had no regrets in calling Mandy. It had been fun and despite my less than stellar appearance this morning, my head felt much better than it had last night. *Bye, Blaise.*

I checked around for my phone — it had fallen out of my pocket onto the floor. My truck was old, but it was so clean you could eat off of the scratched dashboard. The cracked screen lit up and I checked my messages.

Sure enough, Winter had texted me just after midnight saying she was home and to text her when I got home safe. I sent off a quick message, letting her know I'd see her at the diner for breakfast and sat up. No messages from Blaise, but had I really thought there would be? *Stop thinking about him, Shane.*

My apartment was a ten-minute drive from here, but I decided to head straight to the diner instead. I swapped out my long-sleeve shirt for a black graphic t-shirt and a pair of old running sneakers I had stashed in the truck bed. I grabbed a pack of spearmint gum from the underside of my console and took two pieces. My mouth tasted like I had licked the soles of a pair of shoes.

The sun was peeking through billowing clouds and the autumn leaves were just starting to turn. We had so many maples out here and they turned a beautiful deep red color right around the third week of October. Winter loved them and she made me come out here in matching outfits for a cheesy fall family photo every year. I acted like I hated it, but I kept every one of them in a photo album in my room. Ten years of family photos. I was just waiting her out this year. I knew the ask was coming.

I turned on the radio and "I hate everything about you," by Three Days Grace was just starting. Fitting. I cranked the stereo and drove through our cozy tourist town to Johnson's. The diner was already packed with customers.

Carl's brunch menu was a hit in these parts and Saturdays were never slow. I entered and grabbed the only remaining seat, the same round cracking teal leather one at the bar I sat on yesterday, and waved Janice, the other waitress, over for some coffee. Winter was waiting tables on the opposite side of the restaurant, four plates of food balanced on her arms. She would earn her tips today.

"Hey, man." Drew greeted me as he finished stocking the shelves behind the counter. "We missed you last night."

I sipped the fresh cup Janice had just put in front of me and shook my head. "It was the night of a breakup, man. Needed some air."

"Fuck, sorry to hear. You okay?" He moved just in time before Janice came barreling out of the metal swinging double doors, three orders of pancakes and two plates of toast piled precariously in her arms. He smiled sheepishly at her as she gave him a stern glare, turning her back to serve her customers.

"Will be." I raised my mug of coffee like I was making a toast and downed half of the cooling liquid. "To freedom."

He dipped his head at me in a shallow nod and echoed the words, but his gaze traveled over the diners and landed on Winter. He swallowed and looked at her with clearly more than casual interest. *What had they gotten up to last night?*

Winter caught me looking at her and gave a harried wave, hair coming out of her bun in frazzled wisps. This place was busy. I didn't miss when her eyes traveled to Drew's face, a small smile tracing her lips. *Yup, something definitely happened.*

Camden Lane reached over the counter to grab Drew's attention. The richest man in Cascade Falls by a landslide, it was rare to see him at Joe and Eileen's.

"Can you get Joe to call me, son? He hasn't gotten back to me and we have an important matter to discuss." He tapped a finger on the fiberglass bar top. "I wouldn't want him to miss out on an opportunity for misplaced pride."

Drew looked confused, but he nodded, and Camden turned toward the door. "Tell him today, please."

It was a request that really wasn't a request at all. Drew stared out the door long after he was gone, lost in thought. Camden didn't say much, but it was obvious in what he didn't say that something was going on with Joe and the business. How could Drew not know about it, when he'd been helping run it for the past two years? Was he just playing dumb?

He didn't look like it and, from what I knew of Drew, he was a really terrible liar. He was the one who got the team caught when we "decorated" the football field on Halloween. He had been a senior and I was a freshman at the time. Coach could see right through his terrible cover up and we had to do suicides every practice, all practice, for a week straight. Drew had led the charge on the prank, so he got in the most trouble anyway.

So yeah, terrible liar.

I wasn't supposed to overhear Camden, and it really wasn't my business. I was about to change the subject when Drew turned his attention back on me.

"While you're here, I was hoping you could do me a favor. Do you still have that old Triumph hanging around?"

He was referring to the midnight blue 1960 TR120 Triumph motorcycle handed down to me from my father. It was in pristine condition, a point of pride for the Quicksilver men. With any luck, I'd pass it down to my future son one day.

"Sure do." I dug into the delicious-smelling grub that Janice just put down in front of me. I had ordered Carl's Creation — a bacon-weave basket filled with fried dough balls, dusted in vanilla sugar. *Incredible.* "Why, what's up?"

"I ended up snagging one for cheap at an auction, but it's pretty much a write-off and I'm trying to make it work with different parts — would you mind if I came by to give it a look over? It'd be easier to see what I'll really need if I have a completed one in front of me."

Right. Drew was a hobby mechanic and had been tinkering on one thing or another since we were teens. I didn't know what happened to the vehicles when he was done — I assumed he sold them, since I hadn't seen him drive anything other than a gray Toyota Camry. You could tell a lot about a person by the car they drove. Drew's screamed "responsible dad."

"I'll do you one better," I said, licking sugar dust off of my fingers. "Why don't I bring it by tomorrow night? It needs a good ride before I store it for the winter. You can keep it in your garage as a muse if you need it until I put in lockup."

"Really?" His eyes lit up with excitement. "That would be great, man. I've never had a chance to work on one of these before and I'm a bit stumped. I really appreciate it. Tell you what, lunch today is on me." He grinned and stuck out his hand for a shake. I took it and grinned back.

"In that case, I'll take another coffee." I held out my mug to him and he chuckled, taking the old school glass carafe off the warmer and poured a generous cup. He placed it on the bar top and called out to Janice.

"Janice, Shane's meal is on me today." She nodded her dyed blonde curls in acknowledgment and waved a hand as she took the orders of another full table of diners. It was no wonder Winter stayed here when she could be doing a ton of other jobs in town. The tips here were killer.

I kept trying to meet her eye so that she would make it over to me for a quick chat, but she was so busy it wasn't going to be in the cards for me today. That was probably a good thing; I didn't want to have to lie about Mandy, and I really didn't want to talk about Blaise.

I swallowed the rest of my coffee and got up to leave, leaving a generous tip for Janice since my meal was now free, and walked over to give Winter a quick peck on the cheek before heading out.

"I'm looking forward to hearing all about your night with loverboy," I murmured in her ear over the noise, winking when she turned an adorable shade of pink at the mention. Sated and now starting to really feel the night's sleep on a truck bench throughout my body, I left the diner and headed home to crawl into bed.

CHAPTER 4

DREW

*H*ow *is the till off again?* It was the fourth time this month, and it wasn't short, it was over. Really over. *Why would someone stuff the till full of cash?*

I shook my head and decided to recount for the third time tonight. Normally I didn't count the till; the closing shift took care of it and put the money in the slot in the safe in the back office, but Janice had called in sick tonight and Winter and I were covering. Thankfully, she got out of classes early on Tuesdays and Ryker's was close enough to the diner that she could bail me out this evening. Tuesdays were a busy night at the diner and while I was a decent manager, I was not a great server.

Speaking of great servers, my gaze followed the movements of the graceful waitress deftly scrubbing the memories of dried ketchup and mayonnaise off the vintage glass countertops. The diner was already closed for the night and she had her headphones in as she finished her cleaning duties.

I had offered to count the till so the two of us could get out of here faster. It had been a crazy night thanks to Carl's latest Creation: white chocolate infused chicken chili in a cornbread bread bowl. We were both exhausted. This place needed more staff. I made a note to get some ads up in the local paper next week.

I watched her discreetly bob her loose curls to the music, hips swaying enticingly, her orange polyester uniform shirt looking impossibly attractive. Winter was captivating in an old-timey beauty sort of way.

Mom and I would watch old black-and-white movies every time we went to our family cabin in the woods on the ancient, turn-dial TV. Every time I saw Winter, I thought of Audrey Hepburn in "Breakfast at Tiffany's." They kind of looked the same; dark auburn hair, big, captivating eyes, sensual lips, delicate features. She was graceful, beautiful, and charming; a sensual woman in an innocent package.

I had always felt drawn to Winter but until Sadie broke up with me, I never allowed myself to see her in a different light. I can remember the day the switch flipped; I had run into our local grocery store to grab some last-minute snacks for a guy's night, and she was in the chip aisle. She had no makeup on her lightly freckled face, dark hair swept up a messy bun, a loose casual sweatshirt draping off one shoulder, and cut-off jean shorts.

I hadn't known it was her at first; her back was turned. All I could see were long tanned legs, the curves of sexy hips, perky ass, slender neck, and when she turned around and smiled at me with recognition, it hit me like a transport truck. Winter was not just the good-looking girl I had known most of my life. Winter was the *hot* girl I wanted to get into bed with. I should have asked her out then and there, blew off guys night, and bridged that gap between us.

But I didn't, and I still couldn't, but I couldn't stop thinking about her. My cheeks flushed with heat as I reached down to adjust myself. Ever since our shared kiss at Après over a week ago, I couldn't stop replaying the moment over in my mind, an endless repeating loop. The way her body had melted into mine as I pushed her into the booth cushions. The way she moaned into my mouth as I sucked on her tongue ... *Shit.* I was either going to have to step into the bathroom to relieve this growing hard-on in my pants, or distract myself.

Distraction, I decided. I looked at the money in front of me — crumpled bits of green paper, subtly covered in the sins of each owner. Still $202 over.

What's going on?

I left a note for Dad in case a mistake was made this morning and someone forgot to ring in a few orders properly. It was rare, but it happened. I had been pressing him about the discussion he and Camden had last week, but he predictably continued to be closed-lipped about it.

"It's nothing to worry about, son. Camden wants to buy us out, and I told him no. We've worked too hard to see this business bulldozed for a set of new condos."

Why did it feel like it was more than that? Why would that need to be a secret? Camden tried to buy everyone out. He was the richest man in Sequoia County for a reason. I couldn't help a suspicion there was more to his request than that, but Dad wouldn't say anything more about it.

His words were a blow to me too. How was I going to tell him and Mom I really didn't want the diner? That I *never* wanted the diner?

From the time I was thirteen, I never had a choice over my own destiny. Drew was going to inherit the family business. Drew was going to continue the family "legacy." Drew was going to go to business school and put Johnson's on the world stage of diners – *is that even a thing?* – but Drew never had a chance.

I had implemented some good changes in the time I'd taken over the diner management. Carl had been my hire, and the residents of Cascade Falls loved his creativity in the kitchen. I spent the money to upgrade the exterior facade that was as dated as the inside of this clean but tired "ode to the past" with a government grant for business improvements. *Thank you, college education.*

In that same time, Sadie had left me, I was working 70 hours a week for a job I never wanted to do and pining for a woman who I couldn't even talk to with a straight face since I kissed her last week. I sighed, rubbing my palms over my short beard. *My life is a pathetic clusterfuck.*

I broke away from the endless vortex of my thoughts and assessed the restaurant. There would be so much work, so much money, needed to bring this place into the 21st century. We kept the place lovingly clean, but clean did not detract from the ripped and cracked seating – one booth looked to have been torn apart by Jack the Ripper it was so battered – or the scratched tables, the yellowed blinds, the bruised drywall, and the flooring so faded you could barely identify the pattern that had once shined in the seventies.

Mom had brought the charm of the diner to life with the right lighting so it looked clean and cozy as opposed to the dump a few fluorescents would make it, but it really needed upgrading if we wanted to compete with some of Logan's new tenants. My stomach turned. I liked Logan as much as

I liked chewed bubble gum left out in the sun too long. I didn't see the point of his existence and he mildly repulsed me. Harsh, yes. Earned, yes. And after the shit he pulled at Après the other night...

My blood boiled. I didn't say a word, like a fucking coward, when he spilled cider all over Winter's lap. I had immediately wanted to caveman it out and come to her rescue, but something stopped me. Our history, maybe? Fear of retaliation through the business?

I didn't know what had come over me, but it wasn't the side of me I wanted to show Winter. I wanted to protect her, defend her honor, do *something*. Instead, I handed her her coat and let Logan walk away. *Fuck. I really need to apologize.*

I looked up from the counter, eyes searching the space for her beautiful form. I frowned when she wasn't anywhere in sight. She must have gone to the storeroom to finish stocking the shelves before she left for the night.

I looked at my silver Timex. It was nine already. She'd be out of here within minutes. While I was feeling particularly brave, I needed to man up and tell her I was sorry. I didn't want to continue the awkward smiles and questioning glances between the two of us after that incredible kiss at Après.

I followed the brightly lit hallway to the navy steel door of the storeroom. It was left ajar and I peered in. Winter was by the commercial-sized cans of stewed tomatoes, reaching up to the top shelf for a sleeve of coffee cups.

"Oh my god!" she exclaimed, a delicate hand hitting her chest. "You scared me!" She popped an earbud out of her ear, tinny music streaming from the small speaker before she broke the Bluetooth connection. "Sorry, I didn't hear you coming."

She smiled at me warmly then, and I couldn't help but return it. Even in the dark storeroom, her smile was stunning, straight white teeth and kissable lips calling to me.

"I think the lightbulb in here blew out today so I'm using the hall light to see. Good thing I have this place memorized, huh?" She turned back on the step ladder, about to grab the sleeve of coffee cups again, when I simply stretched an arm up to grab the crinkly plastic tube from the top shelf.

"Thanks." She beamed up at me, our height difference still present even with her on the rickety ladder. It was dim in here and I couldn't make out much other than her body and a few items on the shelf immediately next to me.

Her mouth was so close to mine again, body heat searing into me. The smell of her lavender body wash filled my nostrils and I couldn't help myself from reaching for her.

She turned and her breasts brushed against my chest as she moved to grab for something behind me. "I–"

I cut her off with a searing kiss, my mouth closing over hers with such force I surprised myself. The week of daydreams and years of longing from afar came out in that one fluid press of our lips. She gasped in surprise and then started to kiss me back, her hands coming up to the back of my neck and pulling me closer.

I put my palms on her hips and gripped tightly as her body melted into mine. Then I reached under her ass to lift her up and she wrapped her legs around my waist.

The kiss deepened, my tongue battling fiercely with hers. The need to be inside her exploded within me. I moved her up against the storage shelf, hungrily exploring her mouth and tasting her lips, her jaw, her earlobe. I nipped at the space under her ear and she released a breathy moan that hardened my cock to steel. *Fuck.*

She ground herself against me, lips trailing kisses down my neck. She pulled up the hemline of my shirt contacting the skin beneath. She brushed the palms of her hands over the muscles in my chest and swiped lazily over my nipples. Shivers lanced down my spine, directly to the head of my cock. My pants were too tight and, if she didn't stop, I was going to come right there in my boxers.

I pulsed my hips into her grinding pussy, the clothes between us irritatingly in the way. Removing one hand from under her ass, I reached down to grab my belt buckle. Doubt crept in and I abruptly stopped.

"Winter, I–"

She interrupted me with another searing kiss, biting my bottom lip and then sucking it soothingly.

"Drew," she whispered breathlessly. "Don't stop."

She continued to grind against me; I hesitated for just a second more before giving in. When she reached down and pulled the clasp on my belt buckle, clumsily unbuttoning my jeans, I pushed her harder into the shelving.

We were frenzied now, practically fucking with our clothes on in the dark, but I had never felt so aroused in my life. Hastily, I shoved my pants and boxers down in one go, freeing my erection to bob against my stomach, teasing her still clothed core.

She reached down to palm me, but I released her from my hold to pull one leg of her leggings down, my hand stroking along the underside of her panties. I couldn't see the color, but I could feel they were soft and silky. And soaked, so soaked.

Knowing she was this wet for me made me impossibly harder and I couldn't wait any longer.

She moaned into my mouth when I stroked her again, up her slit to the hood of her clit beneath the fabric. I rubbed in small, gentle circles as she nuzzled breathy groans into my neck, before tearing her panties aside. I lined myself up with her pussy, and thrust in, hard.

"Fuuuuuck," I groaned at the same time she cried out my name.

We settled for a moment, adjusting and enjoying the feel of each other. She was so hot, wet, tight. My cock was in a delicious vice grip while she ground her clit into my pelvis.

"Please move, Drew," she begged, her shallow breaths feathering against my ear. "Please. Move. Now."

My resolved snapped in that second. I pulled out and thrust back into her, no longer in control of my body. Her moans of encouragement spurring me on, I thrust harder and deeper. Her wetness spilled out between us. Her long legs wrapped so tightly around my waist there wasn't more than an inch between our bodies.

Within minutes, her pussy walls tightened around me and my balls grew tight, a deep tingle working up my spine. I had seconds to make her come before I exploded. I slid my right hand between us and pinched her clit. She immediately convulsed around me, arching her back, breasts pressed against me as she came.

Her throaty voice moaned my name and set me off, one thrust making me explode inside her. My legs turned to jelly as she settled into me, our bodies relaxed and satisfied.

"Fuck, Winter I–" She cut me off again with another kiss. The passionate, slow burn made the aftereffects of my orgasm fade out into a state of bliss.

I tried again. "That – that wasn't what I came in here for." I smiled sheepishly, realizing I was still inside her and we hadn't moved a muscle for minutes.

"I know." She smiled softly, caressing my jaw as she peered into my hazel eyes like she was searching my soul for something. "But I'm not sad that it happened."

She kissed me again, just a peck, and pulled away from me, untwining her arms and legs to shakily stand back on the step ladder.

I reached out to grab some paper towel from the rack behind her and realization hit me.

"Fuck! We didn't use a condom. Jesus, Winter – I wasn't thinking, I – what can I do?" I asked a little frantically.

I had never, *ever* had sex without one before. Sadie had been adamant we weren't risking the one percent chance of getting pregnant while she was on birth control, and we had used a condom every single time.

Now I knew what sex felt like without one, I never wanted to go back to the latex penis prisons. But I also never wanted to put Winter at risk, and it had been stupid to get too caught up in the moment to care.

"Well, I have an IUD," she replied, adjusting her panties and pulling her leggings back on after she wiped the evidence of our storeroom sexcapade off her body. "If you can confirm that you're clean, I'm not going to stress about this."

I looked at her, a little shocked by her casual stance on surprise unprotected sex. Was it really that simple to her?

"Okaaaay," I drawled slowly. "I've never had bareback sex before, so I'm pretty sure I'm clean." My cheeks blushed a little in the darkness. Did admitting I was a novice at this make me less of a man?

"Okay." She smiled at me, and then stepped into me to wrap her arms around my waist in a comforting hug.

"I've been interested in you for a while, Drew. If you want to explore this further, I'm here for it. If you want to keep this as our little secret in the storeroom, that's okay too. Don't stress about it, alright? I'm okay with being just friends too."

She reached up to give me one last quick peck, and walked out the door, sleeve of cups in hand.

I stared after her, a bit stunned. By the time I had gathered my thoughts enough to lock the battered steel door, I heard the distant sound of a door chime down the hall. Winter had left the building for the night and I had never felt so confused.

CHAPTER 5

WINTER

"**W**inter, wait up!"

I turned around slowly, heavy book bag in one hand, paper coffee cup in the other, a delicious blueberry muffin precariously balanced on top of the lid. I was the Queen of 'do not make a second trip at all costs' and taking some major risks today in potentially ruining my favorite cream-colored blouse.

"Hey, Raven." I smiled at the petite, perky, blue-haired woman rushing toward me.

Raven and I had met at Ryker's during a first year business ethics class when we had to form opposing arguments for a small-business embezzlement case. It turned out we both had a penchant for creating dramatic debate bloodbaths and, after equally eviscerating each other's opinions over the one-hour period, we were instant friends. She was spunky, confident, and whip smart. The kindest soul I've ever met.

With rare hooded violet eyes, a Monroe piercing, apple cheeks and hair always in pigtails, she was a cross between a cherub child and punk badass. Today she was wearing a spiked leather jacket, a pink plaid pleated skirt, and Mary Janes, with upside down crosses for earrings. She was the embodiment of 'I don't give a fuck and you'll love me anyway,' and it was true.

"Are you all set for tonight? Tom wants us to do the new set." Raven snapped her pink gum noisily as she grabbed my muffin from the top of its perch and took a bite. How she could chew gum and eat a muffin at the same time was intriguing.

"Yup, I've been singing in the shower for days." I grinned down at her five-nothing frame. "Good thing I live alone, or I'd have some explaining to do."

I would have some explaining to do. Other than Raven, none of my other friends knew about my little side project. She and I had taken a road trip to Carlisle for some back-to-school shopping before second year. As we drove through the winding roads down the mountainside, we had belted out early 2000s classics — *are they old enough to be considered classics yet?* — and Raven practically pounced on me when she learned I could sing.

"Can you sing in public?" she had demanded as we finished a butchered duet of Britney Spear's "Toxic."

"Umm yeah. I've sung in choirs and shitty garage bands all of my life." I had laughed, thinking it was a weird question.

"Can you play any instruments?"

I shrugged. "I play piano and beginner clarinet. Why? Are you starting a band?"

A few weeks later, she presented me with an opportunity to earn some extra cash. Raven was a bass player who moonlighted in a jazz trio at one of the Speakeasy joints in the next town over, Sheldonville. Their last singer, Lilah, had a falling out with her and Brody, the percussionist, and they were scrambling for a replacement for their next set. She had begged me to fill in, just for the night, to help them out. I had never been to a legitimate Speakeasy before and so I agreed.

I had been hooked from the moment I walked through the dark staff entrance into the club. Bourbon & Blues was a step back in time to the Roaring 20s; beautiful dark cherrywood paneling lined the walls, with crystal chandeliers hanging low every few feet. Deep emerald green velvet curtains framed the center stage and a sole spotlight lit up the wooden floor.

The audience lighting was so dim and intimate, you could easily hide in the matching emerald-cushioned booths with dark round tabletops so varnished they were practically reflective.

The place exuded a dangerous air, like you were participating in an illicit activity just by attending the club. Strangely, I found it comforting, a setting calling to those little bits of the rebellious darkness inside of me.

It only took one song on the stage for me to agree to become part of the Mellowtones full time. As I belted out the last chorus to "At Last," by Etta James, the wolf whistles and genuine applause from the audience warmed my insides like a shot of good whiskey, and I got addicted to the feeling.

We now were a band staple at B&B, playing a set of twelve songs every other Thursday night. When anyone asked what my plans were, I told them I had to study. I wasn't embarrassed, but I wanted this piece of my life to be just for me.

That, and I knew full well that Georgio Carlos, the resident local crime boss, owned the bar. I had only met him twice in passing; he was a handsome man in his early fifties, salt and pepper short hair with ice blue eyes, lean build and a mega-watt smile. He was charming, so charming you knew he was up to no good, and so I kept a careful eye out for him when we were working.

He was deceptively clever, and at a first glance you would never know he ran drugs, laundered money, and organized an underground fight ring for a living. I might be an idiot to work for him knowing these things, but I loved singing in the jazz bar so much I decided to overlook his illegal transgressions. I was just working for a paycheck at one of his legitimate businesses, after all, entertaining the ignorant public as they sipped on cognac and rye in a hazy dark room.

It was an innocent transaction, or so I kept telling myself.

Raven laughed, having eaten half of my muffin at this point, a smushed blueberry crumb caught between her lips. "I think this is the best set we've come up with, I'm really excited about it. Brody's been keeping me up all night practicing." She grimaced, exaggerating a swoon in the middle of the sidewalk.

Brody was her live-in boyfriend and an amazing drummer. While Raven and I were there for fun, Brody was trying to turn drumming into a full-time gig with two other bands in the area. He had the talent for it, but Cascade Falls wasn't a town where musical stars were made.

"Right, I'm sure *that's* what's been keeping you up all night," I teased, stealing the two bites of muffin remaining from her and popping them into my mouth. "What song are we starting with?"

"'Good Morning Heartache'," she replied. "We'll start slow and build up to 'Chicago'."

I winced. I'd have to find time to practice the final number a bit more on my drive there tonight. The high C soprano notes were killing me.

"Tom wants us to start doing longer sets by the way," Raven said as we walked the tree-lined gravel path leading out to the campus parking lot. The leaves had fully turned to a deep brilliant red, and a beautiful autumn carpet crunched beneath our feet. I made a mental note to arrange a time for our annual fall photo with Shane.

"I told him the max we could do is fifteen songs right now, across two sets a night. I don't know how we'll find time to practice any more than that. And I told him we'd rotate songs in the set list every month, so that the line-ups were fresh but we wouldn't have to learn thirty new songs every thirty days."

Raven was our unofficial band manager and worked out all the playing arrangements with Tom, the club's entertainment manager. Brody and I trusted her to speak on behalf of the band and keep our schedules in mind when doing so. She did a stellar job.

"Good call." I smiled gratefully as we reached Basil.

Basil, the 1997 stoplight green Volkswagen Beetle, was my baby. I had scraped, pinched, and saved every penny from my diner tips over two full years in high school to buy him off of our elderly neighbor, who had kept him in pristine condition. The beige leather interior had been lovingly cared for and the car maintained its 'new car smell' to this day. Raven helped me offload my books and turned to leave.

"Can you meet us there fifteen minutes early tonight? I'd like to try a new variation of 'Straighten Up and Fly Right' before we get on stage. Nothing that'll change the piano or vocals, but I think you'll love it!" She wiggled her delicate brows at me before heading to her own car, a brown 1992 Nissan Sentra sedan. "Later, babe!"

I waved her off and took a generous gulp of my now-cold vanilla latte, smiling at my reflection in the rearview mirror. I just loved Thursdays.

I arrived at Bourbon & Blues with twenty minutes to spare, cramming in an accounting – *bleh* – assignment before coming tonight. If I never had to balance a general ledger for the rest of my life, I'd be thrilled.

I took a deep, steadying breath as I walked through the rear entrance. Every time I entered the club, I got stars in my eyes. The atmosphere here had a low thrumming electricity to it; all of my veins buzzed with adrenaline, the anticipation and stage nerves keeping me sharp. I wiped my sweaty palms on the skirt of my flapper dress.

The Mellowtones had invested in a few costumes once we had signed on for a full-time slot, and tonight I was wearing a rose-gold knee-length dress with spaghetti straps and a low neckline, with two inches of fringe lining the bottom. The dress shimmered with every movement and swayed seductively around my hips; I felt incredibly sexy.

I had pinned up my hair in loose curls and kept my makeup light and feminine tonight. Shimmery rose gold pumps completed the outfit, a far cry from my usual slip-on sneakers.

I was especially nervous on new set nights. We didn't switch up our repertoire very often, and despite years of practice, each time I had to sing a new song in front of an audience I felt frazzled until it was over. I decided to grab a drink at the bar before meeting Raven and Brody out back.

A lean 40-something gentlemen in a bowler cap and suspenders was playing a soft ragtime tune on the piano to the growing crowd and I smiled at a few of the regulars as I walked over to the beautiful mahogany monstrosity housing hundreds of bottles of very expensive liquor choices. The multi-colored bottles sat atop a mirrored, soft yellow back-lit countertop and the setting looked like it was out of a magazine, not a club in a town of less than ten thousand people. Georgio had spent a lot of money on this place. I guess crime *did* pay.

My heart stuttered when I saw who was working the bar tonight. Travis Balcom had to be one of the most gorgeous men I had ever laid eyes on. He had the body of a basketball player, tall and lean, but well muscled, not an inch of body fat that I could see. *And I'd like to fully inspect him head to toe, just to be sure.*

His chestnut brown hair was shorter on the sides, long on top, and he styled it to fall just below his ear on one side in soft, sexy waves. His green eyes were the unique color of kiwi fruit, with shimmering gold flecks around the irises, long dark eyelashes highlighting their depths. His high cheekbones framed a very sensual, very full set of pink lips, and his smile was almost perfect, except for one tiny chip in his front tooth. He wore small black plugs in each ear, a black lip ring, and colorful tattoos poked out of his long-sleeved black button up. He was, in short, my ultimate wet dream.

"Hey, beautiful." He flashed his incredibly sultry smile at me as I shimmied up onto the tall metal bar stool. "What can I make the beautiful lady tonight?"

"I need some liquid courage," I admitted, returning his smile with a heated wink of my own. "Make me something that'll give this audience a good show."

He laughed as he reached for a highball on the back shelf. "In that case, I'll just give you a water. Your voice is stunning, beautiful."

I loved that he called me beautiful. I'm not sure if he even knew my actual name, he had never called me by it, and I had never bothered to say anything to the contrary. This gorgeous hunk of a man wants to call *me* beautiful as my nickname? Yes please, give me more, thank you very much.

I blushed lightly at his praise. "Why thank you, good sir, that may be the confidence boost I'm in need of this evening. But can you give me something good and stiff, just in case?" I laughed openly at the double entendre when his grin turned lascivious.

"That's not what I meant – or maybe a Freudian slip? Make me a whiskey before I confess anything else, please." I covered my eyes with my hands and peaked out between my fingers, smiling innocently.

He burst out laughing and I relished in it. He was walking, talking, sex-on-a-stick, but when he laughed, he was enigmatic. I was like a moth to a very hot flame and I had no cares about getting burned.

He lightly booped my nose and handed me a drink. "A whiskey sour – known to provide courage and cause the occasional bar brawl. Drink up."

Conspiratorially, he winked at me before moving on to the next customer. I gazed longingly at his tight ass in the dark denim he was wearing, then left him a generous tip and went off to find the rest of our band.

Why nothing had happened between us was a bit of a mystery to me. We shamelessly flirted every time I saw him, but we never exchanged numbers or made any effort to get to know each other beyond that.

Maybe he was that way with everyone he met. He practically oozed charisma and sex appeal; the perfect combination for a bartender. I had no doubts he did very well for himself here.

Thinking about Travis inevitably made me think of Drew. Drew was another deep mystery to me. It was like he had decided to go from zero to a hundred overnight.

First, the incredible kiss at Après, then the literal fucking in the storeroom at Johnson's. I was reeling when I left my shift that night, my body tender, but incredibly satisfied. I had purple bruises all over my back the next day from the metal shelving unit I had been repeatedly rammed into as he rutted into me like an animal. It was the hottest sex I had ever had, my 19-year-old experimentation year aside, but I had no idea where it – whatever *it* was – was going.

I hadn't seen him in person since that night more than a week ago. Our shift schedules didn't line up, and he had only texted me a few times with awkwardly professional but friendly messages about work and weekend plans. He never committed anything to me and neither had I. I left the ball in his court. For now. I was okay with that, but damn if I had any clue what was going on inside of that sexy head of his.

"What are you doing daydreaming?" Raven called out to me as I made my way backstage to our instruments. "Come on, I want you to hear this before we go on stage."

I hurriedly swallowed the whiskey back in two gulps as she and Brody played the modified bass line with a new percussion solo. She was right, I loved the variation, and it would sound fantastic alongside the piano melody. Tom came back to give us the two-minute warning and we geared up to play to a larger crowd than usual.

As the curtains opened, I looked past the blinding stage lights to survey the crowded dark room, turning on my performance persona to shake off nervous tingles in my belly. It was always hard to see if anyone I knew from

Cascade Falls or Ryker's was in attendance, and that thought always ratcheted my nerves up. Admittedly, the tangy whiskey sour made by the sexiest bartender in the state had helped. *I'm going to make that a permanent part of my pre-show ritual.*

I stepped up to the mic and put on my best smoky voice. "Good evening, everyone. We're the Mellowtones, and tonight, like a good bourbon, we're going to mellow you out."

The first chord on the bass kicked us off. For the rest of the night, I didn't take my eyes off the silhouette of the tall brunette at the back of the room and sang straight into his sexy soul.

CHAPTER 6

TRAVIS

"I expect you to get the money out today, Travis. Do not disappoint me."

I thrummed my fingers on the glass table top of a diner that had seen better days as my last conversation with Georgio continued to repeat in my mind.

I was on drop-off duty today, one of the many money mules he had working for him in the seven towns surrounding Sheldonville. I didn't like drop-off duty — I preferred working the bars at Bourbon & Blues and making my living off of the excellent tips.

I had been mixing drinks for a decade despite only being legal age for the past couple of years, and bartending was my happy place. Running money was not something I ever volunteered for, but Georgio was my boss, and my boss had me by the balls.

It's what I deserve for making a deal with the devil.

I surveyed the drop-off point. I didn't usually do runs in Cascade Falls, instead covering Granite Springs and Taylor's Peak to the north of Sheldonville, but Georgio's Cascade guy wasn't available today. Whether "wasn't available" meant alive and home with a cold, or dead in a cement coffin in Georgio's basement, I didn't know. Either were legitimate possibilities. Internally, I shuddered at the thought. I would get myself out of this one day, but today would not be that day.

The owner wasn't in yet and my instructions were clear: deliver the money directly to the owner. It was early on a Friday morning and I had no idea when the usual guy typically showed up to offload the cash, but I had to do my route in the other towns this weekend too, so I was getting a head start. Georgio only allowed us to take one bag of money at a time; he trusted no one to handle any more than $5,000 cash in one transaction, so I would have to go back to the club another seven times today before my job was done, and I was bartending tonight.

All in a day's work, I guess.

I sat down for a coffee, the gray gym duffle bag tucked tightly underneath my arm as I leaned into the worn leather booth seats. They were comfortable at least. A hipster menu on burlap-colored paper lay on the table in front of me. I wasn't overly hungry, but I needed to pass the time discreetly until the owner arrived. Besides, I didn't know when I would get another chance to eat today.

Surveying the restaurant, I looked for a server. I had seen the ghosts of two women working the opposite end of the building, tending to a large group of senior men who laughed and joked while they sipped cheap diner coffee. Regulars, no doubt. This place looked like it survived off of regular customers, beige paint peeling in some places on the walls and puffs of cotton batting peaking out of ripped leather stools at the bar. Not exactly a tourist trap like so many of the other places in Cascade.

"Hi, Travis!"

My head snapped up in surprise. The beautiful waitress had dark auburn hair swept up in a ponytail with two short pieces framing her face, her face sporting significantly less makeup than what I was used to seeing on her, but there was no mistaking it; she was the woman I'd been watching unashamedly at Bourbon & Blues for months. And now she was standing in living color in front of me.

I scanned the starchy orange uniform, a poor ode to the past, for a name tag. "Winter" gleamed back at me from a stainless-steel nameplate pinned to her left breast. *Winter, huh?*

It suited her. Unique, but unassuming. In all of the time I had seen her at the club, watching her perform in those sexy period costumes and listening to her sultry voice, I had never learned her name. That likely made me an asshole, but I'd had a lot going on lately and chasing ass at work had not been a priority. It was too bad, because I was attracted to her — really attracted to her — and chemistry like that didn't come along very often.

"Hey, beautiful." I gave her a flirty wink. "I see you have other talents besides singing." I raised a teasing eyebrow at her and she shushed me abruptly.

"Shhhh. That's my little secret. No one here knows about my double life. Coffee?"

I nodded, and she poured me a steaming mug. "No cream or sugar for me, thanks," I told her before I took a long sip. *Surprisingly delicious.* "How long have you worked here?"

"Since high school. All in a day's work and all of that." She smiled softly, tucking a strand of hair behind her ear. "Are you eating anything?"

"Yeah, I'll um—" I quickly skimmed the menu and looked back up at her. "You know what? Surprise me. Whatever's good today."

She grinned, a devious look in her eye. "One boiled shoe coming up. It's our specialty."

She winked at me, sexy long eyelashes hiding one gorgeous blue eye for a second before grabbing my menu and turning away. I discreetly checked her out from the convex security mirror mounted to the corner of the room as she walked back to the counter with my order. Even in that uniform, a far cry from the outfits she wore at the club, she was attractive.

I continued to sip my coffee and observe my surroundings as customers came in and out of the diner. The place was busier than I expected.

Cascade Falls had changed a lot since I was a kid. What was once a quiet ski hovel was now a bustling tourist town, with high priced shops and fancy eateries taking over the downtown core. Mom used to take us here for back-to-school shopping. Cascade Falls had been closer than Sheldonville to the trailer park I grew up in. The trailer park I still lived in.

Mom had been a continuing care worker before she was diagnosed with MS. I had been in my last few months of high school. As the disease progressed, I stepped in to help out around the house, taking on more work to pay our bills when she couldn't work any more. As a single mother to two teenage boys and the mounting healthcare debt to go along with that, she didn't have many options and it killed me to watch her suffer.

I had put my college aspirations on hold and after three years as a gas station attendant, I finally got the job bartending for Georgio when I turned 21. It was the first slide down the very slippery slope of working for Georgio. Which was how I was sitting here, waiting for a man with a bag of $20 bills, carrying a heavy handgun in my back pocket.

A hot plate slammed down in front of me, jarring me from my thoughts. Winter plopped herself down across from me in the booth and smiled wide as she nodded her chin toward the plate.

"Carl's Creation of the day." She leaned in and wiggled her eyebrows suggestively. "He can make boiled shoes taste incredible."

I looked down at two slices of toasted sourdough bread, slathered in some kind of white spread, topped with a layer of roasted tomatoes, a fried egg, and a drizzle of black something over top. I gave her a dubious look and held up a piece.

"I guess this place doesn't serve burnt toast and dried eggs huh?" I sighed. "I may not be fancy enough for this shit."

She scoffed at me and smirked. "I've seen you in a dress shirt, Travis. You're absolutely fancy enough for this shit."

I may not have known her name, but she knew mine, and I had to admit I liked that. A lot. We didn't wear name tags as bartenders, so she would have had to ask someone since I had never officially introduced myself. A small smile traced my lips as I assessed her.

Why were you asking about me, beautiful?

I lifted the toast to my lips and took a bite. Flavor exploded in my mouth and a little groan escaped me as I took another. "Shoes are going on my grocery list," I said, mouth half full of food. I sucked down the last dregs of my coffee. She laughed as she got up and left the booth, but before I could ask her to come back, she returned with a full pot and refilled my mug.

"If you can cook this meal, you'd make the perfect wife," I teased, finishing one piece of toast, and moving on to the other.

She snorted and placed a hand on one perfect hip as she raised an eyebrow at me. "If that's all it takes, you can marry me tomorrow. I want a guarantee that you won't complain about my messy apartment, my taste in music, or my excessive hat collection. I also snore, eat snacks in bed, and won't rub your feet. I may be getting the better deal here."

I laughed loudly, not expecting that response, but loving it. Who was this woman? She was sexy, funny, and interesting as hell. Our nameless banter had gone on for months, and I wanted to have an actual conversation with her. It was too bad that between Mom and Georgio, I had no fucking personal life at all.

"I don't think so, beautiful. I would definitely be getting the better deal." I took my time looking her over in what I hoped was an appreciative, not creepy, way and she blushed slightly before winking and leaving me for another table to serve.

Ding.

My eyes snapped to the front door as the hulking frame of Joe Johnson walked into the diner.

Bingo. Hastily, I threw my napkin down on my mostly finished plate and grabbed the duffle bag beside me as I made a beeline for the back hallway, before he headed there. It would look too obvious otherwise. I pretended I was headed to the bathroom before ducking past it into the office he had just entered. Quickly, I closed the door behind me.

Joe's head whipped up when he saw me, mouth open to ask who I was no doubt, before he eyed the heavy bag and sighed heavily.

"You Georgio's new guy?" he asked with resignation, running his hands nervously through his balding blond crew cut before reaching for the bag with a wary shrug of his shoulders.

"Just a fill-in today," I answered in a cool, emotionless tone. "The usual amount's there, and someone will be back in two weeks with the next drop-off. Georgio is going to start upping the amounts next month, so be ready."

His mouth set in a hard line and he snatched the bag out of my hands before I could hand it to him properly. "Yeah, okay. Well, you've done your job so get out of here. I don't want any of my staff getting wind of this."

I nodded, opening the steel door and letting myself out quietly, heading back to my table to pay the bill before getting on with the rest of my shitty day. Before I could sneak out with cash on the table, Winter's small frame was blocking my way.

"Leaving a bride at the altar? That's a dick move, handsome." She grinned, all teeth, freckles bouncing off her nose as she looked up at me.

I barked a laugh. "Never. I just really like playing hard to get." I reached out to tuck a rogue tendril of hair behind her left ear. I didn't want to continue running into her at our workplaces. I wanted to see her someplace casual, where we could banter all night long.

Yeah, like that was all I wanted. I scoffed internally. This was a bad idea, but I was going to go for it anyway.

"Do you have plans next Friday night? Want to stay after my shift and I'll make you a drink? We can grab a booth and ... get to know each other?" Damn, that was lame. I've got excellent game when it can't go anywhere, but the minute it counted, I turned into a 15-year-old with a vocabulary problem.

She beamed at me, eyes wide, perfect lips turning up into that beautiful smile again. "Why future-husband, I thought you'd never ask." She grabbed a napkin from the front counter and scrawled seven digits on it with her order pencil. "There, now you have my number. Text me, okay?"

I walked out of the diner with a goofy grin on my face. As I continued to play money-mule for the most powerful man in the county for the rest of the day, my mind kept gravitating to thoughts of the beautiful brunette. I was going to make that drink one to remember.

I whistled to myself as I rolled a large wooden keg up the steel ramp to the back double doors of Bourbon & Blues. I was offloading our latest shipment of booze before my shift started. My first official date with Winter was tonight and I was in a great mood.

"What are you so happy about?" Cam asked as he rolled another keg out of the delivery truck. Taller than me, with a boxer's build, Cameron was an underground fighter by night, construction worker by day, and had already offloaded two of these fuckers in the time I had done one. He hadn't worked at B&B for as long as me, but I had taken an immediate liking to him and counted him as one of my best friends.

"Hot date tonight." I grinned broadly and turned to haul the final keg into the bar, trying desperately not to get too sweaty. I hadn't brought a second change of clothes — *idiot* — and I really wanted to come across as the suave and sexy bartender, not the suave and stinky bartender.

I smiled, thinking about the message she had sent earlier. It was a cute photo of her in her apartment sipping a mug of coffee, surrounded by a ton of houseplants hanging from the ceiling. All she said was "See you tonight *winky smiley face*" but it could have been a naked photo with some graphic sexting the way it made me feel.

There were people in life you automatically felt a connection to; friends who felt like brothers from the get-go, like Cam, and women who could turn your head long before you actually saw them, like you could feel their presence in your soul somehow. That was how my mystery-girl felt to me. The end of this shift couldn't come fast enough.

Luckily, it was busy as hell, the evening a blur of Tom Collins and gin and tonics. Familiar faces faded into the shadows as memories of Winter's voice carried me through the evening. She had such a natural stage presence, calm and charismatic, at ease in a room solely focused on her. It was getting harder to stay on task, and I had never rushed so much to clean up after the bar closed in all my life.

Before loosening my tie and heading over to the table where we had agreed to meet, I made her the promised drink: a Black Cat cocktail with cherry Brandy, cola, and cranberry juice. I took a hurried sip to make sure it tasted alright, while grabbing a bowl full of candied bar nuts. It was, admittedly, strong as fuck, but I figured that might not be a bad thing; I could actually use some liquid courage now that I was going to be able to spend some real one-on-one time with this gorgeous creature.

Quickly, I checked myself out in the glass wall behind the bar. My wavy brown hair was curling at the ends from the sweaty evening, but my black dress shirt was stain-free and my face looked decent — normal, at least.

The last call for the bar had been an hour ago, but the club still stayed open for another two hours under its cabaret license. A sole male singer playing an acoustic guitar was now on the mic, crooning softly. About a quarter of the club goers still remained and the atmosphere was relaxed and unhurried. Hopefully, the perfect setting for a first date.

She was scrolling through her phone as I approached the most private corner booth in the club. Her curled auburn hair hid her face in shadow. She looked up from her seat and a wide, open smile lit up her face. She had dressed down in a short, black dress and tights for tonight. She looked like the girl next door meeting my sexiest fantasy, and my pants felt a little tighter all of a sudden.

I put the drinks down with a flourish and with a smile handed her the pretty crystal highball glass with the cherry red twizzler straw. I slid into soft velvet cushion across from her.

"Hey, beautiful, I believe I owe you a drink." I gave her a soft wink and a smile as I settled into my seat. "You look stunning, by the way. It'll be hard to take my eyes off of you tonight."

A small blush crept up her apple cheeks. "Hottie bartender wants to check me out all night? It's hard being me," she teased before she took a sip and licked her lips appreciatively.

"Holy fuck, that's good." She took another long drink and closed her eyes as I took another sip of mine. "You have a talent, hubby."

I snorted a laugh as she continued on with the husband joke from the diner. I don't know how I'd feel if anyone else continued to push a *marriage* line of teasing, but somehow, she made it adorable.

"Careful with that one, it's a little strong," I warned, plucking the maraschino cherry garnish from my glass, and popping it in my mouth. "But it's a bartender's job to be able to read people's drink preferences, and you looked like a cherry girl."

Winter's eyes widened and she looked up at me through her long, dark lashes. "It's my favorite flavor," she admitted on a laugh, one eyebrow raised in question. "Pretty impressive — what other assessments have you made about me?"

I sized her up, taking my time to scan each part of her, then I blew out a dramatic breath. I was good at reading people, an unfortunate by-product of my upbringing. I had been thrown into responsibility for others at a young age, so it became survival more than skill.

I couldn't pinpoint how I knew the things I did. It was like I could read the clues with no recollection of how I learned the language. It made for great tips as a bartender, but somehow I was shit at judging girlfriends, if my last two were any indication.

"You're an only child of accomplished parents. You have a ton of hobbies, but still haven't found your passion. You're going to school for something that will keep all of your options open even if it's not something you really care about. Your favorite color is green and your favorite sex position is ..." I paused for effect and eyed her up and down one last time before settling on, "...reverse cowgirl."

I wiggled my eyebrows at her suggestively and smirked as she threw back her head and laughed hard. I loved the sound of it. I wanted to keep making her laugh that way the rest of the night. The rest of the year.

"That's actually pretty accurate. You were right that my favorite color is green. Almost the exact color of your eyes, actually." She winked at me and a small dimple formed on her right cheek.

Be still my aching cock.

"I knew it!" I said smugly, folding my arms across my chest. "That was a test. So, elaborate. Parents, school, passions ..." I let the last word trail off, waiting for her to pick up the conversation. I genuinely wanted the answers and my tight pants would just have to wait.

She shrugged a shoulder and smiled softly. "Only child, yes. My parents tried to have more, but were only graced with me. Good thing too, because I was a bit of a handful." She grinned ruefully. "Do you know who Miranda Wallace is?"

I quirked an eyebrow and shook my head. "Should I?"

"Not likely. Unless you're a 40-year-old man with impotency issues," she joked. "My mother happens to be the leading authority on sexual health and therapy in the country. She's written a bunch of books and does tours all over the world promoting sex positivity and advocating for contraception rights. Dad is an engineer — his consulting firm is based in Carlisle — but they work on projects all over the state. Mostly bridges and infrastructure stuff."

I whistled, definitely not expecting that combination. I had pictured her to be a lawyer or doctor's daughter, sure, but my lowly family was now paling in comparison to the life she would have lived.

"Holy shit," I said breathily, incredulous. "How come you seem so normal?"

"Stick around a little longer and then make that assessment." She took a final suck of her drink and licked her deep red lips contentedly. "I'm ordering this one next time. What's it called?"

"A Black Cat," I said smoothly as I moved closer to her in the booth. Color me intrigued, I wanted to know more about this girl. "And don't change the subject. A hot-blooded man like me has a million questions about being the daughter of a sex therapist, but I'll leave those alone for now. School? Passions?"

"Well, you nailed the school part. I'm taking business, but I have no idea what to do with it. I'm in my final year. I'm paying for my own education, and I wasn't willing to throw money away to become something I have no interest in, so at least this will get me somewhere."

She sighed, fiddling with her straw in the now empty glass. "I really hope I figure it out before I waste away at the diner for four more years. It's fine when I'm using it to work toward something else, but it's going to be damn depressing if I have nowhere to go after I graduate."

I was impressed. After hearing what her parents did for a living, I had my doubts she would have had to work hard for much.

That was my own bias talking; she worked at a shitty diner and sang here, didn't she? Not exactly the M.O. of someone with a silver spoon in their mouth. Although I highly doubted her childhood home looked anything like the tiny trailer where I grew up. Knowing she didn't have her life figured out made me feel better about my lack of direction. Kindred, flailing spirits.

"As for hobbies," she continued, "like everyone around here, I ski, I paint, I read, I sing, but no one really knows I do this, and I've always wanted to try something badass, like kickboxing." Her wide grin is infectious and I can't help by grin back.

"No one knows about this? Really?" She had said something to that effect at the diner. "You have a gorgeous voice. Why would you keep it a secret?"

"I guess I just want a piece of the world that's just for me, you know? When you grow up in a small town, everyone knows everybody, and everybody knows your business. You don't have the luxury of experimenting with who you are and what you want without the entire world watching you as you do it. It's like Facebook on steroids but you don't get to choose what content is put up — it's all there. When I got pulled into this, I just wanted it to be for me. And because of that, it's my most special piece of my existence. Untouched, untarnished, just ... mine."

Layers of emotion lay behind her words that I just couldn't place. There was a story there and I knew I wouldn't get it tonight, but I wanted it. Date two? Date ten? Fuck me if I wasn't already totally into this woman, yet I was only one drink and one superficial backstory in.

"Okay, now I'm going to try and read you." She flashed me a beautiful toothy smile as she not-so-subtly changed the subject and I laughed.

"Sure, shoot." I folded my arms and settled into the cushions, a wry grin tugging at the corners of my mouth. I read people for a living, but maybe the waitress had some skills of her own.

My grin faltered for a millisecond as my mind went to my one secret, the one thing I didn't want her to know. Now that I'd taken her on this date, I would do everything in my power for her to never find out. Winter wouldn't understand why I did what I did; why Georgio had me by the short hairs and the things I'd had to do for him to pay back my debt. The things I'd have to continue to do.

No, I would be keeping this version of me completely separate from *that* version. The only one who knew that version was Cam, and that was only because he was in the same predicament. Two desperate guys doing desperate things because life dealt us a shitty hand.

"You have siblings — one or two, I'm not as good as you are at this. One parent. Mom, maybe? Well, I guess there are only two options, so I'm saying Mom." Her assessment snapped me out of my thoughts as she laughed self-deprecatingly while gazing at me critically.

"You bartend to save money for something important. You like the color red but you're secretly all about hot pink, and *your* favorite sex position is reverse cowgirl." A satisfied grin traced her lips as her eyes never left mine. The sexual tension between us that was a match flame at the beginning of the night was now a roaring bonfire on my senses.

I pursed my lips, trying to decide how much more talking I could handle before I kissed her. A little longer. I knew once I broke that seal, I wouldn't be able to stop, and I hadn't learned all I wanted to learn about Winter Wallace just yet.

"One brother, younger," I conceded. "Single mom, and has been most of my life. Her health isn't great, so I bartend to help her out, and I'm also saving to go to community college at some point. I like working with my hands, so I want to learn a trade, but I haven't decided which one yet."

I lowered my voice conspiratorially. "I actually love the color purple, not hot pink. None of this lavender or lilac shit, either. Real Crayola crayon purple."

I slid out of the booth to sneak back to the bar to mix us another drink. "I'm keeping the position a secret for now. Ask me later and I might demonstrate." I winked, giving her a purposeful view of my ass in my jeans as I walked away.

When I got back to the booth, fresh drinks in hand, we kept talking about everything and nothing. Favorite books, favorite movies, family life, childhood stories. I kept Mom's illness and Devon's issues to a minimum, sticking to safe topics like school sports and hobbies. After the fastest hour of my life came and went, the sexual tension had become an entire forest fire. Finally, I couldn't take it anymore.

I leaned into her warmth, my hand reaching out to caress her cheek. "I've changed my mind, beautiful. I think any position with you will become my new favorite."

Winter bit her lower lip, her eyes never leaving mine, as I shuffled my body around the curve of the booth, reaching for her hands and tugging her toward me. I pulled her sideways onto my lap and wrapped my arms around her waist. She draped her arms loosely around my neck and snuggled in closer to me.

Despite the dim light, her eyes were bright and piercing, speckles of green dancing around her irises. My gaze dropped to her lips, lips I had wanted to kiss, suck on, be sucked on by, for days. I leaned closer, my lips ghosting hers.

I didn't need to bridge the micro-distance between us; she was kissing me before I could start another sentence. I dove into the kiss, unleashing all of the desire she had stirred up in me from the moment she agreed to this date. Her lips were soft and pliant, and she was taking me hostage as she led the kiss the way she wanted, forcing my lips open to suck and nip at my tongue.

I pulled her closer, letting her dominate me before flipping the script, forcing her lips to open wider and deepening the kiss as I explored every part of her mouth. She ground her ass against me. My cock immediately hardened in my jeans as a small moan of pleasure escaped her lips. Her hands left my neck and slid down my chest to the hem of my shirt, sneaking underneath to trail along my abs and toy with the fine hair below my belly button.

My body was getting hotter, the burning need to be inside her impossible to ignore. I brushed my lips against the soft patch of skin behind her ear, sucking gently before moving to nip her earlobe. Her whole body shivered, melting further into me, and I traced my lips down her neck to the sensitive nerves at the arc of her shoulder, shallowly biting the skin and sucking the pain away, determined to leave a mark to remember in the morning.

She released a long slow breath on a groan that would have made 15-year-old me come in my pants. Before 24-year-old me could do that same, I pulled back from the kiss abruptly, catching my breath as I peered into her lust-lidded eyes.

"Where do you want this to go?" I asked, trying to remember how to use my voice after the most mind-blowing kiss of my life.

"I really, *really*, want this to go exactly where this is going," she said breathlessly, giving me a soft peck on the cheek. "But, well, fuck, I'm on my period, and period-play on the first date really isn't my thing so ..." She bit her lip nervously with this admission and my brain fizzled.

Oh. *Ooooohhhh*. Okay, well that definitely puts a wrench in things. Not that I had ever done 'period play' before – I was going to have to Google that one when I got home – but I didn't think anything could have pumped the brakes for me tonight unless she did.

Which, I guess she just did. *Fuck*.

"Okay," I agreed, nipping her lip lightly as I brought her head back to mine and brushed the freckles along her nose with my finger. "In that case, I really need to stop now, or I'm not going to be able to. You're like a Lay's chip, Winter Wallace."

She snickered, her eyes brightening at my attempt to turn our sad situation into something laughable. I mean it was, if not for the extremely blue balls I would be sporting for the rest of the night.

"Thank you." She smiled, tracing her fingers along my jawline as she snuggled back into me. "I wasn't going to turn down this date with my hottie bartender for anything, and I mean, you could have been secretly repulsive with a wenis fetish or something, and then it wouldn't have been an issue at all. Saved by the period!" She chuckled into my chest, and I couldn't help but laugh along with her.

"What the fuck is a wenis?" I asked incredulously, stuck between amusement and confusion.

"You know that flappy skin on the elbow joints of old ladies? That's a wenis. And yes, there is an actual wenis fetish. I looked it up once. Reddit is a cruel, cruel place."

71

She shuddered, and I couldn't tell if she was joking. Tonight, I would be looking up period play and wenis fetishes with blue balls in hand. My search algorithm was going to be a nightmare in the morning.

The brilliant glow of the house lights broke us out of our cozy stupor. Ted, tonight's bouncer, motioned to the few remaining patrons at the front of the club that it was time to leave.

"Why don't I make sure you get home okay?" I kissed her lightly and pushed her delicately from my lap. "I'll grab you a cab outside."

I pulled her out of the booth and we grabbed our coats, walking hand in hand out the large wooden doors of Bourbon & Blues into the chilly November night air. She left me with one blood-boiling good night kiss, with a promise to text me when she got home. I watched her drive away into the night, my erection still throbbing against the seam of my jeans.

When I finally made it home, I fucked my hand under the spray of a hot shower, thoughts of Winter's swollen lips gliding over my cock spurring me on until thick ropes of cum sprayed all over the white tiles. It would have to do until she would give me the real thing. It was only a matter of when.

CHAPTER 7

WINTER

"So, when do I get to meet this guy?" Shane asked, breaking his concentration on the TV screen for a microsecond to give me an interested side-eye before turning his full attention back to Mario Kart.

It was Friday night and we were in his bachelor apartment, lounging on his well-loved black leather couch in front of a massive flat screen, battling it out for dominance on his Nintendo Switch.

I was not a gamer. It wasn't that I was anti-game, but I lost the genetic lottery when it came to operational opposable thumbs and a brain that could comprehend 3-D on 2-D landscapes. Simply put, I sucked. Mario Kart was the only game I agreed to play and I often joked that it was under duress.

Our fall photo edits had been sent to me for review this morning and I wanted Shane and I to choose the best photo together for our prints. He always made it out like he didn't care which photo was chosen, until it was game time. We argued for twenty minutes over three damn photos until he finally conceded to let me choose the final print.

Of course, it came with a string attached. My payment? One full hour of Mario Kart. And as usual, I was getting beaten. Badly.

Shane's apartment was one of the units just off of Oulten University grounds on the other side of town. It took a full forty-five minutes to walk here from my place, which I usually did in the summer time to get some exercise and enjoy the mountain sun.

Today, Basil and I made the trip together. I loved the snow when ripping down the mountain in fresh powder, but I wasn't a fan of trekking through slushy streets for almost an hour, only to have to endure another hour of pain playing Mario Kart.

The apartment was small but cozy. Every game, book, and hobby of Shane's was meticulously positioned in a specific spot, nothing out of order. It was cute, this big bear of a man who wore rugby clothes more often than street clothing, being so anal about the cleanliness of his space. Of the two of us, I was the definite slob.

It had a very masculine feel. Walls painted white and covered with jerseys of famous players I didn't know crisply pressed into wooden frames. All of the windows had been covered with velvet black curtains. His oversized leather furniture was black, and his queen bed was shoved behind a huge cabinet of white IKEA bookshelves to offer some privacy in the open room. His bed featured the only pop of color in the space, a deep red comforter glaring brightly against the Alice-in-Wonderland tapestry.

I threw my controller at him as Princess Peach died a fiery death from a mobile pit of lava for the third time in as many minutes.

"You want to meet him, huh?" I teased as he set up another round of turtle-bobbing torture. "Three dates in and you think he's ready to meet my other half?"

Three incredibly sweet dates. After the first one ended with my unexpected twist, I wasn't sure if Travis would want to take me on another date. I wasn't opposed to sex on my period, but I wasn't willing to be that vulnerable with someone I was just getting to know. History had taught me that lesson the hard way.

Surprisingly, he texted me the next morning, asking if I wanted to go for coffee and a walk. We meandered through Cherry Park with lattes and chocolate glazed donuts in hand, and it was in no way awkward. He was warm, funny, and next-level flirty. Then, two days later we met up for a late lunch after my last class of the day. It was all pretty innocent, considering he had been ready to take all of my clothes off and grind me in the club that night, but I liked it, and I liked him.

I hadn't seen him in over a week due to our conflicting schedules and I found myself missing his presence. My gut instinct told me to curb my enthusiasm before I got bitten, but I couldn't help the way I felt. He was interesting, funny, sexy, kind. I wanted more of him.

People had a tendency in life to be afraid of enjoying the moment, abandoning the joy they could experience out of fear it won't last forever. I didn't want to lose out on any joy with Travis just because it might not pan out. I was going to enjoy this for as long as it lasted, whatever that ended up being.

"Are you kidding? You've had what — three dates in a week? You realize that's borderline obsession, right? I definitely need to vet his potential serial-killer psycho-stalker status."

I rolled my eyes dramatically. "You're such a drama queen. I wasn't saying anything when you invited Blaise over to Easter dinner after two dates." I poked him in the ribs, partly to break his concentration, but mostly to be an ass.

He grunted and pushed me back into the couch, grinning triumphantly and throwing his hands up in the air as he won for the thousandth time.

"Yeah, exactly. There was a fantastic happy ending to that story. Not the best example there, Snow." His relaxed stance immediately stiffened.

I grabbed his hand to stop him from setting up another game, finally calling it quits on our date with Mario.

"Hey," I said softly, looking deep into his pewter gray eyes. "Do you want to talk about it?"

"Nothing to talk about. It's over, it's a good thing, and now I'm just ... lonely? Not even lonely, just craving some companionship, I guess. It's nice having someone you care about around."

He sighed and ran his large hands through his dark tresses. "I miss his presence, more than I miss him. Does that make sense?"

I nodded, understanding exactly what he meant. I wrapped my arms around his waist and snuggled into him, squeezing tightly. "I'm sorry, Quick. I know I can't be a replacement to hunky Blaise, with his strong biceps—" I paused to tickle him in his ribs and he grunted in surprise, trying, and failing, to push me away.

"—and his manly man-thighs," I teased, clinging to him like a koala, digging my fingers into his armpit as he laughed and thrashed to get me off of him.

"—and I know I don't smell like a spicy ocean breeze, or sweaty gym socks, or whatever he smelled like," I continued, even as he successfully pushed me off of him and threw my body back onto the couch seat, leaning over to pin me with his hips and his impossibly large frame.

I stopped talking and grinned up into the face of my handsome best friend as the light came back into his eyes, a wide smile now gracing his full lips. He leaned down over me, his gaze mirroring Satan. Then he stuck his tongue out and obnoxiously licked the side of my face from chin to hairline.

"Gross!" I desperately tried to push him off me. "That's disgusting, Q! Get off, you germy fucker!"

His booming laugh took over the sound of the Nintendo music in the background and he relented, moving off of me and pulling me up from the couch cushion with an evil grin.

"Fair's fair, Snow. There's a price to be paid when you start a tickle war." He chuckled as he made his way to the small galley kitchen off the living area.

"Pepperoni or Three Cheese?" He called out as he took frozen pizza boxes from the freezer. A gourmet cook, he was not.

"Pepperoni," I hollered back, as my phone dinged with a message from Travis. My heart skipped a beat every time we talked, like I was fourteen again with a new crush. It was exhilarating, if not a little disconcerting.

Hottie Bartender: *Hey beautiful, what are you up to tonight?*

WW: *Hey! ☺ Getting my ass handed to me in Mario Kart. You?*

Hottie Bartender: *It's my night off. Cam and I are just hanging out at his place.*

WW: *Cam from B&B? He's a bouncer, right?*

Hottie Bartender: *Yeah, he's a good friend. Want to meet up and hang out?*

"Are you seriously sexting Travis when you're hanging out with moi?" Shane had finished putting the pizza in the oven and was now hovering over me, mock indignation coloring his tone.

"Yup, and I'm considering ditching you to go see him, tough guy. That'll teach you to lick my face, you sicko."

His eyes lit up with devious excitement. "Invite him over! Then I can properly vet him on the serial killer scale."

I bit my lip, hesitantly. Did I want them to meet this quickly? Did I want to combine my two worlds? Shane didn't know about my singing gig, and I wasn't ready to divulge that information. I had told him that Travis had asked me out at the diner and that I met him at his workplace for our first date. I felt dirty lying to my best friend like that — well, it was more an omission. I would look like an absolute asshole if the real story came out now.

Face it, when the truth comes out, you're going to look like an asshole no matter what.

"He's at his friend's and he invited me over there," I hedged, torn between the two options. Shane and I hung out all of the time, granted, but he was struggling to move past Blaise more than he was letting on, and I wanted to be there for him. On the other hand, I really wanted to see Travis again.

I blew out a strangled breath.

"Give me a sec," I mumbled as I texted Travis back.

WW: *Why don't you guys come over here? We just put a pizza in the oven. Quick wants to meet you.*

WW: *PS - he still doesn't know about me singing at B&B. Could you maybe not mention it?*

Hottie Bartender: *No pressure then (tongue out face) Sure. Send me the address.*

Hottie Bartender: *Yep, secret's safe with me*

I sighed with relief and sent him the details. I hollered for Shane to put another pizza in the oven. He and I could share one as a snack, but each of us could easily put away a frozen pizza in a single sitting.

I frowned as I looked over my outfit. I was not one who usually dressed to impress, and seeing as I hadn't been planning on seeing Travis tonight, I had just thrown on an old pair of black leggings and an even older high school sweatshirt with a Panthers logo across the back. My hair was in a bandanna-style headband and I wore fuzzy panda socks with black pompoms. I sighed. Oh well. If this was going anywhere, he'd be seeing me in my comfy-casual ensemble eventually.

He arrived twenty minutes later, beers and canned cocktails in hand.

I looked passed him expectantly. "Cam didn't come?"

"Nah, he decided to call it a night."

I didn't bother being discreet and let my eyes wander over the map that was this delicious man. His hair was tucked under a navy beanie, his lip and ear piercings on full display. Snowflakes still dotted his eyelashes as he came inside from the cold.

"Hey man," Shane stepped up to introduce himself. "I'm Shane." He clapped him on the back and brought Travis into the small foyer. "Nice to finally meet you." He grinned wolfishly as he winked at me, purposely being a deviant.

"I had a feeling your parents didn't name you 'Quick'," Travis grinned back, taking off his coat before setting his drinks down on the counter in the kitchen. "Thanks for the invite. It's hard to resist pizza and Mario Kart."

"My kind of guy!" Shane beamed, bringing two pizzas out onto the coffee table while I grabbed glasses and napkins.

We settled into a surprisingly comfortable rhythm, eating and joking about everything and nothing at all, when Shane started talking about his project at work.

"Logan's being a pain in the ass about it too," he remarked as gobs of stringy cheese streaked across his chin. "He's not even working for Eccles and he seems to think he can show up to project team meetings and offer input. That guy's ego is the size of Jupiter."

I snorted. "Takes one to know one there, Quick." He gave me an indignant glare and flipped me the middle finger.

"Seriously though, why would Stanley even let him into project meetings in the first place? Aren't there privacy laws or non-disclosure agreements with these sorts of things?"

"It's a major government contract, and he's technically a shareholder in the company, so I don't think so," Shane said thoughtfully, rubbing his chin. "Regardless, everyone at WAQ wants to kick him in the teeth every time he opens his mouth."

"I know the feeling," I mumbled between bites, thinking of my last two encounters with the devil himself.

"Logan Eccles?" Travis cut in, looking back and forth between us. He had settled into the sofa beside me. Shane had taken the chair opposite us behind the coffee table. "That's who you're talking about?"

"Yeah, how do you know Logan? We had the misfortune of growing up with the guy. He was a couple years ahead of us in school. And he and his 'fiancée'—" I straightened my shoulders and drawled out the word like that famous *Seinfeld* episode. "—are always at the diner driving us crazy."

"Logan? Yeah, he's a regular at Bourbon & Blues, but only on weekends though, so you —" He cut himself off abruptly. "So you'd never see him when you come visit me." He covered. I snuck a glance to see if Shane caught the slight slip. He hadn't, or at least he hadn't appeared to. Phew.

"I think he thinks he's a bit of a Casanova with the waitresses, but he doesn't say much to me," Travis continued, picking his olives off of his pizza. I snatched them off his plate and popped them into my mouth. No one was throwing out the delicious salty morsels on my watch.

Interesting that Logan headed to Sheldonville on the regular. I filed that away to contemplate later. Three delicious vodka seltzers into the evening was not the time to consider Logan's comings and goings. I also had to consider why I cared about Logan's comings and goings in the first place.

Shane reset Mario Kart as I cleaned up the pizza remnants. Then I settled between the two men as an epic battle between Luigi and Mario began. I couldn't think of a more perfect evening.

CHAPTER 8

LOGAN

My skin was on fire. It always happened when I needed a boost. The deep, aching longing sat low in my abdomen, soon to turn into a gnawing hunger until I got my hands on more. I'd deny it for as long as I could before inevitably giving in. This was the way it always was. I just needed a little taste to feel better.

Sweat dripped down my spine as I continued my work out, trying like hell, and failing, to distract myself until I met up with Tom later. He'd soothe this pain before it got too raw, before Hillary or anyone else could even guess something was wrong.

It helped to be a miserable cocky fuck on the best of days, so no one expected me to be any different when the withdrawal symptoms hit. I pounded into the heavy bag harder, shifting position on the balls of my feet and jabbing with all the power I had left before collapsing to the floor. I took a long drink of my water before wiping my brow, and gulped in huge breaths of air as my heart rate came down.

I cursed the day I took my first hit. It was meant to be a distraction, a party trick. I should have known Dad's closet alcoholism meant genetics weren't on my side. It wasn't an instant addiction, not by a long shot, but money and access to the coke made it a hell of a lot easier to speed up the process. Now, I couldn't go a day without it. Not without the pain, the depression, and the terrible, terrifying dreams.

I stood up from the mats, moving my way through my home gym to grab a shower. Hillary wasn't home and I was grateful for that. We didn't want to be in each other's presence anyway.

People didn't think arranged marriages could happen in the 21st century, but they were wrong. Dad and Camden had practically pushed us together when we were twelve, giving no indication there were other options. Hillary had no problem cozying up to me and filling the role everyone expected of her, but I couldn't care less. I was in it for the money, plain and simple.

If we got married before her 25th birthday, Hillary would get access to the multi-million-dollar trust fund her grandmother set up for her when she died. Camden expected me to use that money to fund his infrastructure projects. Dad expected me to use that money as a cash infusion into Eccles Engineering. I planned to use that money to buy up the rest of the real estate in Cascade Falls, and eventually out from under Camden's thumb. The reality is, it would be Hillary's money, so I had to stay on her good side. At least for now.

We had made it work while I was at Harvard and she was at Barnard College. We flew out to see each other once a month when a weekend in each other's company was enjoyable. The sex was good, the conversation decent. Then it was over and we could both get on with our lives, until the next tryst. I certainly wasn't monogamous, and I had my doubts she never strayed.

For all her faults, I think she actually did care about me, and I supposed I did too, but not in the way she wanted. Not in the way I ever could. I just wanted to get this wedding over with so we could move on with this fake charade, and finally have what we both wanted. Power, money, and a controlling say in our families' assets.

I showered hurriedly. I had things I needed to do before I headed over to Sheldonville. I pulled up a few emails, getting them out of the way; I now had eight businesses in my portfolio, along with multiple properties, and I was going to have to hire another assistant before I took on anything else.

Beth was great at her job, but even she couldn't take on any more. She had made it very clear from day one she wouldn't fuck me, and I respected that, although she really didn't have anything to worry about. I didn't shit where I ate, and I take my work very seriously. Hard work meant more money, and more money meant more freedom. I wouldn't be under Stanley Eccles' thumb for much longer, the prick.

I left our modern condo with the stunning mountain view and stepped into my Audi. I had chosen my blue suit tonight. I may have been going to Sheldonville for personal pleasure, but I always kept up appearances. Tom would hook me up with a couple of grams, I would indulge a little in the private bathroom, and then I would stay and listen to some music before calling it a night.

I usually headed out on weekends, when I was less likely to look out of place, but I was in a bad way and needed something to take the edge off for the next few days. I couldn't risk falling too far down the rabbit hole and Hillary getting suspicious. I had hid this from her for years, and I had no intentions of getting caught now.

Admittedly, the need to feel good was getting worse and hiding it was getting harder.

I couldn't think about that right now. I tapped my thumbs irritably on the steering wheel as I drove through town, parking in the lot at Bourbon & Blues. It was busy here tonight. I guess Thursdays were just as hopping as Saturdays, or so it seemed.

I walked past the bouncer with a $20 bill in my hand and headed directly to the bar. I'd have an Old Fashioned and then meet up with Tom at our usual spot in the back of the club. I could wait a minute before getting a hit. A chill swept up my spine in anticipation.

Travis handed me my drink and I turned toward the stage, hearing an unfamiliar voice singing in the background. I nearly choked on the alcohol when I saw Winter-fucking-Wallace on the stage. She wore a red 1920s flapper get-up and looked hot as hell, singing about blue birds as she swayed her hips.

What the fuck?

Winter was the one I'd beg on my knees to have but would never get. I knew it and she knew it. I was an ass to her every chance I got to drive the point home, and she never took my bait, which goaded me even more.

I would love to have fucked her in high school and then rubbed it in Daddy Darren's face. He and Dad had been rivals my whole life, and Darren made it no secret he considered me the devil's spawn. He was right, I was, and I would have leapt at the opportunity to prove it. Carson

Baker got there first, though, and I wasn't going to be able to do any more damage than he did, so I dropped it.

Winter wasn't a cute freshman anymore. She had grown into one smoke-show of a woman and, despite my feelings on her father, I wanted her. I would take her if she'd have me, but she was too smart for that. *Too bad.*

I sipped my drink with interest, no longer in such a hurry to see Tom. She was hot and she was good. I caught Travis watching her the same way I was, and I almost felt bad for the guy. He wouldn't have a chance with her either, the poor schmuck.

Eventually, the need to make myself feel good again became too great and the ice in my glass had melted. I sent Tom a text to meet me at the usual spot and headed toward the back of the building, going behind the rows of velvet curtains.

Tom met me in the stairwell with a baggie and an envelope.

"Boss says he wants to see you tonight," the big man said, folding his arms across his chest.

My mouth was suddenly dry, and it wasn't from withdrawal.

"Tonight? He's here?"

I absolutely did not want to see Georgio tonight. I figured I'd be able to avoid him for at least another few weeks. "I actually have to be somewhere tonight, I'll come back this weekend."

I turned to walk away, but Tom's heavy arm wrapped around my shoulder and stopped me moving forward.

"No. Tonight." His grip tightened as he steered me into a dark hallway, up another flight of stairs into a large office.

"Hello, Logan." Georgio smiled at me like we were old friends and my heart sank. I knew where this was headed.

"Hi, Georgio, what can I do for you this evening?" I refused to look nervous, so I stood tall and looked him dead in the eye.

"For starters, you can pay me what you owe me. We're at what ... a hundred thousand? Two hundred thousand? What's the figure now, Janet?"

Janet, his mousy assistant – *what was she still doing here at this hour?* – looked up from her tablet and pushed her glasses up her nose. "$175,674.36, sir." She hastily went back to whatever she was doing.

"Thank you, Janet." He turned to me and grinned like a shark. "When am I getting my 176 thousand dollars, Logan?"

I blew out a breath. I shouldn't have borrowed the money from Georgio, of all people, but I wasn't going to lose on this deal. I had two businesses go belly up in the past two years and bankruptcy was not an option with my reputation, so I had made a deal with Georgio to get me through. My other ventures were doing quite well, but the only way I could pay him back was when Hillary's trust fund kicked in.

"We get married in six months, Georgio. You know that's when I'll be able to pay you back. In full, in cash. Full interest included." I looked him in the eyes and didn't back down, like he was expecting.

He nodded. "I'll have a revised bill for you shortly. You know full well my interest rates aren't cheap. And I expect you to help move the money through your businesses, if you don't want this brought to anyone's attention."

His loose threat hung in the air. I sighed and nodded my head once. "I agreed to your terms, Georgio. Nothing has changed. Just wait for me to secure my financial future, and you'll be swimming in pennies in no time."

Georgio barked a laugh and clapped me on the back. "You could do worse," he mused, on another chuckle. "I look forward to your wedding. I am getting an invite, aren't I?"

He was. His underground businesses went undetected by most of the town, but his construction companies built half the county and all of Camden's projects. They were known friends, and Camden certainly wouldn't let us get away without inviting him.

"You'll see our invitations shortly. We couldn't agree on a print," I deadpanned and shrugged my shoulders nonchalantly, heading toward the door.

"Have fun," Georgio called over my shoulder. "Don't let that stuff kill you before I get my money."

I waved my hand goodbye without looking back and made my way back to my favorite bathroom to scratch the itch now creeping through my entire body. The rest, I could worry about later.

CHAPTER 9

SHANE

"Come on, Quick, we're late!"

I looked at my best friend dubiously. Cocking one eyebrow, I assessed her outfit. She was classically dressed to impress in a black sweater-dress and lacy tights with her hair in a high ponytail, and every man in the bar was going to be drooling over her.

Good thing she had three bodyguards to keep her protected tonight, not that she needed it. I had once witnessed Winter throw a Bloody Mary on a frat boy's white cashmere sweater for trying to grope her on the dance floor.

My little Snow didn't need a savior, but I liked playing one for her sometimes.

Apparently, she *did* need a time-keeper.

"You mean, *you're* late. I just spent the past hour waiting for your slow ass to decide what shoes you were going to wear."

"You're exaggerating," she grumbled, tugging on her jacket as she attempted to speedwalk out of her apartment door.

"I am *not* exaggerating," I teased while trailing after her at a snail's pace, intentionally trying to irritate her now. "You'd think you'd look like a pageant queen with how long it took you to get ready. I guess some of us were blessed with natural beauty, and some of us have to get it from a foundation bottle."

I outright laughed when she tackled me in the dingy apartment hallway, her small frame holding on to my large one for dear life like a little turtle backpack. I spun her around to my front and proceeded to tickle the life out of her, until she collapsed into a fit of giggles on the stained, carpeted floor.

"Come on," she wheezed, as I pulled her up from her fetal position. "I'm really excited for tonight. Can we go now, please?"

I refrained from stating, once again, I wasn't the reason we had been held up. Instead, I directed her to my truck as we made our way across the slushy parking lot.

"I feel like we haven't been to Après in forever," she mused as we buckled our seatbelts. "I'm going to be on the dance floor all night."

"You mean, you're going to be grinding on Travis all night," I retorted, giving her a knowing smile. "Let's call a spade a spade, I know you haven't fucked him yet. That sexual tension is going to suffocate all of us."

"You're telling me," she groaned, picking at her nails the way she always did when she was nervous. "It's definitely been a lack of opportunity, not a lack of interest. That man is fucking *hot*. It's more than that, though. I–" She looked up from her hands, her eyes meeting mine in the dark. "I really like him. I can't remember the last time I really liked a guy, you know?"

I reached to grab her hand in mine, interlacing our fingers. "I get it. I like him too, or I've liked what I've seen so far at any rate. And he is hot." I wiggled my eyebrows with a grin. "Let's find me someone like that tonight. I'm in the mood for a dirty one-night stand in a bathroom stall."

I was. I took Blaise's breakup way harder than I should have, and I was ready to move on with my life. Maybe have a little fun before settling into something serious, with someone a few degrees hotter than I was, and who was only in it for the sex too.

"Maybe Cam is into guys? I've never met him before, so I honestly don't know. Raven swears he's sex on a stick, though, so at least you'll have some eye candy. I also volunteer as 'wing bitch'."

"That's a terrible title, you know. It makes you sound like a trashy chicken wing waitress during Happy Hour." I laughed at the imagery; Winter in a Hooters uniform slathered in barbecue sauce. It was oddly erotic.

Huh.

I cleared my throat. "If anyone catches my eye, I'll sic my 'wing bitch' on them, okay?"

We got to Après only a few minutes later and the bar was already packed. Winter was texting on her phone as we waited in the freezing line to pay our cover.

"Travis got us a booth at the back," she said, tugging on my hand to pull me through the dense crowd on the dance floor in the center of the large room.

It was dark and foggy, strobe lights dancing across the walls and a smoke machine filling my lungs with the slightly sweet vapor, having turned from a skier's bar into a dance club once ten p.m. hit.

"There they are!" Winter shouted into my face, barely audible as we passed by the huge speakers blasting The Black Eyed Peas latest hit.

I couldn't see much until we were right in front of the half-moon booth. My tongue stuck to the roof of my mouth when I took in the two men sitting there.

Travis was dressed in a black button-up shirt, two buttons undone and his sleeves rolled up, exposing his colorfully tattooed forearms.

Winter once told me a great business model for porn sites would be pages dedicated to shirtless men in gray sweatpants and men with their forearms on display – fully clothed, just forearms. I had laughed incredulously at that, but she insisted women were far more turned on by those traits than dick pics. Looking at Travis now, I could kind of see it – maybe?

Nah, I'd still take a dick pic.

Raven, the little blue-haired spitfire Winter had befriended at Ryker's, had undersold Cam by one thousand percent.

'Sex on a stick' didn't do this man justice. Even sitting in the booth, I could tell he was tall, maybe a little taller than I was, and his chiseled muscles were clearly defined under a tight white t-shirt and blue jeans. His skin was the color of a latte, with piercing blue eyes that could be seen even in the dark club, and a shadow of stubble outlined his jaw. His hair was so short it looked like it was freshly shaved that morning. His lips were pillowy, and I immediately wanted to kiss the shit out of him.

If he wasn't gay, I'd bow down to the straight woman who would take this man.

Winter let go of my hand and slid into the rounded leather seat. Travis pulled Winter into his side, kissing her deeply and she melted against him. It was nice seeing Snow so taken care of. I had filled the role most of my life, not that she had always needed it, but it was comforting to know that someone else was able to be there when I couldn't be.

I slid in beside her, nodding at the two guys. "Hey, Travis, good to see you, man."

I looked directly at Cam, trying to stay cool. My gaydar wasn't working at all tonight. "Hey, I'm Shane."

"Cam." He stuck out his hand and gripped it in mine with a genuine smile, flashing bright, straight teeth. "Good to meet you."

Fuck me, he had a southern drawl too. I could not be pining after a potentially straight man tonight. I was going to have to find someone on the dance floor and get laid, or I was going to self-combust.

"Cam works at Bourbon too," Travis explained as he raised his arm to call over a server.

"I do." Cam smiled again and my heart skipped a minor beat. I was acting like a fucking 10-year-old with a crush on One Direction; I had to get my shit together. "Construction by day, bouncer by night. I live the life of luxury."

The server showed up and we ordered our round of beers, settling into a casual conversation that was natural and relaxing.

Travis had been working a lot of overtime at Bourbon & Blues, a bar in Sheldonville I had heard of but had never been to. Cam was working on one of Georgio's latest apartment buildings and preferred finish carpentry to framing. No one liked the last season of Game of Thrones, but we all could agree *Seinfeld* was the best show ever written in the history of television. I was having a great time.

Travis and Winter had this easiness I had never seen her have with anyone else. It was fun to see her light up around him, the two of them all snuggled up and joking in between chatting with the two of us.

I then realized we had never done this before. Winter never really dated; she was the third wheel to my dates, but it had never been the other way around. This night was full of revelations.

"I'm going out for a smoke." Cam pushed himself out of the other side of the booth and stood up, and I held in a breath at the sight.

He was even hotter standing. Thick thigh muscles bulged from his jeans and the shadow of swirling tattoos on his ribs were only slightly hidden underneath his shirt. Why he was in construction and not a model, I had no idea.

"I'll join you." I slid out of the other side, leaving the canoodling couple to have at it. The last time I had left Winter at the bar, she had a spicy moment with Drew – her words, not mine – and now she was sucking face with another hottie. That girl had way more game than me these days.

We made our way to the rear smoking deck and stood under the stars. Someone had put out an exterior heater recently, and I was grateful for it. My jeans and thin wool sweater didn't match the crisp mountain air.

Cam took out a pack of menthols and lit one, offering me one as I stood beside him. We had the deck to ourselves, which was rare, and I was going to take advantage of the opportunity.

I took the smoke from him and lit up too. Inhaling, I welcomed the head rush. I smoked a joint every other weekend, but rarely indulged in a cigarette. It was a dirty habit but there was no denying how good it felt in this moment. I could think of worse vices.

"So..." Cam broke the comfortable silence with his sexy southern baritone. "What do you play? You're built like a linebacker." He nodded at my broad frame and height.

"Rugby in the school season, and I board." I flicked some ash off the end of the cigarette into the butt box. "I had a shot to go pro, but I decided to do school instead. I teach at the hill though." I took another long, delicious drag. "You? I'd guess MMA, if I was a betting man."

He laughed, the deep throaty sound filling the night air. "Boxer in my off hours. Not professionally or anything, just to let off some steam."

That made sense. He was a bit taller than the boxers I knew, but if it was just a hobby than it wouldn't hinder him in the ring.

"How long have you been in Cascade Falls?"

His shy smile could have stopped traffic. "I stick out here like a sore thumb, don't I?" He stubbed his cigarette and folded his arms across his chest, leaning against the wall like a Camel poster boy. "Just over a year. My mom was from here, so I thought I would check it out."

I noticed the past tense, but didn't push it. It wasn't my business and he didn't elaborate, either.

"That's cool," I said instead, stubbing the last of my cigarette too, and moving to stand closer to the outdoor heater. I held a lot of body heat, but it was frigid out here. "Is that a Louisiana accent?"

"Georgia. I'm nothing but sweet tea and peaches, I'm afraid. I'm missing that heat right about now."

Fuck, that accent was cute. He opened the door to go back inside and I followed, getting a nice view of that molded bubble butt as we trekked through the dark hallway and back to the masses.

I saw Logan out of the corner of my eye, and turned to see the jack-of-all-asses arguing with a man I had never seen before in the back of the room, the two of them only partially hidden behind a speaker. Whatever they were talking about, Logan was visibly pissed, waving his arms in the air before pushing the guy down the same hallway we had just come in from.

That twat was nothing but gold-plated trouble.

When we came back into the humid, hazy air of the main area of the club and back to our booth, Travis and Winter were missing. I chuckled to myself, thinking she had finally decided to have her way with him in the bathroom, when I caught a glimpse of them on the dance floor.

I nodded my head in their direction. "You want to join them?"

Cam shrugged indifferently. "Sure."

We made our way out to the floor. Body heat and sweat and alcohol saturated the space. Winter was wrapped in Travis' arms, front to back, and their lazy gyrating was sensual and hot; the sexual tension between them was volcanic.

Instead of being my usual obnoxious self, I let them be and chose to dance with a hot brunette girl with dark square-framed glasses beside me.

Cam snuck in behind me and danced awkwardly between Travis and Winter, and me and Whatshername. Winter grabbed his hands and pulled him to her, creating a hot-guy Snowflake sandwich. He hesitated for a second before relaxing into the movements, moving his hands to her hips and swaying in time with the music. Even with a few inches of space still between them, the three of them could easily be the opening scene to a very enticing "Dirty Dancing" themed porno.

So, probably not gay then. Just as well, I hadn't been picking up any "interested" vibes from him all night. Not that he would be interested even if he was gay, but a man could hope. I glanced over at the three of them while spinning Busty Brunette – she was actually really cute and a great dancer – and winked at Winter when I caught her eye. She grinned suggestively and pulled Cam just a tiny bit closer. I choked back a snicker. Good for her. It was time we both let off some much-needed sexual frustration.

Out of nowhere, the shrill clang of a fire alarm sounded before an icy spray rained down from the ceiling. All lights in the club turned on, blinding me as I grappled with what was going on. The sprinkler system; the sprinkler system had been activated.

Screams filled the room as panicked partiers stampeded toward the front doors of the club.

"Come on." I grabbed Winter's hand and pulled her toward the rear hallway, Travis and Cam following right behind us.

We were moving against the crowd and it felt like we were bobbing in a sea of people, but eventually we were spit out into the night air, soaked and chilled to the bone.

"My place is close by," I said to the group and led the way, shivering, to my truck. "Come on over and you can grab a hot shower, and we can order some takeout."

"Thanks for the offer, man." Travis clapped me on the back and took Winter in his arms, rubbing her shoulders as her teeth chattered. "But I've got to work early in the morning anyway, and I'm a half hour from here. We'll just grab a cab to Cam's place."

Cam nodded in agreement, and Winter and Travis said their goodbyes with a heated kiss that made me wish I hadn't left Busty Brunette in the club. I grimaced; that was an asshole move right there.

I had only had two drinks over a few hours, so Winter and I piled into my truck, blasting the heat as high as it would go as our clothes suctioned to our bodies.

"That was fun," she mumbled as she snuggled into her seat for warmth. I may have only had a few drinks, but she was half in the bag, head lolling on the head rest and almost asleep before we reached the parking lot to her apartment.

I carried her into her place, helped her strip down to her underwear, pulled a t-shirt over her floppy head, and tucked her into bed. Instead of heading home, I hopped into her shower to clean the night off of me.

I slid into bed beside her in a set of PJ pants I kept here for this exact purpose. She rolled over and snuggled into my chest and I wrapped my arms around her as I had a hundred times before. I listened to the sounds of her steady breathing and fell into my own deep sleep, comfortable and content for the first time in a while.

CHAPTER 10

DREW

"Thanks for coming over, man."

I doused my greasy palms in coconut oil before scrubbing them with the industrial citrus degreaser and rinsing in the large metal wash basin at the back of my garage. Despite the November temperature outside, the garage was humid, and the dank smell of must and motor oil clung to the air.

Shane stood behind me wearing a set of dark blue coveralls, deeply stained from years of wear. We had just spent the last three hours working on my Triumph, and I was grateful for his help. Despite years of experience as a hobby mechanic, the bike was one tough puzzle to crack, and I would be ten times slower getting the work done without his bike and hands as a guide.

"No problem," Shane said as he stepped up to the sink to scrub his own hands. "When it's done, we can christen it by taking a ride through the mountains. I want to see how she moves on those turns." He grinned wickedly.

"Deal." I shrugged out of my own set of stained coveralls and grabbed my phone from the table by the door. "Want to come up for a beer? I'm just going to order some pizza and throw on Sports Center."

"Sounds good to me. I don't have anything to do tonight." He made a face of disgust. "Well, I'm avoiding my slab design assignment. Beer sounds better."

I laughed, not having a single clue what a slab design was, and headed out the garage door and up the wooden steps to my apartment. I still lived on my parents' property but had turned the old barn adjacent to the farmhouse into a fully functioning double car garage with a one-bedroom loft apartment above.

Dad and I had taken on the project when I was fifteen, knowing that I would end up going to business school nearby and would want my own space. Investing in real estate was the smarter choice than taking on a loan to pay for a cramped dorm room, so every evening and weekend for months we picked away at each section. I worked at the diner for free for a year just to cover the cost of the garage portion, but it had been worth it. Since the place was paid for and I could live here rent free, I had no plans to leave any time soon.

The only downside was the many visits I got from uninvited guests, namely, my siblings. In particular, Rosie, the 17-year-old rebel, liked to sneak into my garage late at night and smoke pot away from our parents, and Dawn, the 15-year-old sneak, ate all of my snacks and watched my big-screen when I wasn't there. The two youngest, Tom and Charlie, stayed away unless they knew I was home and wanted to play softball in the back yard. With family dinner every Sunday evening, I had the chance to catch up with everyone anyway.

For the most part, I didn't mind their company, but after long days at the diner and living a life that really wasn't my own, I didn't want anyone around to disturb my peace. Anyone but Winter, and she wasn't going to happen.

I had been punishing myself over the last few weeks, keeping my contact limited to only what was necessary for work. It killed me to text her and not ask her about her day, and only send her two-word answers, but I had to draw a hard line or I wouldn't have the self-control not to give in. It was harder knowing she was interested. I was technically her boss and what I did – what we did – was a mistake. I wouldn't let it happen again, no matter how I felt about her.

Truthfully, she intimidated the shit out of me. Winter was so self-assured and confident, it didn't matter who was watching or where she would end up, she just trusted her gut. She brightened a room and sparked feelings in my mind and my body I wasn't ready for, regardless if the rushed, closet sex had been the best fuck of my life and I couldn't get the memory of it out of my head.

I was doing a piss-poor job of convincing myself this was for the best.

I shook my head at that train of thought as we walked through the door into my small kitchen. I had designed the apartment to be a true bachelor pad – simple and efficient, with exposed wooden beams, rough wood floors, and large windows overlooking the field and the lights of town in the distance. The decor would be classified as "minimalist," and that was generous.

Other than a small round kitchen table and an oversized cherry red leather sectional with a 70" flatscreen mounted to the wall, the apartment was barren. The only room that had any charm was my bedroom, and that was not a reflection of the action I was getting.

My gift to myself when I graduated college was a custom oversized matching furniture set in deep mahogany wood, complete with the most comfortable king bed known to man. A bed I would give anything to share with the Audrey Hepburn of my dreams, especially now I had had a taste.

Stop it, Johnson.

"Drew?"

I snapped out of my spiraling thoughts and my gaze caught on Shane, who was looking at me expectantly.

"Sorry, brain tired," I rubbed the back of my neck sheepishly. "Repeat that?"

"What kind of pizza do you want to order? I'll call Mimi's." He took his phone out of the pocket of his jeans and cocked an eyebrow.

We settled on their Works special and I grabbed a few local craft beers from the nearly empty fridge — bachelor life — and headed into the living room to watch the game.

The Leafs were playing and while I didn't have a chosen team to root for, Dad had been a Leafs fan my whole life. Shane's too, apparently, if his enthusiasm was any indication.

I was enjoying the time we were spending together. Most of my friends from college had moved away when we graduated, and I hadn't invested any time into a proper social life since managing the diner. I got out to Après every now and again if a band I liked was playing, and there were buddies I could call on to go to the gym or shoot some hoops, but Shane was easy. We could talk cars, or football, or reminisce about some shared high school experience.

The one topic I avoided, of course, was his best friend. He didn't bring her up either, but I didn't know if that's because he knew what we had done and didn't need any more details, or because he didn't think we were a thing.

That's because we aren't a thing.

As Shane yelled at the TV for the tenth time, I watched a pair of headlights light up the long driveway leading to the main house and muttered a curse. Shane forgot to tell them to take a left onto my driveway and my siblings would definitely take the opportunity to snag my pizza with me footing the bill.

"I'll go grab the pizza before Rosie or Dawn grab it first," I explained to Shane as I shrugged on my jacket by the door. "I'll be right back."

My driveway was so dark, I could barely see in front of me as I made my way down the steps onto the gravel. I had been meaning to replace the sensor light on the side of the garage for weeks, and the early sunset hadn't been doing me any favours in the evenings. I cautiously made my way across the icy patches over to my parent's place and froze. Dad was in his robe outside the main house garage door speaking to the owner of the gray Impala that had just parked.

"–fuck are you doing here!?" He whisper-shouted to the stranger, his arms waving in the air in anger. I could make out a few shadows across his face; he wasn't hiding his fury in the least.

"Boss says you're not living up to your end of the bargain, Joe," a threatening deep male voice answered. "You're smarter than this. You know you can't avoid him anymore."

I tucked myself in a deep shadow behind one of the large spruce trees in front of the house, not wanting to be seen, but needing to know what was going on. I didn't have my cell on me to call the police for whatever this was, and I had a feeling I would need the element of surprise if Dad needed backup. This guy didn't sound like he was fucking around.

"I'm doing exactly what I agreed to do," Dad growled fiercely, his anger palpable. "We've run hundreds of thousands of dollars through the diner for years. What more does he want?"

"He needs more, you know the stakes are higher these days. If you don't start accepting and moving the double shipments, you're not going to like what happens to you. Or your family. Georgio doesn't make empty threats."

"How the fuck am I supposed to get away with that? That's an impossible ask!" Dad's face flushed red and he shook his fist in rage. "You can tell him that we're not doing it. We've paid our debt ten times over, and we're done."

He turned to head back into the house before whirling back around. "And don't you fuckers *ever* come to my home again, you hear me? I'll blow your head off with my shotgun." He stormed back into the house, threadbare robe flapping behind him. Even at 55, with a balding pate and a burgeoning pot-belly, Joe Johnson was not someone to fuck with.

I quietly backed away from the scene as the mystery driver ducked back into his car and retreated down the driveway toward the town below.

I had known Dad had been keeping something big from me for weeks. Hell, after that conversation, he had been keeping something from me for years.

How had Dad gotten mixed up with Georgio? The man was the biggest name in construction in the state, and there was no shortage of rumors as to some of his questionable side projects. He was shady at best and a full-on criminal at worst. Is this where the extra money was coming from?

I clearly had no idea what was going on, but now I was going to find out.

The acne-ridden pizza guy arrived just as I got back to the steps of my apartment and I took the order absently. Upstairs, I watched the game through blind eyes, chewing without tasting as I considered what to do.

I wasn't leaving the diner tomorrow until this mysterious package was delivered. It was time to find out what Joe Johnson had gotten himself into.

I waited all day at the diner for nothing. No suspicious people, no suspicious packages, nothing to indicate anything out of the ordinary was happening other than Dad's shitty attitude for most of the day.

Poor Janice was almost in tears when Dad tore a strip off of her for spilling a cup of coffee behind the counter. A 40-cent cup of coffee. I had to give her a free meal and an extra break just to get her calm enough to go back to work. We were short-staffed as it was, and I couldn't have Dad scaring away our only decent employees.

I rubbed my hands down my face and let out a deep yawn. I was exhausted. After last night's mystery altercation, I hadn't slept much, and after a full shift with all of my senses on high alert, I was in need of a stiff drink and a nap.

I had been avoiding Joe Johnson as much as I could; I didn't need to become his next victim. I didn't have much confidence I could look him in the eye without blurting out something to scare him off. He had been denying me answers for so long I knew I wasn't going to get anything out of him without irrefutable proof. Whatever that could be.

It was now 8:05 and I was calling it a day. I made my way back to the bathroom to splash some cold water on my face to get me through the drive home. I heard the muffled sound of Dad closing the office door and locking it behind him, his massive set of keys jangling down the hall. *Why was he locking the door?*

I poked my head out of the bathroom and peered up and down the hall; empty. I took out my own set of keys and quickly unlocked the office and stepped inside. Obviously, this space was mine to use as well, given I was second-in-command around here, but Dad never locked the office. Typical small-town trust, I guess.

I scanned the small, cramped room, bookshelves filled with mish-mashed paperwork and trinkets; sepia-toned photos of Mom and Dad's memories of the diner through the years covered the walls like wallpaper. I didn't see anything out of the ordinary, until my gaze caught on a black strap peeking out from underneath the battered wooden desk.

I pulled the strap with my foot, yanking hard to get it free from the small alcove beneath, grunting at how heavy it was. I didn't know how much time I would have, so I quickly unzipped the unfamiliar Adidas gym bag and gasped internally.

Holy fuck. *Holy FUCK.*

The bag was filled with money, layers and layers of $20 bills, held together with thick beige rubber bands. Not crisp bills from the bank either; unless Dad had recently made a cash sale of a critical piece of equipment – and last I checked we still had a stove to cook on – the crumpled bills were definitely blood money. Pieces were starting to fall into place.

Sometime, somehow, Dad got into bed with Georgio and had been laundering his money. That much was pretty clear. But when? He had said "years" last night to Georgio's muscle. Why?

Where had the bag come from? I had been watching the door religiously all day and I didn't recall seeing anyone with a gym bag, let alone a gym bag *full of money*.

HOW did I miss this?

All of a sudden, I was filled with a deep and engulfing righteous anger. When the fuck was he going to come clean with me about this? When the papers were signed and the diner was officially in my name? I had a *right* to know the kind of shit I was signing my life away for. Didn't he realize he had made my death bed too, if I didn't comply when I took over? What if I flat-out refused? Could a man even refuse Georgio, or did Dad's declaration last night put a massive target on our backs?

Did Mom know about this? I couldn't decide which was worse – for her to be in on the crime, or Dad keeping it from her too. I was furious now for several reasons, and I needed to calm down while I considered my options.

I took several deep breaths and collapsed into the creaky gray office chair. I could confront Dad right now, this instant, but what if there was more he was hiding? A sense of unease grew deep in the pit of my stomach. I couldn't trust him, I realized.

My father and mentor of twenty-four years, the man who had shaped me into the person I was today, had been lying to me; not a little white lie, or a series of lies, but a 'Boardwalk Empire,' highly illegal, 'get-you-sent-to-prison' kind of lie.

I scrubbed both palms over my face and let out a long sigh. There had to be a legitimate explanation, I reasoned. In order to get it from him, I would have to have more evidence. Something concrete he couldn't deny and wash away with excuses.

I zipped up the bag and put it back under the desk in the same position. Then I left the office quickly, relocking the door behind me. I couldn't see anyone close by, so I quickly walked down the hallway and back into the restaurant.

I was scanning the diner searching for the large frame and balding head of my father when my gaze landed on Winter pulling on her puffer coat and mittens, gearing up to face the cold November night outside.

A guy I had never seen before stood beside her, laughing at something she had said, and a stab of jealousy hit me in the gut. He was handsome in an edgy, guitarist sort of way, and I didn't miss how he moved around her, like she was the center of his universe.

My mind was stuck on how I was going to deal with Dad, but I still wanted to know who this guy was. I didn't know how to process my feelings about this new situation when the past 24 hours of my life had been a complete shit show.

"Hey Drew," she called out as she made her way back to the counter to collect her tips from the day. "Are you okay? You look like you've seen a ghost." Her concerned blue eyes gave me a once-over.

"I'm fine, just a long day with no sleep." I smiled at her in what I hoped was a reassuring way, and turned to the new guy who had trailed behind her.

"I'm Drew," I said as an introduction while I handed her the envelope of money. It had been a profitable day by the thickness of it.

"Travis." The man grinned and gave a friendly wave. "Nice to meet you, man." He leaned into Winter in a very familiar way, muttering into her ear. "Better hurry, babe, or we won't be able to get popcorn before the movie starts."

"As if," she scoffed, her smirk highlighting her whole face as she gave him a playful shove. "You should know better than to take me somewhere without feeding me. It's a very dangerous situation."

"In that case..." New-Guy Travis picked her up and put her over his shoulder in a fireman-carry as he walked out the door. "We'd definitely better hurry. I've seen you hangry, Wallace, and it would terrify a lesser man."

"Travis!" She giggled and smacked his ass as she swayed back and forth across his back, shrieking with glee. "See you tomorrow, Drew!"

I gave her an awkward wave as he carried her across the parking lot to her car, my heart sinking into my stomach with each step. I had pushed her away, on purpose, so of course she had moved on. This was what I had wanted. I was having trouble convincing myself of that fact in this moment, watching another man make her laugh and kiss her deeply before placing her in the driver seat.

If I closed my eyes and concentrated hard enough, I could still remember what those lips felt like on mine, what *she* had felt like wrapped around *me*. I was a class-A idiot.

I took my eyes off of the apparently happy couple and refocused. Idiot or not, I was going to need to do a deep dive into the diner's financial records; a full history, from the last ten years at the very least. I would need to be thorough, and I would need help doing it. I could review the numbers from a business perspective, and I had strong knowledge in all of the assets purchased over the past eight years, but I needed someone trained in reviewing data patterns and who could be discreet.

I picked up my phone and sent off a quick text, waiting anxiously for the reply. I could only hope Shane was up for the task.

CHAPTER 11

WINTER

"**A**nnnnnd you're done!" The unbelievably fit and attractive blond female trainer announced as I finished the last sequence of movements of my workout. My online Pilates class continually kicked my ass every week, along with my calves, hamstrings, ab muscles, biceps, triceps... Hell, even my fingers would hurt once Fiona, the celebrity fitness guru, had signed off for the session.

I wasn't a fitness junkie. I enjoyed the absolute bliss that came from biting into a fresh, crackling croissant or a soft, pillowy doughnut too much to claim any sort of health-nut status, but my Pilates class had been a continual saving grace for my mental health since I was a teen. Thanks to the online version, I could fit it into my school and work schedule whenever I wanted and I rarely skipped a class.

Despite my dedication, my thighs were still pocked with cellulite – thanks genetics – and my stomach held a softness that could be mitigated with a few more crunches, but it was what it was. Life was too short to focus on physical perfection, at least while I still had the ability to taste all the goodness there was in this world.

An added bonus was, come ski season, I was limber and strong enough to avoid the "first ski soreness" that always came right after the first day on the hill. Quick and I were going to hit the slopes this weekend, now that there was enough of a base to get some good runs in, and I was excited to feel the whip of wind on my cheeks and the rush of adrenaline as we careened down the mountainside at 40 miles an hour. I grinned at the thought.

We had an annual tradition of racing down the main run at top speed on our first day out. The winner had to buy the loser drinks *and* wear the pink sparkling "loser" pin on their snowsuit all season. Quick had picked it out when we were fourteen, his arrogance betting on the fact he was the semi-pro snowboard star and I the lowly intermediate skier. Despite thinking I wouldn't have a chance in hell at winning, but unable to deny my competitive nature, I agreed to the terms.

Surprisingly, I'd slipped passed him three times since that original bet, and I couldn't wait for my shot to do it again this year. The lovable, yet insufferable, pain in my ass needed a dose of humility every now and again.

I hopped up from my sweaty, worn yoga mat and surveyed my small apartment. Travis was coming over tonight, and I had scrubbed and scoured the place to make it appear I was a neat and tidy person instead of a true slob. I couldn't help it, I liked cramped and cozy spaces, surrounded by my colorful potted plants and my half-drunk teacups and books haphazardly strewn everywhere, the odd fuzzy sock or two littering the carpeted floor of my living room.

When it was this clean, my otherwise welcoming and warm apartment with its antique chairs, mismatched cushions and bohemian curtains felt cold and stark. I didn't like it, but I also didn't want Travis to be scared off by my true nature just yet. I was having too much fun with him.

Tonight, I was confident we were finally going to move forward with sex; at least, I sure hoped so. Our sexual chemistry was spine-tingling, toe-curling magic. With all the time we had spent together in the last several weeks, it was surprising we hadn't taken it farther than kissing. Fantastic, blow-your-mind, soak-your-panties kissing, but just kissing nonetheless.

Despite my apparent physical desperation, it was refreshing to spend time with someone without the sole purpose being sex. I had plenty of experience to be comfortable and confident in the bedroom, but I hadn't dated much. Quick often accused me of having "emotional intimacy" issues, and as much as I denied it, history had proven he was right, at least partially. But being with Travis felt different. I could simplify it to our intense attraction, but I was drawn to him by more than that.

For one, I couldn't remember the last time I had been this physically attracted to someone. This handsome bartender I liked to fantasize about from afar was now so much more.

Travis held himself with such confidence, commanding attention without needing to say a word, yet he could blend in the background to let someone else take the spotlight.

His eyes were permanently backlit, always shining with amusement, like he had just heard the punchline to a hilarious joke and couldn't wait to share it.

His dark, wavy hair framed his face in shadow when he ran his fingers through it, giving him this mysterious allure that called to me.

His pouty lips, his lean and muscular frame, everything about him brought all of my senses to attention.

I bit my lip as I considered my rendezvous with Drew in the storage room almost two months ago. My attraction to that man was no less real, but it was as unique as he was.

Drew made me feel safe and taken care of. Travis had this natural way of putting me at ease, making me feel completely comfortable in my own skin. Drew was the embodiment of a Hardy Boy; clean cut and well-intentioned, through and through. Travis had a nice guy persona but with a dark undertone; kind but with the capability of wickedness, and it intrigued the hell out of me. I wanted to soak up his presence, make him laugh loudly at my jokes, and hold him through life's inevitable sadness and pain.

Perhaps I wanted more from Travis than a companion and sex.

Our schedules hadn't allowed us much time together with finals for the semester starting in two weeks and him having to work extra hours at the club, so I had gone all out for my anticipated evening. My apartment was clean and shiny, I had broken out my sexiest underwear – deep purple lace, in honor of his favorite color – and had even splurged on a wax, something I hadn't bothered to do in a long time. Because ouch, and fuck the patriarchy and its expectations regarding my natural body hair.

But alas, I caved to fit the societal molds of current beauty standards, and gritted my teeth like a badass as I paid someone to bring me pain and suffering. But I'd had to admit once the deed was done, I liked the end result and I felt sexier because of it.

Damn my own brainwashing and internalized misogyny.

Travis would arrive within the hour, so I rushed through a quick shower and blow-dried my hair. I kept my makeup minimal but took five attempts to choose an outfit before settling on jeans and a light green fitted sweater, an outfit I wore every day.

I didn't know if it was a good thing Travis made me want to show him my best, or if I should just settle down and be my authentic, sloppy self. It was *because* I liked him so much that these things mattered, I reasoned. If he was a basic booty call, I wouldn't care what he thought.

There could be no confusion tonight was *not* a booty call. I had invited him over to "watch a movie," a dubious "Netflix and Chill" reference I hoped wouldn't go unnoticed. I had been fantasizing all week about exploring his sculpted body, with a particularly detailed scene of him tasting every part of me, so if he well and truly only planned on watching a movie this evening, I was going to die of need and escape to the bedroom with my favorite vibrator and a dirty audiobook.

A buzz through my apartment intercom made me freeze before my brain kicked into gear and I pressed the button to let him in. I gave one last furtive glance around the space. Finally satisfied with its appearance, I opened the door.

"Hey." My raven-haired date grinned seductively, his eyes molten in the dim light of the hallway as he leaned against the doorframe.

Before I could properly shut the door behind us, he lifted me by my hips like I weighed nothing and spun me around, slamming my body against the door. His hot mouth was on mine in a fraction of a second.

I squeaked in surprise and then instantly settled into the smoldering heat of his kiss. His tongue flicked open my lips and explored my mouth, his lip ring making an imprint on my plump flesh. My arms wrapped around his neck as he lifted me higher, wedging his thigh between my legs to pin me there, my core pulsing wickedly at the firm feel of him against me.

His strong hands groped me, my hips, my waist, my breasts. Then he cupped my cheeks with surprising tenderness. He deepened the kiss further still, until I could no longer think, just feel his presence wrapped around every part of me. All of a sudden, he pulled away. Pupils dilated and chest heaving, he grinned at me sheepishly.

"Sorry, when you said 'watch a movie,' I assumed you meant–"

I cut him off, pulling his lips back to mine, and tugged on his jacket zipper, frantically pulling it off of him and reaching for the hem of his black wool sweater.

"You-were-right," I mumbled in between frenzied kisses. "Dear God, Travis, please fuck me and put me out of my misery."

A primal growl rumbled in his chest as he picked me up fully, wrapping his strong hands around my hips as I swung my legs up to wrap around his waist. He carried me into the living room, lowered me gently onto the couch, and settled himself on top of me while never removing his soft lips from mine, kissing and nipping and sucking me into a puddle of need.

I broke the kiss to pull off his sweater, taking a moment to fully appreciate his gorgeous body. His usually kiwi-green eyes had darkened to a rustic shade of hazel, his wavy hair mussed already with a "just-fucked" look. Those features alone were enough to get my blood pumping, but no, he was so much more.

My fantasies were accurate. He *did* have a sculpted body; defined arms and chest and narrow waist, not from hours spent at the gym but through hard work and daily use. His muscular forearms featured eye-catching watercolor tattoos of two phoenixes in flight, finishing just below his elbows.

A trail of dark hair began at his belly button and disappeared beneath the black boxer band above his pants. The bulge in his pants was impressive, and my pussy clenched on nothing as I gawped at his sheer sex appeal. I was never going to see him at Bourbon & Blues again without wanting to rip his clothes off.

Travis chuckled softly as I openly stared.

"That's not very fair," he tutted with a tease. "I want to stare at you too."

With that, my own sweater was hauled gently over my arms and head and a low whistle escaped his lips.

"Purple just became my favorite for a whole other reason," he murmured with appreciation, his fingers tracing the eyelet lace before flicking open the front clasp to release my breasts.

He gently squeezed my right breast while moving his lips down to my left nipple, sucking tenderly on the hard flesh before biting softly on the tip. My body relaxed into the couch as I lost myself to the sensation. I reveled in every touch, his body fitting into mine like perfectly matched puzzle pieces.

Reaching for his buckle, I undid the belt and unbuttoned his pants, using my feet to push them down his legs. He shucked them off his feet as he reached down to do the same for me. Moving his mouth from one nipple to the other, he alternated between scraping his teeth over the sensitive skin and suckling softly.

Abruptly, he pulled away and sat up, his eyes roving over me lasciviously.

"You're even better than my wildest fantasies, beautiful. I need to taste every part of you." He licked his full lips as he took in my thong, his fingers tracing the outline of the matching eyelet lace once again.

"Normally, I'd rip these off, but they're too pretty to ruin."

Jesus.

He winked at me and bent his head, biting the band of elastic running over my left hip and tugging it down my thigh with his teeth, kissing up the shadow of my groin to do the same to the other side.

Ho-ly fuck.

I was going to self-combust, that move was so hot. My pussy gushed at the attention, wetness beading down the inside of my thigh.

"So responsive," Travis groaned as he saw the evidence of his actions. He flicked out his tongue and licked the collection of my arousal all the way up to my slick cunt.

I gasped. "Fuck." The feeling of his mouth on me shot tingles of teasing pleasure throughout my whole body.

Before I could say another word, his tongue traced up the seam of my pussy, settling on my clit. He started slow, leisurely exploring with soft licks and swirls with the flat side of his tongue before aggressively sucking in a delicious rhythm that quickly made me forget my own name. A slow pressure built low in my belly, my body aching for the delicious release just out of reach.

A finger entered me, curling into the soft inner wall and scraping along the tender nerves, causing my back to arch off the couch with a startled cry. A chuckle vibrated against my clit as another finger entered me, and the two combined set me on fire as a shockwave of pleasure burst from my core.

I cried out, my body spasming as I hurtled off the cliff so fast, I felt weightless. Travis never stopped his inner exploration as I slowly came back down to earth. As the little aftershocks took over, I pulled his face up to mine, kissed him ferociously, and tasted myself on his lips. The sharp, musky tang turned me on even more.

He shoved his boxers down and sat up, reaching for his pants pocket to pull out a foil packet. I watched him

expertly roll the condom over his beautifully thick, pierced
—

Wait, what?

"Travis!" I squeaked, snapping out of my sexually fueled
haze and outright gaping at the curved metal sticking out of
the tip of his cock.

It was a Prince Albert piercing, the bulbed metal tip
protruding from the head of his shaft, glistening with his
own arousal. My body trembled with excitement and
anticipation; I hadn't slept with anyone pierced before; I
doubted many men in Cascade Falls even had one, but I
had heard it made sex feel incredible. I could officially mark
this one off of my sexual bucket list.

As if this could get any better.

Travis just cocked an eyebrow with a deliciously sexy
smirk.

"Surprise?" He laughed, settling himself over my body
once again, nuzzling the underside of my earlobe with open-
mouthed kisses.

"Is that okay, beautiful?" he whispered huskily. "Can
my prince enter your kingdom?"

I burst out laughing at the incredibly terrible analogy.
This man's ability to be such a goof in the middle of such a
hot moment turned me on even more. His confidence was
sexy as hell, and the knowing grin he gave me in response
made my heart skip a beat.

A man who could make me laugh and come in the same
minute? I didn't stand a chance.

I took him in my palm in answer, guiding him to my
entrance, and let out a sharp gasp as he drove himself into
me in one thrust, gripping my hips so tight I knew they
would bruise. The feeling of overwhelming fullness took
over as I adjusted to his girth and another intense feeling of
pleasure shot through me; not quite an orgasm but enough

of a sensation to know it wouldn't take any time at all to get there.

Travis leaned over me again, resting his forearms on either side of me as he bent his head down to kiss me once more. Each thrust pushed me deeper into the couch cushion, my head continually banging against the armrest as he pummeled into me at a punishing pace.

Clearly all of his pent-up desire and sexual angst fueled each pounding stroke as he worked his way to his own release. He reached down and grabbed an errant couch cushion from the floor, pushing it under my hips to change the angle.

I couldn't breathe. The feeling of him between my legs was all-consuming, his weight hovering just above me. His pelvis rubbed my clit with the exact friction I needed, while his piercing continued to hit my G spot with such ferocity, I was seeing stars.

In minutes, I came apart once again, my pussy walls clenching around him with such fierceness he shouted a guttural, masculine cry, and moaned my name into my hair as he pulsed into me.

Our bodies were slick with sweat, the scent of pheromones thick in the air as our pounding heartbeats settled back into rhythm.

Travis pulled out of me and tugged off the condom, tying a knot in the latex and tossing it into the garbage. He settled in beside me, pulling my soft reading blanket from the back of the couch over us and wrapped his arms around me, burrowing his head into the crook of my neck, kissing me softly.

We could have been laying there minutes or hours; time stood still as we both came down from our high, snuggled together like spoons in a drawer.

Eventually, he spoke, his honeyed tenor filling the space that previously held comfortable silence.

"That was ..." His voice trailed off as he unwrapped his arms from my waist and turned my body into his, kissing the tip of my nose with reverence. "...*fuck*, Winter."

I took the moment to look deeply into his eyes, seeing all of the openness, the kindness, the inherently *good* man laying naked in my living room, his warmth radiating through my body and my heart.

"Yeah, you were decent too," I joked, giggling as his hooded eyes went from satisfied to indignant within a split second.

"Decent? Decent!" He whisper-shouted in mock horror. "Holy hell, Winter, here I was thinking this made the list of my top five experiences, and you shoot me in the heart like that."

"I think I need a re-do," I said seriously, my fingertips running through the length of his tousled hair. "I'm not sure this makes the list. Second time might convince me, though. What's your refractory period?" I bit my lip, a suggestive smirk taking over my face.

His eyes lit up in challenge as he flipped me over to my stomach, taking my body to new heights once more.

I awoke in a groggy haze to an incessant muffled ringing coming from the heap of clothes lying on my bedroom floor. As I shifted out of the warm den of blankets, a toned tattooed arm tightened against my stomach to pull me back in.

I smiled softly. The sweet scent of sex and sweat and something distinctively Travis – a blend of fruity shampoo and spicy aftershave – still lingered in the room.

After multiple explorations and orgasms all over my apartment, we settled into my double bed to watch reruns of *Seinfeld* before drifting off to sleep in each other's arms. It was a first for me, keeping a man in my bed to snuggle after sex.

The annoying ringing stopped abruptly, so I snuggled back into Travis for warmth. Within seconds, it started back up again, the continued sound urgently trying to reach its owner.

I glanced over to Travis' sleeping form. We had left the lights on in our slumber and he was captivating in sleep, his face void of any emotion but pure peace as he softly breathed in and out. I didn't want to shatter that peace by waking him up in the middle of the night for a phone call.

I reached over the side of the bed to grab his jeans, fumbling with the tight denim to get the still ringing phone out of his pants pocket. How he hadn't woken up yet was beyond me, given that the caller wasn't giving up. My hands landed on the bulky box of his iPhone, but then felt another, smaller block of metal. *What the hell?*

Pulling both up to the bed, the smaller box was the ringing phone – one of the old-school style flip phones elderly people used to make phone calls but nothing else – a nondescript local number flashing across the screen. The call dropped while in my hand, only to start up a mere ten seconds later.

"Travis," I murmured softly, gently shaking him awake. "Your phone is ringing."

He startled, looking around in a disoriented daze before jolting out of bed and grabbing the phone out of my outstretched hand, leaving me in my bedroom alone and confused.

I laid back down in bed and concentrated, trying to hear the conversation. Eavesdropping might be rude, but a phone call in the middle of the night was usually never for a positive reason, and I wanted to be ready in case I needed to jump in to help with – whatever it was.

Despite my best efforts, all I could make out was Travis' muffled voice through the door.

He stood in my doorway a moment later, a look of apology crossing his features.

"I'm sorry, beautiful, I have to go." He made his way over to my bed and cupped my face between his palms to kiss me gently before pulling on his clothes.

"Tonight was amazing." He smiled with warmth and an emotion I couldn't place in the depths of his green eyes. "I'll call you tomorrow, okay?"

"Is everything okay?" I searched his face for anything that might give the situation away, something to know nothing had gone terribly wrong in the time we had been tucked away in our sexual cocoon.

"Everything's fine. I just forgot something I have to deal with."

I nodded. I had been hoping for an explanation but knew I wasn't owed one, not yet anyway. I knew in my heart this was going somewhere, but one night of passion and a few dates did not constitute me knowing his whereabouts and private conversations. I would just have to trust he was telling the truth.

"I guess round six will just have to happen another day." I grinned sleepily and snuggled back into the covers of my cooling bed. "Can you turn the light off on your way out?"

"Sure thing." He leaned over and kissed my forehead, tucking me under the covers, and turned out the light as he left my apartment.

Shit. I forgot I'd have to lock the door behind him. As I climbed out of bed to do so, my sleepy thoughts clarified. Why had Travis had two phones in his pocket? Who would be calling him at this time of night? What was I missing here?

I received a text from him not two minutes later, telling me to lock the door and to "be safe." A tender smile crossed my lips.

Already he's being a protective bear.

I sent him a kiss emoji before putting my phone back on the charger.

I burrowed back into my blankets. Without another thought, I drifted back to sleep, lost in a dreamland between two handsome men.

CHAPTER 12

SHANE

"Shaaaaaaaaaaaaane!" My sister came barreling out of my parents' living room and launched herself at me like a feral jungle cat.

"Hey sis." I grunted on impact, her tiny form surprisingly blunt as she wrapped her arms around me and my many shopping bags into a bear hug.

I hadn't been home in a while. Between ski school starting back up, finals for the semester, working at the firm, and working through my relationship, or lack thereof, I hadn't put much effort into anything else. Mom was starting to notice.

Thanksgiving dinner for the Quicksilvers was not the same traditional fare of most American households. Given the nature of the meal and the history of our peoples, it certainly wasn't a celebration of sorts, but our family had adopted it as a way to give thanks to each other for their presence in our lives, and to thank nature for its abundance.

My father was the first to go to university and was not only the first in our family, but the first person of our people accepted into a higher education program. He worked hard to provide the same opportunities for me.

I was grateful for everything I was given, and luckily for me, I actually felt the pull to carry on the family legacy on my own, rather than being pressured into a career I would hate.

My sister seemed to be on the same path for success, although she planned on pursuing art history, already studying hard for her SATs despite having two years to prepare.

"Where's Winter? Is she still coming?" Shiloh looked at me hopefully, her jet-black bangs sweeping across her face.

Despite having a fantastic older brother, she had always wanted a sister, and Winter was 'adopted' into the family by the time we were eight for that reason alone. Having no siblings herself, Winter had taken to the role of older sister pretty well, which was heartwarming on most days but a major pain in my ass when they ganged up on me. Usually the case at Thanksgiving dinner.

"She's coming, kiddo. Darren and Miranda are in Washington for a conference."

I sighed internally at that, frustrated on Winter's behalf her parents weren't around for another holiday. Again. It's why we had started having her over for dinner in the first place all those years ago. Miranda traveled the world for her work, and Darren was always visiting tech schools across the globe to recruit new talent for the firm. For a couple that desperately wanted a child, they weren't around much to watch her grow up.

Shiloh squealed in delight, leaving me in the foyer carrying four bags of groceries — *thanks for the help* — and rushed into the kitchen.

I shrugged out of my winter coat and kicked my boots off, happy to be in the home I grew up in, with all of its familiarity and memories enveloping me with each step down the hall. It wasn't a big, lavish house; it would fit into almost every northwestern suburb in America. Two stories, two car garage, brick and clapboard facade. It was a Quicksilver haven and I loved it.

"Hey, sweetie." My tiny five-foot nothing mother stretched up on her tiptoes to give me a kiss on the cheek, her frazzled silver hair tickling the top of my chin.

I dropped the groceries on the counter and scooped her up into my arms, spinning her around; her laughter made my heart sing.

"Hey, Mom." I put her down gently, careful not to jostle her bad leg.

She had been in a major car accident six years ago and still couldn't make it through the day without her cane, despite years of rehab and physical therapy. The whole right side of her body had been temporarily paralyzed, so it was a medical miracle she was able to gain control of her muscle movements at all. I hoped Shiloh had been helping her with the meal.

A sudden feeling of guilt threatened to choke me as I recognized I hadn't come home last night to give her more support.

I'll do better.

"What can I do to help?" I started unpacking the groceries and putting them in the pantry. The overwhelming scent of cedar plank salmon and fresh bread made my mouth water and my stomach grumble.

"You can start by helping Shiloh set the table. Is Winter bringing her sweet potato dish again?"

"Maybe it'll be cooked through this time!" Shiloh's braces-clad mouth grinned widely at the memory of last year's dinner.

The traditional marshmallow sweet potato casserole Winter had brought last year was mushy on the outside, rock hard on the inside, and somehow managed to taste like Easter peeps candy and vinegary turnips. My Snowflake was a lot of things, but a good cook wasn't one of them.

Admittedly, between the two of us, we regularly cleaned out the frozen food section at the grocery store, neither of us having much skill in the kitchen. We needed to add someone to our duo with cooking skills.

I winced internally, thinking of Blaise. That man had created masterpieces in my kitchen wearing only an apron and the little chef hat I had bought for him as a joke. Sexy and skilled, and he didn't want me.

Fuck me, I've got to move on with my life.

"Don't let her hear a word of that," Mom scolded, hands on her hips. "It's sweet that she wants to contribute."

The woman who notices everything turned around to face me and lowered her voice, her honey eyes quizzical and concerned.

"How are you doing, honey? I know you've been struggling. Are you taking your pills?"

I grimaced, not in the mood to talk about Blaise or my mental health issues, but also knowing I wouldn't be able to shake her off.

"I'm fine, Mom. The adjustment is hard and we work together. I can't just walk away and never see him again. And it's not like there was a big blow-up or anything. We just... don't fit." I ran my hands through my dark hair left to hang freely across my shoulders today. "And, yes, I'm taking my pills. I always take my pills. Are you taking yours?"

I turned the tables on her, not wanting to continue a conversation focused on me, and looked pointedly at her. She had a habit of ignoring her pain pills and suffering through the day, claiming the pills made her brain fuzzy and her body lazy. As if chronic pain couldn't do the same.

"Yes, dear." She gave me a soft smile that failed to reach her eyes, and I knew she was lying, but I let it drop. Today was about connection, not an interrogation.

Shiloh and I had just completed our task, all of the porcelain dishes set out on the walnut table as Winter walked into the dining room, her hair covered in melting snowflakes.

"Win!" Shiloh barreled her over with a clinging koala hug just like she had done to me, and Winter laughed with good humor as she detached herself from Shi's suction-like grip and placed her — likely terrible — casserole in the middle of the table.

"Hey, Snow." I pulled her into my arms for my own hug and kissed the top of her head. "Glad you could make it."

She squeezed me tightly, tilting her glistening auburn head up to look into my eyes. "I'm just glad you guys keep inviting me. I would have to cook my own Thanksgiving dinner otherwise."

Her tone was light, but I could hear the longing behind her words. She never spoke about her loneliness growing up. She didn't have to. I had been around to see it firsthand and had tried to fill in the gaps where I could.

I grinned down at her, keeping my voice upbeat to match hers.

"Yeah, you'd definitely starve. I didn't think Delissio made turkey dinners now."

She gave me a playful shove, her blue eyes dancing with laughter despite the pout on her face.

"Shi, you make sure he wears his loser pin this year, okay? Wouldn't want to catch him cheating, *again*." An evil smirk dotted her lips as she reminded me of my loss on the hill for the hundredth time this week.

"Oooooh, you won!?" Shiloh squealed in delight, clapping her hands together triumphantly. "Funny, he failed to mention that."

"I'm sure he did." Winter quirked her eyebrows at me suggestively. "It's about time someone taught this guy a lesson. Don't let him forget it, okay?"

She winked at my little sister conspiratorially before turning to my mother for a bear hug of her own.

"It's nice to see you, Amelia."

My mother had always been a safety net for Winter. She was devastated when Mom got hurt, spending most days after school with me at the house helping to take care of her and Shiloh while Dad was running the firm with Darren. The two started a soft conversation in the kitchen while I went to find him in his study.

Dad had learned years ago that helping Mom in the kitchen was not appreciated or encouraged. He mostly got in the way and annoyed my mother to no end, so he had been officially barred from holiday cooking duties ever since we were little. On the flip side, he cleaned up the aftermath every time, so she was getting the better end of that deal.

He was standing at his large drafting table in the corner of the room, his gray eyes much like my own focused on a massive set of construction drawings, a disarray of manila files littering the floor.

"Hey, son."

At a matching height, with the same build, jawline, and facial features, I was the spitting image of my father. His dark hair had streaks of gray and his brow was lined with deep wrinkles, but we could pass for brothers on most days.

"I have a conference call with Darren and Camden after dinner that I'd like you to sit in on."

"On Thanksgiving? That's weird, isn't it?"

He looked up from the drawings and shrugged his broad shoulders. "We have the deadline for the bridge tender coming up, you know that. Time is money, and we both know Camden will do anything to save a dime."

He cracked a good-humored smile at that, leaving the drawings and walking toward me, his calloused hand outstretched for a handshake. I ignored his hand and wrapped my arms around him in an embrace instead. He stiffened, then chuckled and hugged me back, somewhat begrudgingly. Outward signs of affection were not his style, but I didn't care. If you couldn't hug your parents, who could you hug?

We made our way to the dining room and settled into our usual seats before starting the traditional Thanksgiving prayer of our people. It was a beautiful piece passed down from our ancestors for hundreds of years, and I loved hearing it.

After a good ten minutes of thanks — our people were nothing if not thorough — Dad closed the prayer.

"We give thanks to all that gives us life,
May our hearts be open,
Our burdens be lifted,
Our stomachs be filled,
Our will be calmed,
Our bodies be strengthened,
Our energy restored.
We give thanks to the one earth that is in us all."

We tucked in to a truly delicious dinner and conversation flowed easily.

Sure enough, Winter's dish had succumbed to the same fate as last year's. Maybe it was supposed to taste like that? I ate it with a smile – at least I hoped my grimace came off as a smile — and drowned my taste buds in a dark ale as a chaser.

When dessert was served, Shiloh had to open her big mouth.

"I miss Blaise. Do you think you guys will get back together?"

I shot daggers into her maple brown eyes, willing her to shut up. My sister was fucking clueless sometimes.

Mom, ever the peacemaker, quickly chimed in. "I'm sure Shane doesn't want to talk about that, honey. Would you like more dessert?"

Dad visibly stiffened at the statement, and my stomach turned over, far too uncomfortably, given how stuffed I was.

"Yes, maybe he'll want to try dating a girl this time. A nice girl, like Winter."

I choked on my sip of beer, gasping for air as Winter hit me on the back with her palm, my dinner threatening to come up at both of his comments.

"I don't think you need to be concerned about that, Emmett." Winter smiled, placatingly, rubbing my knee reassuringly under the table. "I'm searching for a nice, quiet, short, bald guy. Really the opposite of Shane in every way!"

That drew a laugh from the table, and I snorted, grateful for her diversion from my father's not-so-subtle lack of understanding. It was a work in progress, but still a painful gap between us.

He had all but ignored my preferences since I came out as a teenager, but he couldn't help throw out a passive aggressive barb every now and then when my chosen relationship was with a man.

He liked Blaise as a person, certainly well enough to bring him on for this project with Eccles; he just didn't want that person dating me. Or me dating him, more accurately. Really, anyone with a penis.

I hoped with enough time and consideration, he would understand this was a part of who I was and not a youthful experiment. We weren't there yet.

After dinner, with thankfully no more awkward conversations to navigate, we made our way back to the study for the meeting. I was so full I could barely move as I settled into the large armchair in front of a series of computer monitors on my father's desk. The computer screen split into four squares and Camden and Darren popped up in unison, having already started the discussion.

"Oh good, Emmett, you're here," Camden's gruff voice filled the room, authoritative and no-nonsense as always. "I was just discussing the projected construction costs for the project before we have to submit on Tuesday. I was speaking with Georgio and I —" He cut off abruptly, noticing me for the first time. "What is Shane doing here?"

"Shane is here at my request, Camden," Dad challenged Camden's brusque tone with one of his own. "He's been involved in the project for years and I'm showing him the other side of the business – a side of the business we anticipate he'll play an active role in when he graduates. Do you have any issues with that?" He hated his decisions being questioned. I didn't know how he and Camden worked together without killing each other.

"Fine, fine." Camden waved a hand in the air, dismissively. "But I think it's best for all of us if we continue this conversation with Stanley and Logan in private, once we review the logistics, yes? Darren?"

Darren, his short salt-and-pepper hair and familiar blue eyes looked up from whatever he was doing on his phone and gave me a small smile. "Hi Shane. Yes, that's fine with me."

Stanley and Logan? Stanley I could understand, we were partnering with Eccles, but why was Logan involved again? Something wasn't adding up here. Unless Logan was way more important at Eccles than I thought him to be, he was a business guy, not an engineer, or even a project manager. I failed to see how he was valuable here. I didn't think Logan was valuable in any situation, though, so I was biased.

Fucking twat.

We continued to go through mundane project details and deadlines before I was asked to leave the conversation to bring in the others. Dad gave me an appreciative look as I got up to leave, closing the door behind me. I couldn't just walk away though; after weeks of suspicious activity, I had to know what was going on. I hung around outside the door, listening in to the muffled voices through the hollow wood. They were faint, but I could get the gist of most of it.

"—*Georgio needs assurances that he'll have what he needs to proceed with the work.*" Camden, I think. Probably Camden, given he's the only one in cahoots with Carlos Construction.

"—*give assurances when he's giving us nothing in return.*" Logan, definitely Logan's entitled twat voice.

"—*agreed to keep the connection private.*" Darren.

"—*will make us very rich, what other assurances do you want?*" Stanley? Maybe Camden.

"—*start-up cash for other enterprises. – financial backer, not partner.*" Dad. Definitely Dad.

"—*already too deep, - can't back out now without consequences. – hired protection for -*" Logan.

"—*grease the right palms. - already done.*" Camden? Stanley? They sounded too similar through the door.

"—*questionable legalities. – protected?*" Darren?

I wasn't able to hear the answer to that, or the muffled partial answer, anyway. Shiloh's voice carried down the hall as she and Winter turned the corner to her room. I straightened quickly and ducked into my old room, now the guest bedroom, before I could get caught shamelessly eavesdropping.

Sitting on the white duvet, I ran my hands through my dark strands. Whatever this was, it didn't sound good. It certainly didn't sound legal. Drew had texted me last week, asking for my help to go through some financial information for the diner, Georgio's name front and center in Drew's suspicions of money laundering. I had gone through a few spreadsheets from over a decade ago, but I hadn't found anything out of the ordinary. At least, not yet.

Were all of our parents caught up in Georgio's shit? What even *was* Georgio's shit? We had nothing to go on but questionable conversations and mysterious money popping up, but it was time to get serious and find out.

I took out my phone and texted Drew.

Shane: *New development with GC. Let's meet up this weekend.*

Drew: *Diner, Saturday night. We can go through the system. I'll bring dinner.*

Shane: **thumbs up emoji**

I put my phone away and went to interrupt whatever Shiloh and Winter were up to. I had a feeling my life was about to get a lot more interesting.

CHAPTER 13

WINTER

"**A**t laaaaaaast," I sang into the retro microphone, starting the last verse to the final song of our set. My love for Etta James carried me through as I put my all into her beautiful music, the words and melody transcending time.

As I crooned one of the most soul-stirring songs ever written, I couldn't help but ogle the sexy bartender serving guests and sending me outrageously dirty looks at every opportunity. Since we had finally broken the sex seal, it had been incredibly difficult to keep our hands of each other. It was cringy behavior more worthy of horny 15-year-olds, but I fucking loved it.

I caught his eye when he leaned against the black granite bar top and I put an extra sway in my hips and sultry tone in my voice. Reaching into his pocket, he pulled out a red tootsie roll lollipop, popping it into his mouth between his sinful lips. He sucked on the candy, his eyes wickedly suggestive.

Fuck me.

He ran his hands through the longer wavy locks of dark hair on the top of his head and then started to slowly unbutton his shirt sleeves, rolling them up his arms to expose those beautiful tattoos. This man was playing dirty.

I don't know what his workout routine was, but even from this distance I could see how his shoulders and biceps filled out his shirt. He wasn't bulky or ripped in the traditional Men's Health Magazine way, but his lean body was solid. It was masculine and protective, and hotter than hell.

He continued to roll the Tootsie Pop between his teeth, his full lips sensually sucking in ways I knew intimately. I felt my body flush and my underwear became a whole lot less dry. I tried to subtly squeeze my thighs together for some brief relief. We weren't able to hang out tonight after the show since Travis worked the late shift, but I wondered if Basil could handle a backseat quickie in the dark parking lot on his break.

I belted out the final few notes of the song and waited for the applause to die down as the house lights brightened to signal the end of the set.

"That's all for tonight, ladies and gentlemen. Thank you for listening to the Mellowtones!"

I flashed my best performance smile to our sold-out crowd and walked off stage, my red backless silk dress slinking around my calves. Once behind the thick velvet curtains, I made a beeline for the staff washroom just down the hall of the backstage Green Room. After that little sexy showdown with Travis, I needed to freshen up before cleaning out my dressing room table for the night.

The staff bathroom was just as luxurious as the guest washrooms. Georgio never seemed to half-ass anything — there was no "toilet in a broom cupboard" here like at the diner. The walls were embellished with shimmery cream and gold damask wallpaper; the towel bars, mirrors, and accessories were all gold plated; and a small crystal chandelier hung from the ceiling.

I was leaning over the marble countertop to splash some cool water on my blazing cheeks when the door handle jiggled.

"Occupied," I called out, hoping for a few moments of peace to gain some composure. Other washrooms were down the hall if they were desperate.

The door handle jiggled more insistently this time, and irritation crept up my neck. I was coming down from my performance high, I was horny as hell, and this asshole wasn't leaving me alone.

I yanked the door open, about to chew out the mannerless prick, when Travis barged through the space, picked me up by my thighs and kicked the door closed behind him. I squeaked in surprise, too stunned to react as he spun me around. My back hit the solid door with a thump while his mouth captured mine in bruising kiss. He tasted like the sweet and tart cherry of the Tootsie Pop, my favorite flavor.

His mouth trailed hot kisses down my neck. I managed to catch my breath long enough to speak.

"We've got to stop meeting like this, you know. I'll never be able to open my door without expecting an orgasm."

His deep, throaty laugh vibrated through my shoulder when he bit the soft skin and ran his tongue over the mark with a lazy, sensual kiss.

"I've wanted to rip this dress off of you from the moment you walked out on that stage tonight." His words came out on a panted growl, the need in them raw and evident.

Without warning, he spun me again, dropping my legs down to the floor and pinning me against the washroom vanity counter, my back to his front.

His kiwi-green eyes caught mine in the reflection of the mirror; his gaze gleamed with pure lust and his lips were red and swollen from our frantic kisses. If I hadn't already been hot and bothered, I would have self-combusted by now.

He traced my breasts through the soft fabric, kneading them until my nipples were at risk of cutting through it. Moaning softly, I relaxed into his strong arms, loving the heat of his body against mine; the feel of his erection digging into the small of my back. I loved that I affected him in the same way he affected me.

I felt wanted; worshipped and powerful.

His hands slid down to my waist, caressing my hips, and down to the hemline of the fringe of my dress. He hesitated, his eyes searching mine as if asking for permission. I wiggled my hips into the length of him behind me in invitation and raised a perfectly filled-in eyebrow at him.

"Don't stop now, Travis," I chided him, breathlessly. "You can't tease if you won't deliver."

The look he gave me was pure fire as he roughly yanked my skirt up and palmed my bare ass cheeks. He paused with his gaze steady on mine through the mirror.

Our fixation was primal; predatory. I could pretend to be his prey, but we both knew I was his equal in this jungle.

"Is that what I'm doing to you, beautiful? Am I teasing you?"

His fingers gently trailed down the line of soaked fabric barely covering my pussy, rubbing gently over the outline of my opening.

I groaned, wishing I didn't feel the need to push him and endure this torture, but I relished in it and knew my sweet relief at his hands would be worth the wait.

"Nope, I'm just not that interested, sorry." My retort came out on a very shaky breath, and even the fly on the wall knew it was a blatant lie.

A wicked smirk filled his face and he ripped the lace aside, plunging two fingers into me. He immediately curled them inwards, going for gold by striking my G spot with deadly accuracy, causing my whole body to quake in pleasure.

"How about now?"

His teeth nipped the sensitive patch of skin behind my earlobe, scraping his lip ring across my flesh. His thumb brushed my clit in light circles over the fabric still covering it. I almost collapsed in his arms at the touch.

"Nope," I croaked out. My legs trembled when he added a third finger. The pressure and perfectly placed thrusts were driving me into madness.

"That's a shame." He winked at me, his reflection in the mirror downright dirty. Then he suddenly withdrew his fingers, popping them into his mouth to lick them clean.

Holy. Fucking. Shit.

I had truly self-combusted. My poker face sucked because there was no way I could maintain my nonchalance, if I had even succeeded in the first place. I was too busy watching my sexy bartender to worry about how my face looked.

"I guess I'll just have to break out my secret weapon, then, since my performance is so lacking. He's a prince, you know."

I snorted as he sighed theatrically, reaching into his pants pocket and pulling out a square foil packet. His eyes never left mine as he unzipped his dark jeans, tugging the pants and his black boxers down his thighs. He was about to open the condom wrapper when I decided to take my power back.

"Are you clean, Travis?" My voice was sultry; soft and suggestive.

He visibly gulped, one hand on his impressive, pierced cock, completely taken by surprise at the question. He paused, staring into me with an honesty that couldn't be faked.

"Yes."

"So am I. I've been tested recently and I hate those things."

I had gotten tested right after Drew, as a just in case. I trusted him, but one could never be too careful. I waved at the condom dismissively.

"You can use it if you want, but not on my account."

He knew I had an IUD, so that wasn't worth mentioning again. His eyes turned a deep emerald, his dark eyelashes flashing as he threw the condom wrapper to the floor.

In one fluid movement, he bent me over the counter with one hand on my back, the other on my hip; he lined up perfectly and drove into me with one beautifully agonizing deep thrust until he bottomed out inside me.

The hours of foreplay on stage made our movements frenzied. I hauled the dress up further and pushed my hips back into each thrust, forcing him to go deeper. His Prince Albert piercing rubbed deliciously across all of my nerve endings, enhancing each thrust to the point of oblivion.

My body was taut, strung so tight, and the tingling warmth started low in my belly. I was so, so, deliciously close.

"I looked up period play, you know," Travis whispered into my ear, his breaths harsh and labored. "And we are definitely doing that."

That did it. The thought of Travis wanting to dive into the exciting and erotic world of dirtier sex with me pushed me over the cliff.

He clamped his hand over my mouth as I cried out. The hot wave of incredible bliss filled all of my limbs as he continued to drive into me, lengthening the pleasure. Seconds later, his entire body shuddered and hot spurts of his cum filled me. His body collapsed over mine as our breaths evened out, our heart rates coming back down.

Travis slowly stood up, a lazy, languid grin filling his face. His eyes sparkled, and I turned around to see the real image in front of me, not the reflection.

He was so breathtakingly beautiful, sporting his post-sex glow. Despite me not even touching it, his hair had the rumpled "just fucked" look, his cheeks were pink, and his lips puffy, his black lip ring sticking out on a slight angle.

I took a picture with my mind to go back to later.

I had slept with hot men before. Many hot men if I were being honest. But Travis — he had this spark I hadn't experienced with anyone else. He lit me up like a bonfire, knowing just what to throw on the fire to make me burn, and the sex was mind-blowing. Abso-fucking-lutely mind-blowing.

Travis held me by the chin and kissed me reverently, saying so many things in that one gesture that we couldn't speak out loud. I knew he felt it too, this connection. There weren't words for it yet, but there might be someday.

He grabbed some of the luxurious cotton napkins from a gold decorative tray on the counter and ran them under warm water. He cleaned me up gently before taking care of himself and putting his clothes back in order.

"You may not be able to watch my performances anymore," I joked, as we snuck out of the bathroom and walked down the hall toward the backstage area. "Colin's going to kill you if you disappear on him every set change."

"Colin's fine," Travis scoffed, as he wrapped me in his arms for a goodbye kiss. "But yes, I should get back before he makes all of my tips tonight."

He kissed me lightly on the nose, deeply on the mouth, and then gently on my temple. "I'll text you later."

I watched him disappear through the thick green curtains and quickly threw all of my makeup and change of clothes into my purse before heading down the private hall toward the staff entrance.

"Winter?" An unfamiliar voice called my name down the hall, and when I turned, I nearly gasped out loud.

Georgio was walking toward me with Tom by his side, a beaming smile on his handsome face.

I had never actually been formally introduced to the man before. Tom had hired us to play gigs and, technically, he had never hired me at all – Raven already had a singer when they were hired, and I had been the replacement.

Of course, I had seen him around his club, and everyone in this area knew who the man was, but I didn't think he would know me. Why would he? I was a lowly college singer performing one set a week for $100 and two free drinks; hardly someone of importance to know.

When he reached me, he held out his hand to shake. "It's nice to officially meet you, Winter. Tom here has been telling me all about you. I managed to watch your performance this evening, and I am very impressed."

"Thank you, sir," I stuttered out the words, truly in shock this was happening. What a weird and unexpected Thursday I was having.

He held out a gold embossed business card to me containing the name Janet Lindross and a phone number and email.

"This is my personal assistant's contact information. If you're ever interested in taking on additional work for me, please don't hesitate to call."

Was he… propositioning me? The look on my face must have betrayed my inner thoughts because he laughed loudly, a knowing grin overtaking his face.

"For service or performance jobs strictly, Winter. You're an attractive woman and I hear you're already a server. You could make great money here with those attributes."

He was surprisingly stoic with this statement, not a hint of lechery or sleaziness in his tone or on his face. The man had the most unsettling way of putting you at ease, while making you deeply uncomfortable at the same time.

"Thank you, sir. I'll certainly consider it." I smiled at him politely as he nodded and turned to go back down the hallway.

"Oh, Winter?" Georgio called out as I stood dumbly by the door. "Don't tie up our best bartender during set change next week, please? I have a business to run."

I blushed a deep crimson to match my dress and hurriedly left the building, sinking into Basil's comforting warmth as I came down from my orgasm high and that odd encounter with the most powerful man in the state. My life was just getting weirder.

CHAPTER 14

TRAVIS

I woke up to the sound of retching in the toilet bowl, the small bathroom in our trailer directly across from my bedroom. I groaned into my pillow, not thrilled at being woken up from an incredibly dirty dream featuring a certain auburn-haired vixen, but equally pissed my brother was on another bender.

"Dev," I called out, struggling to lift my head from the pillow. "Are you okay, man?"

The lack of response was concerning, but not unusual. If he was at puke stage than he likely wasn't at coherent stage anymore. I had gone through this with him far too many times to count. Despite the many stints of rehab, no amount of therapy stuck. I couldn't think of two more terrible diseases than the ones my family suffered from under this roof.

"Dev?" I called out again, hoping at least for a grunt of acknowledgment to put my mind at ease.

I should have known this weekend would be a bad one. Dad walked out on us on Thanksgiving when we were just little kids, and Dev had taken the abandonment the hardest. Thanksgiving dinner was usually the Drunken Devon Show, when he pushed his liver and my mother's patience to their limits. It was why I hadn't invited Winter over; I really didn't want her to see that.

Fuck. No answer. I shifted my weight and pulled myself out of bed, the warm covers calling out to me as I stumbled my way to the bathroom in a sleepy haze, hoping he was all right so I could get a few more hours of rest before starting the day.

My hopes of a mild alcohol poisoning episode were dashed when I opened the bathroom door.

"Devon!"

I rushed to the small toilet, taking in the blood, so much blood, covering the toilet bowl and his head. I had learned the signs of a drug overdose through Devon's many experimentations, and excess blood like this was not one of them.

My eyes landed on a wide misshapen gash on his forehead, and the imprint of the same shape along the side of the porcelain toilet bowl. It was going to need stitches, for sure. Provided I could keep him alive that long.

He groaned, a deep pained sound, and his chest rose and fell rapidly, his breathing ragged and disjointed.

"Devon! Open your eyes, man. Can you hear me?" I slapped his face as gently as I could but hopefully hard enough to jolt him awake. His eyes remained closed, his heart pounding beneath his ribcage.

He was having a heart attack or a stroke, I was sure of it.

I ran to my room to grab my phone to call for an ambulance. We didn't have health insurance, and I couldn't get Mom to pay for an ambulance on top of everything else she was struggling with, but I had another option I always carried in my back pocket. An option that screwed me more than anybody, but these were the kinds of things you did for family. I wasn't confident I wouldn't hurt him by lifting him in this state.

I held him gently in my arms on his side in case he puked again, so he wouldn't choke, and stroked his blood crusted hair. My heart ached for my little brother, the man who couldn't get out of his head and into his life.

"What did you take, Dev? What pushed you to do this to yourself this time?" I murmured into his hair, keeping a close eye on his breath and pulse rate as I held him close.

I was getting covered in blood and who knows what else, but thankfully his fear of needles was a saving grace in this situation. I knew I wouldn't find any on the floor and I was banking on the fact he hadn't contracted any blood-borne diseases since the last time he had a screening at the clinic. It was no joke, loving and caring for an addict.

"Travis?" A soft voice called out from the other side of the trailer. "What's going on?"

Mom's room was on the other side of our small home, and she likely couldn't hear much over the whir of the machines by her bedside. Thank God for small miracles.

"I've got to get Devon to the hospital, Mom. He's – not well." My voice cracked at the lie, but I was confident she couldn't tell in the dim light of morning within her own sleep-smothered haze.

Mom had a blind spot when it came to Devon. She refused to see how much he was hurting and colored her stories of his rehab as "an adolescent with a penchant for drinking."

Right.

She had been a nurse before going off work for her own health issues, so she knew better. I loved the woman more than anyone on this earth, but I also resented her for never being the firm hand we needed to get Devon's issues resolved at the early stages. When a sixteen-year-old was caught doing cocaine in the school bathroom on a Tuesday afternoon, that wasn't "rah-rah, party-time" behavior.

The great irony became I was stuck doing a job for a man I hated in order to cover Devon's expenses for the ongoing – and seemingly useless – help he needed, by offloading the proceeds of such drugs sales in the first place. It made me feel disgusting and dirty, yet I couldn't see a way out. I could justify my behavior six ways from Sunday, but I was no innocent man here.

The paramedics arrived four minutes later, their mobile overdose unit taking a tox screen of his blood right then and there. Due to the skyrocketing increase in overdose deaths over the past few years, the local healthcare authority implemented the new unit in hopes it could save more lives on the spot. I was saying a prayer to every god who would hear me that Devon would benefit from that tonight.

Thirty minutes later, Devon had been pumped full of medical counter-agents and was stable enough to be taken to the local hospital for further examination.

The culprit? Opioids and methamphetamine. The crazy kid was hopped up on both. The paramedics' best guess was he continued to take more of each because the two combined couldn't create the "desired effect."

I was at a loss here. Four rehab stints at a cost of thousands of dollars a pop, money I sold my soul to pay for.

No amount of counseling or talk therapy had worked. This man was determined to die in his misery and take me along with him.

I rubbed my palms over my face, thoroughly exhausted from both the surprise adrenaline-fueled wake up and this whole Groundhog Day situation. I wasn't able to protect him any more. I had to come to terms with that.

I walked into the house and moved to my mother's bedroom. Her usually delicate face was etched with worry lines, the wisps of her thinning, graying hair falling around her cheekbones.

"He's going to be okay." I breathed out and, just like that, I deflated like a released balloon. I hadn't realized the tension in my body until I collapsed on her bed. The unreleased tears were burning through my eye sockets.

"Your brother is strong, Travis, he just needs some time to adjust. His drinking problem will get better."

I failed to comment, so spent by the ordeal I didn't have it in me to argue or explain for the fiftieth time Devon's issues could not be reduced to a simple "drinking problem." It didn't matter anyways. Stress was a killer for autoimmune diseases, and I wouldn't be the one to add to her stress tonight, even if it wasn't my actions causing her harm.

Mom held my hands for what seemed like hours as I just lay there, lost in my own feelings of guilt, fear, and futility over Devon, her illness, and my lack of a promising future. By the time I got my thoughts together, she had fallen back to sleep, her wrinkled hands hanging limp in my own. I kissed her brow gently and tucked her beneath the covers, knowing my day ahead wouldn't be a fun one.

"I'm going to need another job to make some quick cash."

I was seated in Georgio's stereotypical "mob-boss" cherry-paneled office on the upper level of Bourbon & Blues, an hour before my shift was to start on the legitimate side of the business.

Georgio, who, despite my hate for all that he stood for, had been nothing but accommodating given my set of circumstances. He steepled his fingers and assessed me critically from behind the large desk separating us.

"What did he do this time?" It wasn't a question of who the money was for, Georgio was aware of my situation. In fact, he had banned a few of the local dealers from selling to Devon, an act both confusing and relieving at the same time.

"Overdose. I have to pay for the ambulance and the hospital bill."

I was keeping my responses short and to the point. I hated leaning on this man for financial support, but I had nowhere else to turn, and Georgio always delivered.

If he wasn't the leader of a crime syndicate, I might have liked him. I had never seen him be cruel or even rude, and he presented himself professionally in every encounter. He was never lewd to the female staff downstairs, and I rarely even heard him swear.

There was the unsettling feeling in my gut, though. Georgio was a wolf in sheep's clothing, so I was always on guard around him. I was a sitting duck, but maybe I could protect myself in the reeds a bit better – or something. I wasn't great at analogies.

Georgio sighed and leaned forward in his chair. "I'll need you to take on the Cascade Falls route permanently. The previous runner is no longer with us."

Yup, definitely a wolf.

I'd have to be even more careful around Georgio Carlos if I knew what was good for me.

"I've got a few events coming up downstairs," he continued thoughtfully, removing non-existent lint from his perfectly tailored suit. "You could bartend for me there, and keep an eye out for any suspicious customers."

I quirked a brow. "Suspicious customers?"

I knew what he was referring to. "Downstairs" meant the lower-level fighting set-up only accessible through a hidden panel in a side room at Bourbon & Blues. He hosted fight nights there once a month, and rumor had it high rollers from other areas of the state came in to place bets on the fighters. Thousands of dollars changed hands through the evening.

The only indication they were happening on a club night was the beefed-up security inside and outside the building. If you concentrated hard enough, you could hear the muffled sounds of cheering below over the din of music.

"Yes, the police have been upping their interests in my businesses. We've got to protect ourselves from any wayward customers who shouldn't be there. We can't afford to have anyone caught red-handed, can we?"

The threat was clear. By "we" he meant "me." *I* couldn't afford fancy lawyers and post bail of any sort, unlike him and his associates. If he was going down, I was going down; all of the desperate guys who were just trying to get a leg up in a truly shitty situation would go down. The working poor didn't stand a chance in this country.

"The first fight you can work is New Year's Eve. There will be some important people at this event, and I'll need all the extra eyes and ears we can get. You in?"

It wasn't a choice and he knew it. I swallowed all of my pride, my convictions and every screaming feeling in my gut telling me 'no', and reached out to shake his hand.

"I'll do it. Thank you, sir."

I walked out of his office feeling sick to my stomach and cursing my brother, my mother, my dead-beat father, and all of the shitty choices I made in my life that led me to this fucked up situation.

I brightened suddenly, remembering I would see Winter in a few hours. At least I could end this day on a high note.

"Definitely salt and vinegar," Winter said emphatically as we decided on our snack selection for tonight's movie night at her place.

I didn't plan on doing a whole lot of TV watching, but she insisted we were actually going to watch it this time around.

Her favorite fantasy series had just come out with a sequel on Netflix and it was very important we watched it the very night it came out, so she wouldn't see spoilers all over the internet.

Her excitement over the simple things in life was adorable and refreshing, given my past week of trying to keep Devon alive and myself sane.

"Yuck." I made a disgusted face at her in the chip aisle. "That flavor is for old people with false teeth and no taste-buds. Sour cream and onion all the way."

"Gross. Then I'll have to suffer through onion breath when you kiss me," she joked, her eyes alight with mischief as she leaned in to grab a – currently onion-free – kiss.

"Ahhhh, the things we do for love," I teased. Immediately, I choked on my words. "I mean – that's not what I meant, I –" I stammered awkwardly, not wanting to insult her but not ready to throw the L-word out in the middle of the grocery store, regardless of how strong my feelings were becoming.

I was rapidly losing all game with this girl.

"It's okay, sweetie, I love spending time with you tooooooooo."

She intentionally made her voice breathy and high-pitched, mimicking the famous *Friends* episode where Ross's girlfriend wouldn't say "I love you" back.

I laughed with relief, grateful for her ability to make light of a potentially critical relationship error at this stage of the game, and swept her up into my arms for a fierce kiss.

She kissed me back, deeply and unabashedly, not caring we were standing in the chip aisle for everyone to see. As she pulled away, her goofy smile froze on her face, a look of fear flashing in her eyes, and her entire body stiffened as she gazed at something behind my shoulder.

I turned around, hands still on her waist, trying to see what had changed her mood almost immediately. Nothing jumped out at me, only an unassuming guy about my age dressed in chinos and a tailored wool coat, looking at the wide array of popcorn selections a few lengths over. Winter tugged my hand urgently, silently pulling me to leave as quickly and quietly as possible.

The guy looked up then, and I could see he was handsome in the classic, rich-kid sort of way; put together with confidence in his stance. He had a muscular but lean frame, sandy brown hair and light blue eyes; eyes that followed Winter's movements.

He quickly walked toward us, and Winter once again froze like a deer in headlights, her fingers gripping my hand so tightly it was starting to hurt.

"Hey, Winter." His smooth baritone said her name with intimate familiarity, like they were old friends, or even – lovers. "Long time, no see."

His previously friendly face curled into a cruel mask and a blind man could sense there was no love lost between them.

Winter took a deep, subtle breath and spoke, her words strong despite the fact she trembled beside me.

"How long are you home for, Carson? I thought Cascade Falls got rid of all its trash years ago."

He laughed, a harsh, condescending tone that instantly got my hackles up. I didn't like this guy, regardless of their history. Now he was closer, his body language screamed "entitlement."

"That's not a very nice thing to say to an old friend, Winter. I thought you'd be happy to see me. So many memories, hmmm?"

His blue eyes gave her a once over, clearly trying to make her uncomfortable.

It's virtually impossible to check someone out in a knee length puffer coat, so he'd have to use his imagination if that's what he was looking for, but the effect and intent were not lost on either of us.

"With friends like you, who would need enemies?" Winter's voice dripped with false sweetness, her nails now digging crescents into my palm. She turned to me with a pasted-on smile, her eyes pleading. "I don't want to be late, sweetie. Let's get going."

"Not going to introduce me?" Carson laughed again, as she turned on her heel and dragged me down the aisle at warp speed.

She left our basket by the door, abandoning our snack selections for some poor teenage kid to put back, and practically raced out to the car, anxiously waiting for me to unlock it.

We'd taken my car today, and the old black two-door Dodge Daytona needed to be unlocked manually. I'd call her a classic, but really, she's a piece of junk that got me from point A to point B. Right now, Winter really wanted to get to point B, wherever that was.

I unlocked the doors with my keys and we got in the car, sitting in a suffocating silence for a few minutes. She avoided eye contact and fixed her gaze on a light pole in the parking lot outside the car window, hands twisting in her lap, her body still tense and trembling. I was determined to wait her out and let her open up to me, but the silence stretched out so long I was concerned she'd never talk again, so I spoke up.

"Do you want to talk about it?" I tucked a strand of her hair behind her ear and gently tugged her chin toward me so I could see the emotion in her eyes. "Who was he?"

She let out a deep sigh, unshed tears sitting on her lower eyelids, taking a full minute before responding.

"Carson and I dated briefly in high school. Shortly after, things turned south and I ended up being bullied pretty badly by he and his friends. We had to get the school involved and I had to do summer school to make up for all of the classes I missed. I lost some friends because of it. When he went away for college, I was able to get my life back and by some miracle, I haven't had to see him since. I didn't realize – I didn't realize he would still have that effect on me."

The words opened up a dam inside her and the tears started falling. Fat drops splashed on her cheeks in a torrent. I wrapped her in my arms, held her for a while, and tried to be a comfort. Something she could hold on to so the memories wouldn't drown her.

When she had calmed, I drove out of the parking lot to her apartment. The mood of the evening was killed and she wanted to be alone. I walked her up the three flights to her door, and after a gentle kiss and a concerned "good night," I reluctantly left her to battle her demons alone.

Every fiber of my being screamed at me to go back there and cuddle the shit out of her until she fell asleep in my arms, but she had been kind, but clear she needed some space to work through the grocery store encounter.

Outside of her apartment building for a while, I sat in my car, looking up at her windows until the lights went out. My heart ached for her. I had never been bullied and I didn't know what kind of bullying had to take place for an other-wise level-headed person to run scared in a public setting years later. I hoped she would feel comfortable enough to open up to me about it someday, and we could face those demons together.

I realized in that moment I was falling in love with this woman. Just hours before, I had a mini-panic attack over accidentally inferring it. Now, after witnessing her fear and pain and wanting to be the person who took it all away, I knew it was true.

I was in love with Winter Wallace.

I let out a deep sigh, both relieved and scared shitless by that admission. I knew we were headed in this direction; I didn't need to know everything about her and her life to know my feelings were real.

I also couldn't deny that loving her complicated things. Loving her meant I would have to introduce her to Mom and own up to Devon. I would have to find a way out of Georgio's shit before it ended up ruining the best thing I've had in a long time.

Could I even dare to hope for the possibility of happiness?

Deep in thought, I pulled out of the parking lot and headed home. This was the kick in the ass I needed. I was going to find a way to save my skin and build the life I wanted. I longed for a future with someone who could soften all of the hardness around me.

I could only hope she felt the same way about me too.

CHAPTER 15

DREW

"Eureka!" Shane crowed triumphantly, fist pumping in the air like the obnoxious asshole he was. I laughed at his antics, relieved and exhausted by what we found.

I wiped my hands down my jaw, savoring the moment and wishing it didn't have to exist. After a few weeks of searching through accounting spreadsheets and computer files, Shane had found a trend of falsified inventory starting nine years ago.

Coupled with a buried computer folder that tracked the exact numbers being dumped in each month, $847,356 in total, I had all of the evidence I needed to confront Dad.

I couldn't keep the grimace off of my face. I would have to do the deed sooner rather than later. It had been hard enough keeping a straight face and a cool head around him these past couple of shifts, knowing he was outright lying.

Shane's grin immediately turned somber when he saw my expression. He put his hand on my shoulder and gave me a strong squeeze.

"I'm sorry, man. We've solved this puzzle, but I know that puts you in a whole world of shit right now."

Whole world of shit was right. I had looked up the penalty for money laundering last night. He would get a minimum of ten years, and an accomplice could get up to fourteen years.

I could get a fucking jail sentence for this shit. I was known for my levelheadedness, but every time I stopped to consider the consequences of his actions, my blood boiled.

I gave Shane a half-smile, my gaze returning to my computer as we sat in my living room, surrounded by old paper files and cardboard boxes.

"Thanks. We still have your puzzle to solve at least. I just don't know how I'm going to be able to confront Dad without decking him."

My blood heated again, and I knew that was the truth. Could someone learn how to meditate successfully in twenty-four hours? I might need to try.

Shane plopped down on the couch beside me, mismatched papers crunching underneath his considerable weight.

"It's not going to be pretty," he agreed, as he organized some of the sheets around him. "And I'll be honest, knowing what your parents are mixed up in makes me nervous about mine. I'm almost afraid of what else we'll find, you know? It's like everything in this town is tainted."

I couldn't disagree. Finding the proof my parents or Dad, at least, was mixed up in some serious criminal activity was souring the memories of my childhood in our sleepy town. Charlie would have just been born when all this started – what would make him take a risk like this?

I helped Shane get all of the papers back in order. "I'm going to do it tomorrow. We all know I'm shit at lying and I can't avoid him anymore."

It was true. I couldn't think if a single solitary instance where I had successfully hidden something of substance from anyone. I usually went with my go-to back-up plan, avoidance. I wasn't going to be able to pull that off any longer.

Shane boomed a laugh in agreement. We both grinned, and I knew he was thinking about the high school football prank where my terrible poker face had royally screwed the team.

"Hey, we can laugh about it now, right?" He winked, stuffing manila folders back into the boxes. "I don't envy you, man, but I'll do whatever I can to help."

I knew he would. The last two months had been miserable, watching Winter from afar and digging into my parents' criminal past and present, but I could admit that hanging out with Shane on a regular basis was nice. I had forgotten what it was like to have consistent guy friends around, and I didn't want to lose the feeling.

"I wouldn't have gotten this far without your help. As shitty as this is, that" — I faltered, not wanting to sound cheesy— "well, just ... thanks. I'll return the favor and we can tackle your project together. I know something will come up."

His gray eyes gleamed with mischief, and he clapped me on the shoulder. "It's okay, man. It's been great hanging out with you again. It's been a good distraction for me too, despite the circumstances. Let's keep it up, yeah?"

He took one box from the shelf and put it by the door to load up my car. We had to get all of the boxes back to the diner's storerooms before tomorrow morning. Dad hadn't noticed anything missing, yet; I doubted he visited the basement frequently. Still, better safe than sorry.

We loaded up the last of the boxes, idly chatting about Shane's snow school classes and my lack of a social life. Together, we left the house, going our separate ways into the night. Whatever happened tomorrow, it would bring more answers, and that could only be a good thing.

Right?

I walked into the diner the next morning, prepared for a day of chaos and corruption.

Winter had taken the next two days off to study for finals, and Janice had a family emergency. I was left with two junior wait staff, Carl, two line cooks, and Dad and I on the first Friday of December, when tourists and locals were officially in Christmas shopping mode.

We were going to be fucked.

I was still determined to confront Dad today, but that would have to wait until the breakfast rush was over. Probably lunch rush too. Supper would be fine, I had my usual evening crew scheduled, so we just had to make it through the next eight hours.

I was questioning my life choices as I downed my third cup of coffee a few hours later, when Winter's boyfriend – Trevor? No, Travis – came around the corner of the bar top.

"Oh, hey." He gave me an uncomfortable smile as his eyes searched the diner, seemingly looking for something.

More like someone; a sexy auburn-haired someone who wasn't mine and was now apparently his. I internally groaned at my caveman thoughts. She wasn't a *possession*.

And she wasn't mine because of me. Although, Travis was likely the more attractive of the two of us, with his edgy good looks and easy grin. I didn't have arm tattoos or piercings or any kind of bad-boy energy. I was as white bread as they came.

But does she come as hard for him as she did for me?

That memory stirred my cock into gear at the most inconvenient time and I had to immediately shift gears.

Okay, caveman thoughts are over, *right now.*

"Hey," I returned. "Winter isn't here today, she's off to study."

"Yeah," he answered, attention still focused elsewhere. Was he avoiding me on purpose? "I just came to grab a Carl's Creation. She's got me hooked on them."

"Cool." Carl's Creation today was a stack of raspberry buttermilk pancakes with peach salsa and sour cream whip. That man was a culinary master.

The silence lengthened between us. I gave an awkward cough. "Welp, I'd better get back to it. See you around."

"Yeah, see ya."

I pretended to go back to my coffee and paperwork while there was a mild lull of patrons, but I watched him from the corner of my eye. He turned away from me and picked up an old Adidas duffle bag I hadn't seen from the floor. Then he rounded the corner toward the back hallway of the diner.

No. Fucking. Way.

I knew that duffle bag. It was the same one I had found tucked under the desk of the office just weeks ago. Travis – Travis had been the one to leave it here?

I had no idea who the guy was; if he was a student at Ryker's with Winter or someone she met at a bar, or online even. I had avoided asking because I really didn't want to know, but now, now I had wished I had asked at least one question about him.

Did Winter know? I banished the thought as soon as it filled my brain. No, she absolutely did not know. Not a chance.

I was flooded with a white, hot rage as I considered this situation. Today, of all days, the day I was confronting my father, Winter's boyfriend – of all people! – was the lackey dropping off Georgio's cash. It made me murderous and nauseous all at the same time, my urge to scream and puke warring with each other.

I took a few deep, calming breaths. I was not going to barge in on them in the office, not yet. I didn't want Travis knowing that I knew his dirty little secret. I'd have to sit on that one until I knew what to do with it.

Once I saw him leave the diner through the chiming front door, I made a beeline for the office. I wouldn't catch Travis red-handed today, but I wasn't going to grant the same grace to old Joe Johnson.

I stopped right at the half-closed door, listening to the muffled sounds of rustling papers and plastic. I would need to play this cool. I willed myself to remain calm; if I barged in there with even a fraction of my anger, I wasn't going to get any answers at all, and the restaurant was half-full. I didn't want to cause a scene either. Whispers went everywhere in small towns.

I slowly strolled into the small space just as dear ol' Dad was stuffing the beaten black bag underneath the metal desk frame.

"Oh, hey, Dad." I said the words as casually as I could muster and settled myself into the ripped brown and yellow tweed office chair across from him. "What are you up to?"

Joe Johnson straightened in his chair, perspiration dotting his thinning hairline as his light blue eyes appraised me. I was looking at my future, I realized. A once handsome man with big dreams, trapped in a business with criminal ties, a consequence of his own making.

Did Joe have everything he ever wanted? The high school sweetheart, the five children, the modest but nice home, a thriving business, a legacy of his own? Or somewhere along the way, had he realized this was not the dream, and he needed something to break up the mundanity of his life?

I shook off the thought as soon as it had come. My father was a kind, humble man. He wasn't a money launderer to spice up a boring life. He was no innocent party here, but I refused to believe that this clusterfuck of a decision was for shits and giggles.

"Just tidying up, son. It's been a busy day out there." He shifted uncomfortably in his seat. "We should get back out there before supper rush."

"Yeah, we should. But first I wanted to talk to you about something."

I reached down to the shoulder bag I had tucked by the door, filled with the folder of evidence for this very moment. I took out the beige file and lightly dropped it on his desk.

"Can you take a quick look at this for me? I need to know your thoughts on it before I make a decision."

"Can it wait? This doesn't seem like the time for –"

"Nope, has to be now, Dad. Please, just take a look." I sat back into the hard seat, hands resting behind my head, doing my best to feign casual interest.

He grabbed the folder and flicked it open. A heavy silence came over the room as he thumbed through each printed spreadsheet, his gaze never leaving the paperwork as each beat passed.

"Well?" I prompted. "What do you think? What should I do about this, *Dad?*" I couldn't keep the sneer out of my voice at the end, the anticipation of this moment finally getting to me.

I let the question hang in the air instead of speaking further. It was his turn.

"Son —" He stopped, not finishing his sentence; his eyes never left his hands, now clasped on the desk in front of him. His skin had turned a sickly pale and sweat fully coated his brow as he grappled for the words.

"I'd ask how long, but I know how long. The proof is right there. What I want to know is why? Why would you get in bed with Georgio? Why would you risk the business? Why would you risk Mom? Why would you risk *me*?"

What had started as a measured question was now being whisper-shouted across the cramped space. I couldn't keep the hurt, the anger, and the betrayal out of my voice.

"The fire — the grease fire we had ten years ago — the one that nearly destroyed this diner? It"— he took a deep breath — "It was no accident."

Okay. That was a completely new piece of information.

"Your mother and I were deep in debt. The diner had some steady support, but the town didn't have nearly as many tourists as it does now, and we weren't able to cover our bills most of the year. We had just found out she was pregnant with Charlie and we were desperate. A failing business, another kid on the way, and no savings to speak of."

"Your mother and Georgio were — together — when we first met in high school. He still had a soft spot for her and at the time, he was doing really well. Two construction companies successfully started, making a name for himself all across the state — we went to him for help. I won't lie to you and say we didn't know about his other businesses, because we did. His family was no stranger to walking the line."

What the fuck? Mom and Georgio?

My mind was still reeling with that information as Dad took in another deep breath. A deep crimson color filled his features, and shame shadowed his eyes as he looked into mine for the first time since the conversation started. Nevertheless, he continued.

"Georgio arranged the grease fire. We collected the insurance money and covered all of our debts while he outfitted our kitchen with all new equipment. We could start fresh. The agreement was that we would run some excess cash from his businesses into ours, and eventually the debt would be repaid. That time has never come.

"It was exactly what we needed. Business increased, we made better food and hired more people, and then the tourism boom happened. Had we had some savings, we probably would never have needed his help at all. I haven't bothered upgrading the dining room because I'm afraid that if we do anything more to this place, Georgio will expect more in return."

Dad stopped speaking and the truth of his words spanned the space between us. I chewed at the inside of my cheek, the flesh raw from the excess pressure. Whatever I was expecting, this explanation was not it.

I was torn; my emotions ranged from empathy for my parents in a shitty situation to absolute indignation I was only hearing about this now that I was slated to take over entirely in the next few years. If that "time had never come," why would they ever push me into this position in the first place?

"So when," I asked, pushing those thoughts out of my mouth, "do you think you would have told me this? Once the paperwork was in my name and I had no choice? Once Georgio's thugs came knocking on my door in the middle of the night? Yeah, Dad, I got to see that too." He winced at the admission, but said nothing.

"Why would you ever want me to take on this burden? How could any parent want this for their child?" My voice broke on the last part, my hurt overtaking my anger for the moment.

"I was hoping for more time." His pale blue eyes pleaded with me, tears shining on their surface. "More time to figure out how to get out of this. I debated going to the police, but that would incriminate me and your mother. I could handle jail if that's what it took, but I couldn't do that to your mother."

His tears fell freely now. My stomach turned as the man I looked up to fell apart in front of me. I should feel sympathy, I should feel protective, or ... something. But I didn't. He was a coward. A well-intentioned coward, but a coward nonetheless. Before I could interrupt, he spoke again.

"I never wanted this for you, all my life I've been building this business for you. My father could give me nothing because of his own bad choices, and I never wanted the same for you. You're my eldest, my oldest son, the legacy of the Johnson name. Everything I've done has been for you."

"I never wanted this in the first place!"

I exploded out of the chair, its metal legs spinning haphazardly to the floor.

"This isn't my dream, or my legacy. It's yours! Why the hell would I want to run a diner—a *diner* of all things? Do you think I'm passionate about greasy cooking, or tomato inventory, or pretentious Karens who constantly try to ruin businesses like ours? You practically nailed me to this shitty counter and forced this legacy down my throat from the time I could walk, but it was never *for* me. It was for your own dream, and your own ego, and I'm fucking sick of pretending otherwise."

That was it. My anger had risen to the surface and I laid everything out on the table. It wasn't my original intention today, but fuck it. I leaned forward, grabbing the black duffle bag from under the desk and dumped the money out in front of my father. The hundreds of $20 bills wrapped in elastic thudded noisily on the hard steel surface.

"I can't pretend anymore. I can't continue helping you commit serious crimes, I can't work with you, and I can't be here." I spat the words like venom, and stalked out of the room, out of the diner, and out of my personal hell.

My life as I knew it was over and I needed to figure out my next steps, fast.

"I think you should tell her." Shane's voice was sure and steady as he languidly tossed a football up in the air in my garage the next night. "Winter won't hold your parent's actions against you or tell anyone else, that I can guarantee you, but she needs the opportunity to talk to Travis about it herself."

He was right, I knew he was, but it was another shitty conversation in the abundance of shitty conversations I didn't want to have this week. I didn't doubt what I had seen. I was sure beyond a shadow of a doubt Travis was the one bringing in the money.

I didn't go in to work today. As far as I was concerned, I wouldn't be going in ever again. Sooner or later, my parents and I would have to have a serious chat about steps forward, but today was not that day. Tomorrow wouldn't be either. Since that problem was just going to have to hang out for a moment, I decided to focus on my other problem; how to tell Winter Travis was a scumbag.

"You're right," I relented, standing up from the work bench and pacing the concrete floor. "Honestly, bringing someone else into this just makes it that much more real. If you and I are the only ones who know, I can pretend that this isn't my life right now."

He gave me an understanding nod, catching the football and holding it between his fingers. "I get it. It's not going to be an easy one, but I'd do it now before she finds out another way. She pretty big on honesty and it won't end well for you."

"And —" He frowned, throwing the ball up one more time. "She's going to be pissed at me if she finds out that I knew too. I met the guy and I liked him. Who knows what his situation is? But, I don't like the idea of her mixed up with someone like Georgio, even if it's accidentally."

So, Shane was Team Travis. What a softie. I couldn't care less about that endorsement; anyone working for Georgio, putting regular people into terrible situations and blackmailing them into these kinds of crimes, could go to hell. Travis included.

I collapsed onto the old couch in the corner of the room in defeat and took my phone out of the back pocket of my jeans to send her a quick text.

Might as well rip the Band-Aid off.

CHAPTER 16

LOGAN

"I don't fucking care, Hil, alright? It doesn't matter, *none* of this matters!"

I threw my hands up in the air in exasperation and then pushed myself away from our kitchen table to grab a drink. My crystal tumbler was waiting for me on the marble counter, and I poured a generous three fingers of whiskey, neat.

"It does matter, Logan. Everything has to be *perfect*. The Governor will be there. The Senator will be there. We have to keep up appearances!" Hillary's blue eyes flashed angrily; her little hands bawled up into fists.

Good, I liked making her angry. It was the only time she ever had any personality. Any other day she was a sniveling suck-up, doing whatever Daddy told her to make nice with whoever was on his radar in that moment. She was smart as fuck, but a personality airhead.

I hated this marriage arrangement more by the day and kept reminding myself that the money, the power and, most of all, the freedom that would come along with marrying Hillary Lane would be worth it. It had better be. These conversations were sucking the ever-loving *fuck* out of me.

"Then make the damn decisions, and stop asking my opinion. When I say it doesn't matter, it actually doesn't matter. I don't care if the linens are cream or ivory. What the fuck is the difference, anyway? There are so many better things I can be doing with my time." I took a long drag of the alcohol, coating my insides with its soothing burn.

Hillary pouted for a second before switching gears. Turning on her charm dial, she got up from her chair and suggestively swayed her hips, walking over to me like a high-class escort.

"Baby, I just want this day to be everything we dreamed, okay? I want you to love it too." She wrapped her arms around my waist and snuggled into my chest.

I sighed. I could lie and say Hillary wasn't hot; she was a living, walking, talking Barbie with an MBA, and a trust fund that could fuel a small country. It was because she had the looks, was decent enough in bed to keep me coming back, and the money I so desperately needed that I had stuck around.

Did that make me an ass? Sure. Show me someone who wasn't using the people around them to get ahead, and I'd show you a liar.

I didn't hate her. I didn't even dislike her most days. I understood her, which made it easy to live with her. I also knew this game. Hillary wanted to stroke my ego, act like she loved me, and get her way. It usually worked because I couldn't give a fuck about fighting her. You want cream linens? Great. One step closer to my money. You want a ten‑piece orchestra? What the hell, hire a twenty‑piece brass band, if that's even a fucking thing, and call it a day. It's another decision closer to saying a big ol' 'Fuck You' to Stan‑the‑man and moving on with my life.

I set the whiskey down on the counter and wrapped my arms around her .

"I know, baby," I crooned, whispering in her ear and nipping her earlobe, a surefire way to switch gears on the conversation and get my dick wet. "It will be perfect." I moved my hands down to her ass and pulled her into me, kissing along her neck to her collarbone.

Just when I was about to pull down her skirt for a quick fuck right there, my phone rang, the distinct ring‑tone blaring from the table.

"I've got to take that." I gave her a quick peck and pushed her away from me, reaching for the phone. "Make the decision and I'll support it."

I walked down the hall to the spare bedroom for some privacy before taking the call. I spoke in a low voice, not wanting Hillary to eavesdrop. "You're not supposed to be calling me on this line."

"Logan," the authoritative voice clipped. "We need to meet. This evening. Something has come to light, and we're going to need more information as soon as possible."

Fuck. We weren't supposed to meet for another few weeks, and I didn't have much to report yet. My hands were tied though, and this call wasn't a request. Few people had this kind of hold over me, but M was one of them.

"When and where?" I wanted to get off this call immediately.

"9:00 pm, Kirby Park in Sheldonville. I'll meet you by the lake."

The line went dead and I tucked my phone into my back pocket, wondering what was so urgent to push up the timeline. My date with a hot brunette and an 8 ball while Hillary flew back to Washington were going to go to waste.

I drove the Audi slowly through the abandoned parking lot of Kirby Park, wishing I had a more discreet car, like an old-man Corolla, so no one would have a clue Logan Eccles was hanging out in parks late at night in the middle of winter.

Still, I had taken all of the necessary precautions. My life depended on it.

The last time I had seen M was when he surprised me at Après, risking my cover and almost fucking me over when Georgio's number two, Angelo, had walked into the bar at the same time. I had pulled the fire alarm as a diversion. It was probably overkill, but I had panicked. It had cost John thousands of dollars in insurance damage, but I didn't give a fuck. It wasn't my business and that bill could go to the feds for all I cared. They weren't going to get anything from me if I was dead.

M was waiting on a wooden park bench hidden between a large rock outcrop.

"I wish I could say it was good to see you, but I'd rather be anywhere else tonight."

M looked me over with a frown. "I don't like this arrangement either, Logan. If I had my way, you'd be in jail, and I'd be busting bad guys instead of having conversations with them while my balls freeze."

I tsked. I wasn't a criminal. I was opportunistic and probably needed some therapy for my daddy issues, but the bad guy label was a stretch. I was a "caught" guy, which is how I had gotten myself into this whole mess in the first place.

"Well then, let's keep this as short as possible so mine don't freeze along with yours." I smirked, loving how easy it was to rile this guy.

"Careful, Logan. You are nowhere near the safe zone, and I don't have to tell you what could happen to you if you don't deliver."

M's smirk rivaled mine and his words hit home. I dialed back my usual snark and settled for direct. "What do you need?"

"We're hearing rumblings of an insider-trading situation. Thanks to you, we know that Georgio is working with Camden through Eccles and WAQ to rig one of the biggest contracts in the state, and they are fueling the fire by pushing the stock up. We need proof that this is happening."

I considered his words. I knew most of this, but nothing about insider trading. It was no secret that Georgio and Camden were using Eccles and WAQ to gain the government's favor for this contract. I had been attending meetings for months, sitting in on corporate and team conversations and bringing the information back to M. With full cooperation, my drug charges were supposed to be dropped and I could go back to my life.

I could easily pay my bail if I were charged, but I couldn't risk Georgio thinking I had any leverage over him with the feds, especially with the amount of money I still owed him. I wouldn't live to see Christmas if he decided I was a liability or he'd find a way to make me useful; either way I was fucked.

I also didn't want my dirty little secret getting out. I had businesses to run, respectable ones, and I wasn't risking the hit to my reputation. The FBI had convinced me this route was in my best interest and self-preserving fucker I was, I took it.

I get them the information they need; I marry Hillary, I get off the hook and land buckets of monetary freedom. I didn't care about the engineering firm anyway. Other than the few shares I owned myself, that was Stanley's baby, not mine. And he could go fuck himself.

"Why would the FBI be so interested in this? And wouldn't I benefit from the stock going up? This conversation doesn't make sense."

"Ahh, but you're forgetting that we can freeze your assets," the pompous prick said smugly. "If you were to benefit from illegal activities, we'd simply seize it. Not much of a benefit for you, is there?"

Fuck. He had me there. Hillary's trust fund was more important to me than ever. Her grandmother had set it up, so Camden couldn't touch it. It would be the only safe way to get out from underneath Georgio's thumb.

"I'll see what I can find out. You realize that it's Christmas season, right? Everything is on hold until the new year. The tender won't even be selected until February."

"Good thing we're speaking tonight, then. I expect something within the next two weeks. And, Logan? Bonus points for whatever dirt you give us on Georgio. I know that can't be hard in your position."

M gave me a satisfied shit-eating grin and left me standing by the bench in the freezing cold to contemplate my life choices. It looked like I would be hitting up B&B tonight after all.

CHAPTER 17

WINTER

Drew: *Hey, can we talk?*

My brows rose in surprise at his text. Drew hadn't gone out of his way to text me outside of work-related scheduling inquiries since our little surprise tryst in the storeroom.

I continued to try and think about it as just casual sex, but I could admit that it had stung a little when he never mentioned it again. I knew he wasn't faking how badly he wanted me, and neither one of us could deny it was excruciatingly burn-down-the-building-and-send-me-to-hell hot. If he never wanted to touch me again, I could live with that, but I sure as hell hoped he didn't regret it.

Even with Travis now in my life, a man I thought I could love if I were really honest with myself, I couldn't pretend I never thought about Drew. In a perfect world, I'd try to have them both. Some dreams were never meant to become reality.

Winter: *Sure, what about?*

I waited for his reply, confused and a little on edge. Was everything okay? Was the diner okay? I was either about to lose my job, or he was in trouble; those were the only possible scenarios I could think of to drive Drew Johnson to text me at ten p.m. on a Monday.

Drew: *This is a little weird, but I'm close to your place. Would you mind if I came over for a minute?*

Okay, now I was really concerned. Was Joe okay? Eileen? The kids?

Winter: *Ooook. I'll buzz you in when you get here.*

Two minutes later, I heard the familiar metallic buzz that reminded me of television prison gates.

He wasn't kidding.

"Hey." I opened the door and appraised him critically. He looked handsome as ever in a black wool coat and dark jeans, dirty blonde hair tousled from the weather outside. His hazel eyes were fixated on me. He had grown a longer beard in the past few weeks and it highlighted the plumpness of his soft lips and the slight freckles across the crest of his cheeks.

Images of his shorter stubble scraping across my neck and jaw as he pumped in and out of me flashed behind my eyes and I shook my head before they could turn this evening into something they shouldn't. I wouldn't even dream of crossing that bridge anyway, until Travis and I had an open conversation about where this was going and what was okay. Because morals.

"Hey." He gave me a soft smile and motioned to the apartment behind me. "May I come in, or—"

"Yeah, shit, sorry!" I moved to let him inside and closed the door behind him.

He took off his boots at the door and moved further into my small haven. He knew where I lived thanks to employment records and the fact this town was tiny, but he had never been here before. He took in his surroundings and settled himself on my couch in the living room.

"Nice place – I like the boho look. It's definitely a lot prettier than my man cave." He gave me a shy half-smile as he shifted uncomfortably in his seat.

"Would you like a tea, or a soda, or something? I have a feeling whatever you want to talk about isn't particularly happy." I scrutinized his body language, but other than nervousness, he gave nothing away.

"Tea would be great. Can I help you make it?" He immediately stood up from the couch and made his way to my cozy kitchen area, looking for – a teapot, I guess?

I humored him and handed him one of my custom pottery tea pots to fill with water while I searched through my stash for a good quality calming brew. We were going to need it. We shifted in the tight space, and he was so close the heat of his body was all around me.

I wished Drew could just be a guy I worked with, a guy who grew up in my town, but his presence was more. A current flowed between us; not an electric chemistry of wit and words like I had with Travis, but a slow pulsation of calm and tranquility. Drew was grounding. Stable. Too bad he was also so unattainable. He truly was a man of mystery.

He moved at a snail's pace to make the tea, but we finally got back to my living room once I had pulled out some cookies and chocolate to go along with it. He had taken three or four sips of his tea, staring into the bottom of his floral cup without saying a word, when I couldn't take the waiting anymore.

"As much as I love your silent company, Drew," I deadpanned, "can you please tell me what brought you here on this random Monday?"

He winced, a look of chagrin on his face as he finally looked up at me. He sheepishly rubbed the back of his neck, clearly uncomfortable.

"Has Shane said much to you about why we're hanging out?"

The question wasn't what I was expecting, but I clearly had no idea where this was leading, so I went with it.

"Not much. Just that you had asked him to help you with a data project for the diner."

I had shrugged it off, really. Shane and Drew had been friends in high school, both of them on the football team and teaching at the ski hill, so the explanation wasn't a stretch of the imagination. Since I didn't want to be the clingy girl who pined after a one-night stand, especially when I had another hotter-than-sin man in my life, I refrained from asking too many questions about the hottie in front of me. If I was being *really* honest, I didn't care about a diner data project.

"Well, there was a bit more to it than that."

He figuratively laid everything out on the sea-shell chipped coffee table between us. The planned arson. The debt to Georgio. The money laundering. The escalation of thugs at his house. Him leaving the diner.

My mind whirled with the stories he was telling. The wholesome town I called my own looked dirtier and darker by the second, and my heart ached for Drew as he looked more and more dejected with each layer of his tale.

I wish I could say I was shocked but the revelations and I couldn't possibly fathom our little piece of the world was capable of such deception and lies, but I wasn't. A long time ago, I had learned evil had a pretty face and would happily kiss you tenderly while sucking out your soul with a smile.

I reached out and clasped his hands in mine, gently squeezing his rough palms in a gesture of friendship and solidarity.

"I'm so sorry you're going through this, Drew." I spoke softly, with as much warmth and sincerity as I could muster. His eyes, more amber than green in the dim light of the room, stared deeply into my own. For a second, I thought he might—

"There's more."

His serious tone interrupted my focus and brought me back to the moment. "Winter, I know who's been bringing the money into Johnson's."

He paused somewhat dramatically, but I could see he was summoning the courage to say the next few words. Who could we possibly know doing this right under our noses? I had worked at the diner for four years; it was my very first real job. Drew had practically lived there since he was a little kid. Was it Janice? No, it couldn't possibly be the sweet, gullible—

"It's Travis. I'm so sorry, I didn't know how else to tell you, so I wanted you to have all of the facts beforehand and —"

"Wait, what?" I interrupted the tidal wave of words gushing out of his mouth. I was sure I hadn't heard him correctly.

There was no way Travis, my Travis, sweet, fun-loving, tender-kissing Travis; Travis, the man I admitted to almost loving at this point, was a money mule – I didn't know what the technical term was, but we were going with it – for Georgio. It was so ludicrous to even consider. Yet, here I was, sitting here holding a lukewarm drink of tea in my hand, my mouth opening and closing like a landed fish, trying to fathom why Drew would make up something like this.

"Drew, that's *not* possible. I know Travis, he's a good guy, a *great* guy. This has got to be a mistake. I know you're upset right now but—"

"It is not a mistake, Winter." He cut me off, hazel eyes now flashing with emotions I couldn't decipher. Anger maybe? Disappointment? Pain? "I've seen it with my own eyes. He—"

"Wait, so you saw him physically hand money over to Joe, then?" It was my turn to cut him off. "You witnessed Travis commit the crime yourself?" My voice was hard, my patience waning, as I defended the lovable man who had come to mean so much to me in such a short time.

"Well, no." Drew's voice faltered. "I saw him with the same bag that I found filled with cash in Dad's office and—"

"The same bag, or a similar bag? Did you watch him put it in the office?"

"No, but—"

"Okay, so no proof, then." I cut in again, fully angry now. He didn't even have real evidence against Travis.; he was using his subjective suspicions to drive a wedge between us.

"What is this really about, Drew? Is Travis an easy fall-boy because he's someone that I care about? You all but ignore me for months after temporarily wanting me, and now that I want someone else, you're trying to put doubts in my mind? To what, drive me back to you? This is bullshit, and you know it!"

I was angry, likely angrier than I should be given the fact Drew's life was falling apart around him and the diner that was a second home to me — a second, crumbling, grease-scented home with a scratchy uniform that gave me cones for tits, but a second home nonetheless — was now a haven for dirty crimes. But I couldn't help the hot, sweeping feeling of pure fury writhing through me. All of my buried feelings of being ignored and shunted after an intimate moment with someone I had actually hoped to care for crashed through me and I lost it.

"Winter, I – I can't believe you would even think that! I have never, I could never – that's a crazy accusation!" His eyes grew wide with indignation, and his own anger flared to the surface of his pale skin, darkening his freckles and turning his cheeks a deep pink. "I'm trying to warn you about someone who is *lying* to you. He is not who you think he is and you could be in danger. You could be—"

"You need to leave, Drew." I set my tea cup down on the table with an aggressive crack and marched to my door, opening it wide and holding my arm out like a vengeful Vanna White. "I don't want to hear any more. I'm sorry about your parents and your shitty situation, but I'm not going to stand by while you make wild accusations and pretend that it's for my well-being. Go be someone else's knight in shining armor."

He hesitated for a second, fists balled up at his sides, before grabbing his coat and boots and stalking out the front door. I slammed the door behind him and flopped down on my couch, angry tears falling from my cheeks as I replayed the whole scene in my mind.

Fuck him and the high horse he rode in on. The empathetic part of me wanted to give him the world's biggest hug, knowing his world had just been completely shattered. The petty, vicious part of me wanted him to suffer my wrath this evening, knowing he had no actual proof against Travis but decided to tell me anyways. He couldn't ignore me for months on end and then show up unannounced under the guise he was protecting me from my boyfriend. I called bullshit.

If I was being honest — truly, blatantly, Dr. Phil-dose-of-reality honest with myself — Drew had planted a seed of doubt in my mind, one starting to grow with each snap of my synapses. I didn't actually know many things about

Travis, and the two phones, the cryptic calls, the mysterious job I didn't know much about, were now worrying me.

I blew some stray strands of hair out of my face, my tears and snot and saliva coating my skin and making me feel disgusting. I hopped into a hot shower and let the cleansing water wash away the last few hours of the day.

Tomorrow, I would decide what to do.

CHAPTER 18

WINTER

After a full week went by, I decided to be brave and pull up my big-girl pants and ignored the situation entirely. I had finals to finish up my semester, my parents were home and wanted me to visit, and Travis had been busy with work and his mother's appointments, so I didn't have much for mental capacity to throw anything else into the mix.

I managed to make it through two diner shifts without Drew's presence on Friday and Saturday. He hadn't been kidding when he said he was done. To say that we had suffered because of it was an understatement.

Joe had been an intolerable shift manager all weekend, and if I hadn't known what had happened between him and Drew, I would have turned in my hollandaise and gravy-stained polyester apron and left without a second glance after the brunch rush on Saturday morning. Since I had a heart and couldn't leave Janice to fend for herself against the onslaught of hungry Christmas shoppers, I grudgingly slung coffee and potato crunchers — Carl's new take on French fries — all afternoon.

I went home to grab a quick shower and change of clothes, cleansing the shitty day off of my body, before heading out to my parents for the evening. I hadn't seen them in almost six weeks. Mom's fall book launch had taken her all over the continent this year, and Dad had been flat out with the mysterious bridge tender that no one was talking much about.

Not that there would be much for juicy rumblings over a construction development, but still, it was odd for such a major venture to be so hush-hush. Small towns played telephone with private information on a professional level; I knew that better than anyone.

I drove Basil up to the familiar two-story modern glass and wood structure. Dad had designed their dream home in his early twenties. Then, when he and Mom had made enough money to afford the build, they built it into the side of the mountain exactly as drawn.

It was beautiful, tasteful, and eye-catching; one of the simple Scandinavian designs meant to blend into nature. It was one of the most peaceful and lonely places I had ever known.

My parents were wealthy, but they didn't flaunt it like the Lanes or the Eccles. They believed in investing in yourself, your skills, and your education more than anything else in the world. Success meant accomplishment, and growing up as the only child in an accomplished family had been intimidating.

All my life I had felt like an impostor; like I had been switched at birth and the real Winter Wallace, who had a fire under her ass to take on the world to meet and match my parents' expectations, was floundering within the walls of my true family home: the mediocre Jones', satisfied with the split-entry middle class suburban home and nine to five jobs that brought in enough money to make ends meet. My ambition and my intelligence never seemed to align with my genetic destiny. I had swallowed a lot of parental disappointment over the years.

I grabbed my overnight bag and walked through the twelve-foot-high mahogany front door.

"Hello?" I called out into the cavernous space. "Mom?"

"In here, honey." My mother's husky timbre floated to me from somewhere beyond the modern glass staircase that separated the front foyer from the open great room. Her voice was smoky and alluring, like the sexy narrators who read my smutty romance audiobooks. With a voice like hers, it was no coincidence she was a successful sexual therapy author.

In the modern kitchen, my mother stood at the oversized propane stove stirring a large pot of something that smelled deliciously like moose stew, a local staple on this side of the mountain and my absolute favorite. Confusing scents of cinnamon and peppermint mingled in the air and I knew immediately that she had been baking all of our favorite Christmas treats this afternoon.

A fleeting wave of nostalgia washed over me. Mom never had much time over the holidays to spend with me growing up, with Christmas season coinciding with book tour season, but she always made time to bake with me before we decorated the tree, like we were doing tonight. I had missed the chance to make those cookies with her today, and it stirred something within me.

"Hey." I smiled at her and leaned over, kissing her cheek and inspecting the pot's contents. I was right; hearty chunks of moose meat were nestled in a thick gravy with peas and potatoes. "Is that for supper tonight?"

Miranda Wallace's shrewd gaze looked me over before she nodded and gave me a quick hug and kiss back. I had been told more than once I was spitting image of my mother. Dark auburn hair, upturned nose, and a smattering of freckles crossed our cheeks. We had the same build; delicate feminine features with prominent hips and butt, and we stood at the same height. The only notable difference was my eyes; my baby blues came directly from Dad and his northern European heritage.

While Quick's parents had intentionally held off on having kids after college, Mom and Dad had wanted to start their family right away. After nine years of trying and failing to get pregnant, they gave up the fight; the fertility options twenty-one years ago were a far cry from today's available menu, and they had accepted that children weren't in the cards for them. They moved on, continuing to build careers and professional reputations and then, surprise, I arrived three years later.

It was sheer coincidence Amelia had gotten pregnant a few months earlier, so Shane and I had the chance to grow up together. I would have been lost without my adopted family when Mom and Dad were tending to those previously established careers and reputations. The truth was I was their second child — their dreams were their first. It took me sixteen years to accept that fact, but I had, and we had all moved on.

"I know it's your favorite, honey. It's been so long since we've been able to spend some time together. How were your finals?"

"Not bad," I answered carefully, as I did with all school-related questions.

While my parents had encouraged me to pursue my own path, a business diploma at the local community college hadn't exactly been what they had in mind, so I tried not to divulge too much information when it was requested. I could only stand the look of concern and disapproval in their eyes for so long.

"I'm not worried about any of my classes this semester. I've been doing well and I've studied hard, and now I have three weeks off to enjoy!" I grinned and perched myself onto the metal bar stool at the end of the gray granite counter. "Where's Dad? We're still decorating tonight, right?"

"We're still decorating. Your father is just late as usual." She sat on the bar stool next to me and grabbed my hands in her own. Her palms were soft and warm, and I welcomed the touch. I had missed her presence and comfort.

"How is life? I'm sorry we missed you for Thanksgiving. You know how these tours go." She waved her dainty hand dismissively. "What's new?"

"Life is good, Mom. Quiet, mostly. Quick and I have gotten out on the hill a few times, and I've been working a lot of shifts at the diner to prep for next semester's tuition fees. I've been really into why choose novels lately." I smirked at her, falling back on our shared love for obscure romance books as a topic of conversation. "Have you read Rebecca Quinn? Her newest book is fantastic!"

I kept my romantic cards close when it came to my mother. While sexually liberal, she was far more protective over who I chose to give my heart to, rather than my body. She was the exact opposite of a good Catholic.

I would tell her about Travis when I was sure he could handle her scrutiny. Which, if I had my way, may be never. My parents had visited my apartment twice in the three years I had lived there, so chances were he could move in and they would be none the wiser. I took comfort in that fact.

We talked about our latest book finds. She was regaling me with tales of her latest convention in Florida when the front door slammed shut. Darren Wallace – Dad – in all of his handsome glory, strolled into the kitchen, tossed his car keys on the counter, and brushed errant snowflakes off of his winter jacket. He looked up and broke out into a big smile when he saw the two of us sitting at the counter.

"How's my girls?" His salt and pepper hair sparkling under the island pot lights, he wrapped the two of us into a big bear hug. He kissed my temple before pulling away. "It smells great in here. Did you help your mother with the cooking?"

"I had to work today, Dad," I said ruefully, wishing I had the opportunity to help. It would have been nice if Mom had thought to invite me, even if I couldn't have made it. I would have given my left arm to bake cinnamon candy canes and chocolate Andes mint cookies rather than the afternoon I had under Joe's dictatorship.

"I think Mom made enough for the entire town, so she didn't need me today." I nodded over to the racks of cookies cooling in the butler pantry with a grin. "She wouldn't let me touch them until you got home. It's the only reason I'm glad you're here."

"Ouch!" He playfully tousled my hair and swept Mom up into a heated kiss. My parents were never shy showing affection, and it was both heartwarming and mildly off-putting when I was still present in the room. They didn't see me often, but they also didn't see much of each other with their busy schedules, so this tradition was a treat.

"Let's get to it!" Dad said excitedly, rubbing his hands together and marching off into the great room to stand next to the very large spruce tree already set-up in the center of the space.

Cardboard boxes of ornaments had already been taken down from the attic, and Mom put on her favorite Christmas jazz playlist as background music while we unwrapped tissue-paper enrobed glass bulbs and munched on star-shaped Christmas cookies. Dad balanced himself on the ladder while Mom and I handed him strings of lights to wrap around the feathered fronds.

I settled into the familiar rhythm, basking in the glow of the tradition and the feeling of belonging in my childhood home. I only felt this way when the two of them were here, and that hadn't been often in my childhood.

Hours passed by as we talked about everything and nothing at all. We avoided speaking about anything truly deep or meaningful. The heavy topics weren't encouraged around the holiday season, and I was grateful for it. We could superficially enjoy each other's company and then go our separate ways a little bit lighter than before.

When we were finished, I nestled myself into the stuffed leather sectional with a rum and eggnog, enjoying the twinkling colors dancing across the tree. Dad broke the silence from across the room.

"So, sweetie, has Mom talked to you about Christmas Day yet?"

Mom shot him a look that said *really?*

"I was waiting for the right time and I didn't want it to overshadow our evening, Darren." She turned her attention to me, her sharp green eyes looking apologetic, almost.

"Honey, your father and I have some prior commitments that are going to take us out of the country for Christmas. I would have told you sooner but everything was just finalized yesterday and I wanted the chance to tell you in person." She took my hands in hers again, her go-to gesture whenever she was breaking bad news. "We'll be leaving on the 22nd, and won't be back until New Year's."

"Wait — what?" My mind floundered. My parents, the only family I had, were leaving town for Christmas without me and had decided to tell me two weeks before hand. I could predict the next words to come out of her mouth.

"I've already spoken to Amelia, and she said that you're welcome to join them for Christmas dinner. They would be thrilled to have you."

Typical. All of the rosy feelings of contentment from just five minutes before leached out of me, replaced by a cold sense of abandonment.

It wasn't the first time my parents weren't around for a major holiday, but it was certainly the first Christmas. Once I had graduated high school, it was if their sense of responsibility for their only child had been reduced to love and support from afar, when they were available and when it suited them.

I remained silent, willing her to continue her lists of reasons why I wouldn't be invited along and all of the amazing things I could get up to at home without them.

When silence hung in the air and nothing came, I realized another truth. I was an adult now. They loved me in their own way, but they no longer owed me an explanation for living their lives and fulfilling their careers.

This decision was a drop-off point; a parting of ways of sorts. They would now be doing their own thing, and I would be expected to do mine.

My heart squeezed at this chapter closing. This tradition was the send-off; we may not even do it again next year. I put up a figurative shield around my heart and it took all I had in me to keep my emotions under wraps.

"Okay." My voice came out in a shaky breath. "Thank you for telling me. I'll figure out my own plans."

"Sweetie, are you okay? I know that this isn't what you had in mind, but it was an opportunity that —"

I cut off Dad, not wanting to hear any more. I didn't need to hear any more. Their decision was explanation enough. I hadn't been invited to come along wherever they were going, and they were leaving me here by myself, expecting the Quicksilvers to step in and be the co-parents they'd always fallen back on.

Even as an adult, it stung.

"It's fine, Dad. I'm no longer a child, right? I'm making my own way and forging my own path. I don't need you or Mom around to step in and play parent whenever it's convenient."

So much for swallowing my emotions. I drank the rest of my eggnog in one large gulp and pulled myself up off the couch. I gave them each a hard look and walked out of the room.

"I'm going to bed. I'll see you in the morning." I made my way up the stairs, my feet slowly carrying me through the lonely familiar hallways.

My head and my heart hurt. Years of pent-up frustration and denial slowly leaked into my consciousness. I realized then and there, if I truly wanted the family I never had, I was going to have to make one of my own.

CHAPTER 19

TRAVIS

"**W**inter, that set was killer!"

Winter's blue-haired friend, Raven, the bass player, gushed beside us as we all headed out from Bourbon & Blues after one of the busiest nights of the year. One week before Christmas, and I had made almost $1000 in tips.

It couldn't have come at a better time. Mom's medication bills were piling up and I still wanted to get Winter something nice for Christmas. After weeks of working triple shifts at Bourbon & Blues to try and save enough money to start weaning myself off of Georgio's easy cash, Mom took a relapse, and I still had barely enough to make ends meet. I was so sick of being work-your-ass-off poor.

Brody, the quiet drummer, mused, "We could actually make a go of this thing you know." He walked hand in hand with Raven behind Winter and me. "I think the world is ready for the Mellowtones."

Winter threw her head back and laughed; I loved the tinkling sound and the way it made her eyes crinkle.

"I think I'll keep my day job for now guys, but thanks. You'll have changed your tune in January when the club is dead and no one can afford to buy any drinks after the Christmas credit card statements roll in."

We made our way out onto the now quiet street, walking through the silence of softly falling snow. I had driven us there tonight in the old Daytona and I was going to drop her off at her apartment before heading home to check on Mom.

I opened her door like the gentleman of a decrepit chariot, and gently kissed the tip of her nose before rounding the car to the driver's side. We had barely spent any time together in the last two weeks and I missed her spark in my life. Texts and Facetime wasn't the same.

My phone rang and I reached into my pocket to grab it. It was Georgio on the burner phone. I sighed in defeat, counting down the days until this was no longer a part of my daily routine. I took the call outside, walking around the rear of the car to be completely out of earshot. I didn't want to run the risk that my holey rust-bucket of a car would transmit outside sound.

"Hello," I answered quickly and quietly, hoping this call would be a short one.

Georgio's charming voice came through the line, in a friendly, yet inarguable tone. "Travis, there's going to be a disruption with Johnson's deliveries. You can skip the next two weeks at that location. I'll have two extra bags for you to deliver tomorrow to new businesses.

"Oh, and Cam will be fighting one of Drake's best guys on New Year's Eve. I'll need sharp eyes on the patrons. Show up at nine."

That was it. He hung up before I could even agree, because he knew he had me by the balls; I couldn't turn it down if I wanted to.

Which of course, I wanted to. I *needed* to.

I had no idea what was going on with the diner, but my gut clenched with worry for Winter. I didn't want her to get mixed up in any part of this world, and it was getting a little too close to home to be comfortable. I needed to get out as fast as possible, but I'd have to follow through for a little bit longer. I just needed more time.

Knowing Cam would be fighting was even more motivation to show up to my first fight night. Rumor had it that these fights were brutal and I needed to keep an eye on my friend. Not that I could do much if he did end up getting hurt, but there was solidarity in being present for his own fucked up choices.

I shook my head free of Georgio and the mess that was my life, and pulled open the car door.

Immediately, I wished I had never taken the call.

Winter was white as a sheet, with my glove compartment open, and she was holding my Smith & Wesson MP9; the handgun Georgio insisted I have for drop-off duties.

Her blue-green eyes were filled with shocked, unshed tears as she stared me down, peering into my soul with all of the disappointment of an Olympic athlete who just came in fourth.

My heart plummeted. All of my plans to get out from under Georgio's thumb and start building the life I wanted with the girl of my dreams came to a crashing halt in a single moment.

"Tell me this isn't true." Her voice was a cracked whisper, her eyes searching my face. "Tell me that you're just a closet gun enthusiast and you have a perfectly legal permit to be carrying a loaded handgun in your vehicle. Tell me that you are not, in any way, shape, or form, participating in illegal activities that can get you or someone else killed. Tell me that this is not for Georgio!"

Her last words rose an entire octave as she practically screeched them in the small cabin of the cramped car, and I winced.

I went to grab her hands in mine but she pulled away so fast the gun dropped to the floor and she squeaked in panic.

"It's not going to fire, Winter. The safety is still on." I picked up the gun from the wheel well and tucked it safely into my side door pocket, away from her and away from any well-intentioned but irrational thoughts she might have.

"Has this been happening the whole time we've been together?" Her words were no longer shaky, turning hard and resolved.

I ran my fingers through my hair anxiously, cursing my terrible luck and timing tonight. This was not the way I had wanted her to find out. I wanted a chance to make a solid plan, confess my sins, and have her support me as I worked through a terrible situation. I wanted to go to college and have her be my champion as we built a life together.

All of it was vanishing before my eyes because I was stupid enough to leave the gun in my car while I worked the bar tonight.

Stupid, stupid, STUPID!

"Yes," I answered simply, not wanting to add any fuel to this already blazing fire. "You know my mom's sick and my brother needed to be bailed —"

"So, you carry a gun and drop off money to hard-working business owners and turn them into criminals too, is that it? A quick buck to offload all of your issues onto someone else?"

The anger and spite in her words sliced me open like a hot knife. I wasn't some thug on the street. I was someone who was supposed to mean something to her.

Bitter bile crept up the back of my throat as I fought to keep my resentment at bay. How easy it was for her, with her wealthy parents and her lack of responsibilities to judge me for my choices.

"I have a sick mother and a druggie for a brother, Winter. I'm the only one keeping my family afloat right now. Do you have any idea what kind of a responsibility that is?" I took a calming breath before saying something I'd regret. This wasn't her fault, and I didn't want to hurt her more in the process.

She shook her head, shaking off my explanation. "This is a deal-breaker, Travis. Whatever you and I had before this moment is gone."

My heart dropped at the callousness of her dismissal. Then a dark anger overtook any semblance of protection I was trying to offer her.

"Jesus Christ, Winter, you won't even give me a chance to explain," I bit back angrily, heat flushing up my neck.

"We've been together for months, and you're just going to cut me completely out of your life? Does what we have mean nothing to you? Do you think I'm a good enough actor to fake my feelings for you? To what end, huh? Do you have some secret millions I'm unaware of or magical powers that can save the fucking world? It means everything to me. *You* mean everything to me."

"That's rich," she scoffed, her normally bright eyes the color of steel. "This is about lies and trust. Not only did I defend you when Drew accused you the first time, but by your actions you've made me an accomplice, Travis! What if we got pulled over tonight and the police found that gun in your car? What else is in here that could tie you to Georgio's other activities? How could I mean everything to you when you've put me in that position?"

"I —" I was a loss for words on that one. She was right. "I fucked up." I admitted, my jaw clenching at the thought of her getting into trouble because of me. "I was running behind today and I was excited to see you and — it's no excuse, I royally fucked up. I will never do that to you again, Winter, I swear it, I —"

"You're right," she interrupted, "you won't, because I'll never put you in that position again. There are no second chances here, Travis. I don't care the how or the why of it all. The trust is gone and, now, so am I." She turned to leave and I grabbed her by the arm, pulling her toward me.

"Winter, please," I pleaded, desperate for her to understand. "I didn't have a choice here, it's my job. Georgio —"

"It's a job, huh? Show me your employment agreement, Travis. Show me your paystubs, your yearly tax return. You don't have a job with Georgio, you have a fucking death sentence. What's the end game? How do you get out? How would we have been able to move forward with our relationship? You tell me the truth when we move in together? Would you ever tell me the truth, or would I just stupidly assume that the man I'm dating *isn't* a criminal because he didn't goddamn *say so!*"

She slipped out of my grasp, leaving me speechless. I racked my brain for an adequate response. There was nothing I could say.

Before she walked out the door of my life forever, she paused, looking me dead in the eyes, disappointment and pain shadowing her blue eyes in darkness.

"You know what the worst part about this is? I understand desperation, Travis. You could have come to me and told me everything, and we could have tried to get you out together. I cared about you enough to try, at least. But you didn't trust me enough to let me in, and now we'll never know where that could have led, because I no longer care to find out."

"Winter, don't —"

She didn't look back as she left me behind, slamming the car door and disappearing into the night.

"Fuck!" I bellowed to the empty space, slamming my fists against the steering wheel until my knuckles were raw. I couldn't see her any more in the darkness, and regardless of how that conversation just ended, I needed to make sure she got home safe.

I sent a quick text off to Shane, asking if he could let me know when she got home safely. I knew he would be the first one she'd call.

I got a response exactly a minute later.

Shane: *Fuck off*

Yup, she had definitely called Shane. I remained in the car, lost in my tumbling thoughts with my head in my hands when another text came through.

Shane: *She's safe. Now fuck off.*

Well, that was something, at least. When my body was adequately freezing from sitting in an unheated metal box in the middle of winter, I breathed a long-suffering sigh and started the car, leaving the parking lot and all of my dreams behind.

CHAPTER 20

SHANE

"You're doing great, Jordan! Keep that edge up, okay?"

I couldn't help the pride filling my voice as my little seven-year-old student rocked the bunny hill like he owned it.

The hill was gorgeous today. The temperature was ideal to keep the snow crisp; there was no ice or slush to deal with, and the sun was just behind the clouds, so visibility was near-perfect. I couldn't wait to do a few runs down the mountain once our lessons were done for the day.

Nearby, Drew was in his element teaching the beginner skiing class for the afternoon. I had asked him to be a guest instructor today since Shannon was sick. The guy had been alternating between moping in his apartment – not that I could blame him, his life was a bit fucked right now – and frantically searching for more information to get his family out of this mess, despite the fact he told Joe he'd have nothing to do with it. He had the biggest heart of any guy I knew.

I had hoped a day on the hill might lift his spirits a bit, and at least force him to have a shower. I knew a downward spiral of depressing thoughts when I saw one, and I wouldn't let him go down that path if I could help it.

He looked up from his lesson on snow plowing and gave me a genuine grin with a thumbs up in his bulky ski gloves. Good; my plan was working.

"Shane?" My little rockstar of a snowboarder tugged on the bottom of my jacket and I bent down to at look him.

"Can I try Pillar's Peak next week? I'm bored of the bunny hill."

I patted the top of his helmet and smiled, loving his enthusiasm. Dad had gotten me on the hill at five years old and, almost immediately, I had fallen in love with the sport. I spent most of my childhood begging Mom and Dad to take me to the hill, even in the summer time. Jordan wasn't able to do Pillar's Peak just yet, but he had the potential to go far with the sport if he stuck with it.

"I tell you what." I brought his goggles up to rest on his helmet so I could look him in the eyes. "You practice your edging during the next two lessons, and then, if you're ready, I'll take you up there to do a run with me, okay? But only if your mom says it's all right."

He beamed at me, taking his boot out of his binding so he could push off and go back up the ski carpet to start practicing. This was why I taught.

There were moments when I wondered if I had made the right decision turning down my Burton sponsorship and turning my back on training for the X Games. My coaches thought I was crazy, but the pressure had been ruining snowboarding for me and messing with my head too much for it to be any fun anymore.

I had avoided the hill for an entire year before deciding to take up teaching to dip my toe back in the water and see if I could handle it again. Watching kids and adults fall in love with the sport that was once part of my DNA was an incredible feeling, and along with the right medication, I was able to get my life back.

I had invited Drew over to spend Christmas with us, since he was dead against spending it with his family. I knew that had been a tough decision for him. Family was important to him like it was important to me, and I couldn't imagine spending the holidays without the people I loved. I actually had a family who wanted to spend time with me, so that helped.

When Winter told me her parents were taking off to Switzerland for the holidays, I was furious for her. They told her not even two weeks before Christmas they wouldn't be here, and she hadn't been invited, not that she could afford to go on her own even if she were.

I did not understand Darren and Miranda sometimes. What was the point of having a kid if you didn't want them in your life? Of course, Winter was able to spend the time with us; it wouldn't be the first or even the tenth time, but it was the principle.

Christmas Day wasn't going to be a picnic, though. Winter and Drew still hadn't made up after their fight, and it was going to be awkward as hell. Winter could be one stubborn son-of-a-bitch when she wanted, and I had not-so-subtly suggested she swallow her pride and apologize to Drew. From what she told me, her accusations weren't even a little bit fair, and Drew deserved the benefit of the doubt. It wasn't his fault Travis was a liar.

That was something else I didn't want to touch with a ten-foot pole. Winter did what she always did when she was truly hurt; she went numb. She hadn't said two words about him since she had called me to pick her up, and in true Winter fashion she was pretending nothing was wrong. I hated when she got like that; I'd rather a raging best friend than a robot.

I hated that he had hurt her. Dating Travis was the first time I had seen Winter this happy in years, and despite the scenario, I felt for him too. I don't know what I would do in his situation, but I didn't know enough about his life to pass judgment. I know I should have her back and I would always go to bat to protect her; I just didn't believe he was a malicious asshole. Stupid for sure, but not malicious. We knew what malicious looked like.

I wrapped up my lesson and grabbed my board from the rack, strapping my bindings to board down the little trail to the chairlift.

"Let's do a run," I called to Drew as he finished up with his students for the day. "I'm itching to carve in some at that fresh powder."

We headed up the lift, talking and laughing like we had done this for years, and raced down the hill four times before calling it a day. I whooped and hollered as I hit every jump on the trail, sailing through the air like I was a human projectile. The adrenaline rush curbed my anxiety about having to play peacemaker over the next couple of days. No matter what was going on in my life, this hill would always feel like my home.

On Christmas Eve, Drew was already over at the house, playing video games with me in my parent's basement. I felt like I was sixteen again, battling it out with a headset on and eating the snacks Shiloh had brought down to us just minutes before. A sense of nostalgia washed over me.

I heard Winter come down the stairs before I saw her, her soft gait on the carpet unmistakable to my trained ears. We used to sneak down to the basement to watch scary movies any time she slept over as kids, waiting until my parents fell asleep, since we weren't allowed to watch the R-rated ones. We had to get used to each other's footsteps to make sure we didn't get caught. That would have been a cardinal sin to my mother. She took her movie ratings very seriously.

"Hey, Snow." I smiled at her softly, as she sat down next to me on the large gray sectional couch and cuddled into my side. I paused the game and wrapped my arm around her, giving her a light squeeze. Today was going to be a hard one for her and I wanted to take that pain away.

"Hey," she mumbled into the crook of my shoulder, and I pulled back to give her some air. She breathed deeply and then slowly turned to make eye contact with Drew, laying on the opposite side of the couch on the chaise lounge.

"Hey, Drew," she said slowly, as if the words were painful to speak, but she said them nonetheless, and that was a good first step to my peacekeeping mission today.

Drew's hazel eyes softened – another good sign, I hoped – and put down his controller. Shifting his weight to sit on the couch properly, he leaned forward, his elbows on his knees.

"Hey, Winter."

The air thickened and I decided now was the time to cut the elephant in the room into bite-sized pieces. That was a saying, right?

"Okay, before we all enjoy some Quicksilver holiday cheer," I started, not wanting to lose the momentum of this moment, "I think it's time we all had a little chat to move forward."

I folded my arms across my white rugby t-shirt and gave them both a solemn look.

"Um, no offense man, but I think we can work this out without you playing referee." Drew quirked a blond eyebrow at me and nodded toward the door to the next room. "Mind giving us a few minutes?"

That was not a part of my peacemaker plan, but I stood up agreeably and left the room, walking through the door into the small spare bedroom on the other side of the rec room. Mom had banned us from coming upstairs until she and Shiloh had finished all of their food preparations for tomorrow, and I wasn't brave enough to incur her wrath right before Christmas morning.

Maybe it was better to leave them to their own devices. I didn't want either of them to censor themselves because of me. I had no intentions of letting them have a private conversation anyway. I loved the two of them and I really wanted them to kiss and makeup, literally or figuratively, whatever it took. That, and I wanted to know every juicy detail firsthand. I was a nosy asshole like that.

I left the old slab door open a crack and planted myself just behind it, so they wouldn't be able to see me if they looked into the room. I was taking the creepy eavesdropper vibe very seriously. The only disadvantage was I couldn't physically see them or their facial expressions. I'd take what I could get.

"Winter," Drew started, then stopped. There was a long silence and I was regretting not being able to see into the room when he finally continued.

"Winter, it hurt me when you thought I was trying to get into your pants instead of trying to protect you."

Okay, coming right out of the gates with some solid truths then. Good on you, Drew. Let's do this.

"Can you blame me?" Winter's voice was mildly defensive but that wasn't surprising. She really struggled with the words "I'm sorry," when she thought someone else was in the wrong. I had to turn my thoughts off before I missed any of the conversation.

"I would like to think you know me better than that," he responded quietly, almost too quiet for me to hear. I pushed myself closer to the edge of the door.

"Drew, we've known each other a long time. A loooooong time. Before the diner, I had gone to school with you my whole life. My parents are friends with Joe and Eileen. We've never been close, but I've always looked up to you like an older cousin. You gave me college advice and helped me apply for school. You always scheduled me with the best tip shifts when you found out I was paying for it on my own. You had the cooks bake me a high school graduation cake, for fuck's sake. Then we have sex, unexpected, mind-blowing sex. Sex that *you* started, for the record, and then you *ghost* me. I mean, I gave you an out, sure, and I meant it, but I never expected that by giving one I would lose my friend too."

There was another silence. *Fuck, I wish I could see their faces.*

"Winter, I follow the rules, right? I drive the speed limit, I do my taxes on time, I follow other people's dreams for me, and usually keep my complaints to myself." His self-deprecating humor felt flat. "I was your boss when we hooked up. That's a serious HR infraction. Sexualmisconduct-level bad. I panicked and I had to put up walls between us, because the truth is I can't trust myself not to do it again."

Yes! That's what I'm talking about.

I could picture Winter's expression right now. I'd bet a million dollars it was surprised, blushing red, and seriously uncomfortable. It was almost worth risking a peek.

"You have to understand I'd never done anything like that, Winter. Ever. You bring out something in me that I'm not really familiar with, and it's confusing as hell and terrifying at the same time."

Another silence.

"Do you regret it?" Her words were tentative, controlled.

"No." Drew's voice was strong now, emphatic. "I can't pretend I don't still want you; I can't pretend I wasn't jealous of Travis, and I can't pretend that I didn't want to be in his place. But I would never do anything to intentionally hurt you, Winter. Ever."

"Okaaaaaaay," she let out with a long sigh. "Can we try this friends thing again, please? I know sharing Christmas Day is kind of a big step, but let's not overthink it."

That's my girl. Knowing she was able to joke in that moment let me know she was at that stage of forgiveness. I hadn't heard her say, "I'm sorry," mind you, but I'd take the small wins. My peacemaking plan was a smashing success.

"I'd like that."

I heard a muffled shuffling through the door and decided it was time to make an appearance. I waited a few seconds before walking into the rec space again, finding them in a tight hug in the middle of the couch.

Winter looked up at me and cracked a grin. "Are you happy now? I know you heard the whole thing, you creeper." She tossed a decorative pillow at my head and I caught it with one hand.

"No regrets," I said without shame, as I launched myself onto the couch and wrapped my long arms around both of them into a big bear hug. "I'm fully invested in this relationship. We're a friendship throuple now."

She rolled her eyes as Drew laughed and I settled beside them, handing them each a controller to start a new game.

"All right," I said, excitedly, grabbing my controller and turning on the PlayStation.

The serious part of our holidays was over. We could deal with all of our problems in a few days when we were so full from food and alcohol that we had no choice but face our reality.

I wriggled my eyebrows at the two of them and grinned.

"You're going down. Merry Christmas, Mother Fuckers."

CHAPTER 21

WINTER

The diner was quiet tonight; not unusual between the holidays, but quieter than I had been expecting. I still had an hour before I had to close up and, aside from Chad, Carl's underling line cook, Hillary and I were the only ones here. I didn't usually work the night shift but Janice had wanted to take the week off to spend time with her son and I had nothing else taking up my time at the moment, so I had volunteered. I could use the money anyway.

I saved all of my tips for tuition fees for the year, and I almost had what I needed to finish the final semester with as little debt as possible. With my parents' income, I wasn't eligible for financial assistance, so I had to make every penny count. I didn't want to be drowning in debt when I graduated from a degree I wasn't even sure what to do with.

The Christmas present I had bought for Travis sat at the bottom of my dresser and I had taken it out to return ten times in the past week to get my money back. I couldn't really afford the watch I had bought him, but I had wanted to get him something special and it had seemed like the perfect, albeit cliché, gift.

Every time I went to throw it in my purse to bring it back to Saxon's though, I didn't have the heart to do it. I was refusing to look too deeply into those feelings. Denial was the safe haven I had come to know intimately and I welcomed its sweet, unencumbered relief.

I wiped the counter for the thirtieth time in as many minutes. This was a current reflection of my life. Slow, monotonous, and lonely.

I had been feeling a bit better since Quick forced Drew and I to talk out our issues. The guilt for the way I had treated him, when he had only been trying to protect me, had weighed heavily on my heart, but my pride weighed more. It probably would have taken a couple of weeks before I would have stepped up to the plate, so I was grateful Quick always pushed me in the direction that was in my best interest – well, ninety percent of the time. I didn't know what I would do without that man.

I certainly didn't know what I would do without his family. Once again, Amelia and Emmett had taken me in and given me a home when I had needed it the most. I couldn't help feeling like the lost orphan child, though, as I sat around their kitchen table and joined them in their Christmas rituals and traditions. The fact Amelia had sewn me a stocking stirred a well of emotions in me. I don't think my own mother had ever shown me that kind of dedication for no other reason than to bring me joy. I was a sopping mess by the end of the day.

Hillary shifted in her vinyl seat, and the obnoxious creak of the rough material broke me out of my thoughts. I looked around the near-silent space. The dim light was casting shadows all around the room, mimicking a horror film version of *Grease*. It was disconcertingly creepy, like something was off about an otherwise lovely scene, but you couldn't put your finger on it.

I wondered if passersby even knew we were open. It wasn't like it was a nice night out. The snow had been falling for hours, and I knew I would have to shovel Basil out of at least two feet of it before I made it home to my apartment. Good thing I was a Cascade Falls local; everyone who lived here knew you didn't leave home without a shovel and a pair of snow boots in your car. If you by chance forgot and one of our very regular snowstorms hit, you would never do it again. Ask me how I know.

Hillary huffed out a frustrated sigh and her high-pitched voice filled the space. "Do you ever feel like you're trapped in your own life?"

She tilted her head up to the ceiling as if asking the universe, then dropped her head into her delicate, well manicured hands and released a long groan of exasperation.

It was a bit unorthodox, but I was desperate to do *something* to move through this time warp of an hour, so I walked over and plopped myself down in the seat across from her, my orange apron pinching my ribs as I tucked my feet under the table.

"Yes," I said solemnly, nodding my head at her. "All of the time."

She peeked over at me from behind her hands and then grunted irritably. "It was a rhetorical question, Winter."

"Well, don't say things out loud in an empty diner and expect others not to start a conversation, Hillary," I snapped back, annoyed we couldn't talk for two seconds without her bitchy tone coming out to play.

"I'll just go back to cleaning this counter for the hundredth time." I moved to get up, but she surprised me by putting her hand on my arm and squeezing gently.

"I'm sorry." She sighed. Her tone had sounded genuine rueful, so I settled back into the seat for a moment, enjoying the excuse to sit down. "That was rude of me."

"It was," I agreed, assessing her carefully. "That's never seemed to matter to you before."

Hillary was the kind of woman you either hated or wanted to be like. She had the kind of beauty only the wealthy possessed; every golden, honey-blonde hair in place, every inch of her ivory skin clear and toned, every fiber of her tailored clothes rich and form fitting, her makeup flawless, her body language poised.

She emanated a self-assurance that screamed 'money.' She wasn't used to hearing the word no, and wouldn't tolerate it if she did. She was also whip-smart. Logan may own his share of Cascade Falls, but everyone knew Camden was teaching his only daughter everything he knew, and her fancy, likely well-earned, MBA from Barnard was no less impressive.

I didn't hate her or want to be like her, so maybe my assessment of her wasn't true after all. I was indifferent to Hillary. Other than her moments of austere bitchiness, she had never done anything to me, or to anyone I cared about – or didn't care about for that matter. She also had never done anything outwardly kind or selfless, so she was on neutral ground. Other than his looks, I had no idea what she could possibly see in Logan, but we all had our own tastes.

I looked at her now; her blueberry blue eyes were bloodshot with clumps of mascara crumbling along her bottom eyelashes, and if you looked hard enough, you could see deep purple bags under her eyes beneath layers of high-end foundation. She looked like a high class escort the morning after a rough night.

"I know," she said as she rubbed her eyes with the back of her hand. "I don't try to be a bitch, you know. It just seems to come naturally."

I reached over and popped an ice-cold fry into my mouth from her set-aside plate. "Wanna talk about it? I'm not exactly swimming in customers here."

She gave me a dubious look before sinking into the booth behind her, her body language finally relaxing.

"It's what I said." Her thin pink lips pursed into a sour smile. "I'm so stuck. With this wedding, Daddy's businesses, a fiancé that I can barely tolerate on most days – I'm stuck."

My brows rose in surprise. I had not been expecting that kind of confession. I mean, barely tolerating Logan was understandable, and I was a bit relieved to know Hillary could actually see the man for what he was despite all of the evidently fake appearances, but she stood to make a lot of money from this wedding; a minor fortune if the rumors were to be believed.

"Hillary, don't take this the wrong way, but from the outside looking in, you look like the exact opposite of stuck." I gave her a pointed look. "You have an Ivy League education, you grew up with money, and everyone thinks you're going to run the world one day. That's not exactly limiting."

She scoffed, tapping her nails on the scratched glass table. "That's all anyone can see though, isn't it? 'Look at Hillary, her life is perfect, she's got it made.'

"Daddy always wanted a boy and, instead, he got me. Mom died before she could give him anyone else, and so I was it; he had to settle for me to bring forward the family legacy." Her words were bitter, hurt lacing her tone.

"I'm only valuable because everyone on this earth wants a piece of my inheritance. Daddy can't touch it, Logan can't have access to it. No one financially benefits unless I'm around. I'm virtually a well-schooled puppet. I can't trust anyone around me, and that's exhausting."

"I wanted to get married in Barbados, you know that? Simple ceremony, ten people. Instead, I'm planning a wedding for 300 people, most of them I don't even know, and it's going to be covered by the media to help Daddy's ventures. No part of this day is about me. Or love for that matter."

Now this was some fabulous gossip. I wouldn't breathe a word of it to anyone but Quick, but my curious mind was getting carried away with everything she was telling me. Hillary was far more interesting than I had given her credit.

"Do you not love Logan?" I asked carefully, wanting more information but not wanting to risk her clamming up. It was still only us here and I couldn't even hear Chad in the back kitchen, so maybe he had gone out for a smoke break. Now was the time for juicy answers.

She gave me an incredulous look. "Do you think I ever had a choice in the matter? Stan and Camden practically dictated our nuptial agreement when we were twelve. It's why I chose Barnard. I could get away from here and live my own life for a few years before returning to my prison."

Her shoulders slumped as she looked down at her hands.

"Believe it or not, I do care about him. He's brash and he's an insufferable egomaniac sometimes, but he's had his share of bruises being Stanley's son too. When I was younger, I had hoped we could find love in each other one day, but it's never going to happen."

I decided then I would vault this conversation; I wouldn't tell anyone about Hillary's confessions, not even

Quick. Because, girl code. I was willing to give that to her, given her trust to lay it out on the table. Truthfully, I liked her more because of this conversation. Maybe that made me some kind of sadist, knowing someone else was suffering and their life wasn't perfect either. I wouldn't analyze my motivations too heavily.

"We always have choices, Hillary," I replied gently, knowing I was currently in the position to make a few choices of my own. "If this isn't the life you want, walk away now. Once you say 'I do,' this isn't going to go away – from what you're saying, its going to get worse — and then how will you feel? Is it worth it? I don't think you'll ever risk being poor," I joked, turning the unsolicited advice I was doling out into a little lighter diatribe.

"You may have to come down to earth with us other humans and actually worry about how you're going to pay a bill for a year or two, but it sounds better than jail."

Hillary chuffed, looking up at the ceiling again, seeming to count the water stains along the drop-in pieces of cement tile. Her eyes met mine and a small smile traced her lips.

"Thanks for the pep talk, sweets. I don't think I'm ready to make any life-altering decisions just yet."

That was my cue. I started to pull myself out of the booth when she put her hand on my arm once again.

"Thanks, Winter," she said softly. She removed her hand and started gathering her papers.

I walked over to the counter to close up for the night. There was no way anyone else was coming in in this weather, and I wanted to get out of here before I was truly snowed in.

Hillary came over to pay her bill. As she walked out the door, I looked down at the receipt. She had given me a $100 tip. I hoped she didn't think she needed to buy my silence, but I was grateful for the generosity all the same.

Our conversation had brought up a lot of repressed thoughts of my own about my life and where it was headed. I pushed them down, grateful for the first time in my life for the three feet of snow I'd have to spend the next hour shoveling. One couldn't think when they were working themselves into exhaustion. Thanks, universe.

I walked down the slippery concrete steps in my flip flops, my toes chafing in the bitter cold as I made my way down to the steamy lagoon.

Quick had gotten me a month's membership to Haven's Head Hot Springs, the local Nordic spa, and I desperately needed the therapy for my aching muscles after all of my manual labor last night. It had taken me an hour of shoveling and another full hour to drive home through the messy streets, only to find my parking lot hadn't been plowed and I had to shovel out a space just to get in. Good thing Basil was tiny, or I might have passed out right there in the snowbank, only to be found by vultures when the snow finally melted.

I breathed in the familiar lightly-metallic scent of iron and earth, settling myself into one of the deep pools. The natural hot water had been diverted into three separate spaces; one hot, one medium, and one mild – like taco flavors, really, but therapeutic spa bliss. I loved the hottest one of all and usually stayed in it long past the recommended time. If my flesh wasn't slightly boiled, it wasn't worth the entrance fee.

I couldn't even see a foot in front of me as I tucked myself into the rear corner where the best jets were. I nestled into the comfort of the hot water and let out a long sigh, closing my eyes to find my zen.

Drew was taking up most of my thoughts today. I could finally admit to myself, if not to him, that my reaction had been harsh and unwarranted. And selfish really, considering all he had been going through with the shock of his parents' illegal activities and their connection to Georgio. I was shocked myself.

Joe and Eileen, the sweetest, most down-to-earth, *Family Matters* kind of family, had their own *Ozarks* money laundering operation for the baddies of our county. I couldn't blame Drew for walking away from the diner, given that he was set to inherit the mess. I felt uncomfortable working there myself these days, but I couldn't afford to quit.

The diner was still a legal business, wasn't it? Just like Bourbon & Blues. I was an innocent employee making a few dollars to get through school and move on with my life. Why didn't that sound convincing to my own ears? Or ... thoughts. Brain? Whatever.

I opened my eyes and peered into the fog. The mist was thick — the thickest I had ever seen it. It was like the Stephen King film Quick and I watched way too young. Despite the heat of the water, a chill crept up my spine. I was about to laugh at my imagination when a hand touched my thigh and I let out a scream, an embarrassingly feminine high-pitched scream.

"Shit, sorry," a deep voice murmured apologetically. "I didn't see you there."

My racing heart calmed as I squinted into the haze. Piercing blue eyes stared back at me, and I realized I knew the beautiful man sitting beside me. Cameron Chase, Travis' friend. My stomach soured at the thought of Travis, and my face must have betrayed my thoughts because Cam lifted up his hands in a surrender gesture.

"I'm not here to cause trouble, Winter, I just need to soak my pain away, okay? Is it okay if I sit over here with you? It's the hottest spot and my quads could use the heat."

He shifted his body weight a little further from me and settled into his own seat. "I swear I won't say a word, if that would make you more comfortable."

I nodded before closing my eyes and sinking deeper into the water. His southern accent was so wholesome and cute; I could listen to him speak to me all day. I was going to be mature about this and not hold his friend's mistakes against him. A little voice inside my head, the voice I often steamrolled and ignored, told me that I should probably be more mature about Travis' situation too, but I wasn't going to think about that right now. Ignorance was bliss. The irony was not lost on me.

In the brief moment our eyes met, I couldn't help but notice how damn beautiful Cam was. He had one of those profiles that stuck out in a crowd. Tall and muscular, a light caramel skin tone, lips that were pillowy and looked distractingly kissable, and a set of light sky-blue eyes that could stop traffic.

When I had first been introduced to Cam at Après, Quick and I agreed he could easily be a Calvin Klein model. Quick would have given his left arm to see the man in his underwear. I would have too, if I were being honest. With that thought, I realized I could see this man in his swim shorts, which was practically the same thing.

Shamelessly, I cracked open one eye to take in the view beside me, but instead I let out an audible gasp. Despite the mist, and despite the fact I had been staring into his eyes just moments earlier, I had missed the bright purple mottled bruise taking over one side of his jaw.

"Are you okay?" I couldn't help asking, moving closer to examine his face. The water rippled as he moved away slightly, wincing when my fingers brushed the swollen skin.

"Sorry!" I bit my lip, wondering why I had been compelled to touch him in the first place. I'd blame it on animal magnetism.

"Cam, how did this happen?"

"I was on the wrong side of a boxing glove, sugar." His angelic features scrunched into a pained scowl. "Well, knuckles, anyway. A training fight gone wrong."

Our voices carried through the calm waters, and I lowered mine out of respect for the other spa guests, even though we were completely alone on this side of the large pool.

"Have you gotten medical attention, at least? Not going to lie, Cam, it looks bad. Like, really bad."

He grinned but it was more like a halfhearted grimace. "Boxing is a rough sport, honey. This won't be the worst of my injuries."

As if to prove his point, he sank deeper into the water until it hit his chin.

"Are you some sort of masochist?" I joked, trying to lighten the mood. If we were going to sit here for who knew how long, I might as well chatter politely than pretend to ignore him.

"You could say that." He raised an eyebrow and a glint entered his gaze. "The pain helps center me and my demons."

Oh, wasn't that an enticing morsel of information. My thoughts went wicked, imagining his demons coming out to play with me in all kinds of naughty ways, before turning sad as I imagined the demons Travis had been battling. I couldn't help but wonder if Cam was caught up in Georgio's web of crime too.

"I'm sorry, sugar, what that too much information?" Cam's voice turned serious as he watched me carefully. "Where'd you go just now?"

"It's nothing." I waved my hand dismissively through the water, causing ripples to form across the surface of the misty pool beyond.

"Desperate people do desperate things," Cam said quietly, as if reading my thoughts. "Desperate people make mistakes. Compassion can go farther than judgment, if you'll let it."

That comment stung me more than it should have, given the kind way it had been delivered. I shook my head and looked away from him, speaking into the air in front of us. "I don't want to talk about it. Why don't you tell me about yourself instead?"

He smiled sadly before allowing me to steer the conversation in this direction. "Sure, sugar, what do you want to know?"

I tilted my head in thought, the back of my neck settling into the hot water. "What brings a Southern boy like you to Sequoia County?"

"That's an easy one." His pouty lips pursed as he closed his eyes and answered. "My birth-mom was from here. I came to see if I could find any family."

"And have you?" I asked, curious to see why a man from the sunniest area of the country would want to live in one of the coldest.

"Not yet, but I keep tryin'. My adopted parents died a few years back and I don't have much for records, so its slower than molasses."

"I'm sorry to hear that," I said breathlessly, truly sorry for his loss. As much as my parents were absent these days, I couldn't imagine losing them for good. "Any siblings?"

"Thank you. Nope, just me. It's why I left, there wasn't a whole lot to stick around for anymore."

The poor man. In another state, with no family at all for Christmas. Did he even see Travis over the holidays? Did he have anyone else? My heart ached for him, this stranger.

He was likable to be sure, but it was more than that. Our situations were different, but I could connect with his feelings of loneliness; for years I'd also felt like a wayward wanderer waiting for something or someone to bring meaning to my life.

We continued to talk, staying in the pool for far longer than we should have, and he answered every question I asked. From the mundane – his favorite candy was Reese's Pieces, to the existential – he enjoyed philosophy and poetry, to the completely random – he could say the alphabet backwards in less than five seconds, and he proved it.

Our conversation flowed easily, and I could admit that I was enjoying myself. It wasn't the quiet, peaceful day of avoiding my own thoughts I had initially wanted; his company was a better distraction than I ever could have planned.

He was sweet, and kind, and could set even the most skittish man at ease with his deep baritone and sexy accent. I had snuck a peek or two while we were talking. His shoulders and arms were muscularly honed and defined; I would trust him to carry me from a burning building.

A swirling tattoo of intricate symbols followed the line of his hips up his ribs, stopping just below his underarm. It was pretty and delicate, yet masculine and strong; the perfect depiction of his appearance and how he carried himself. Every few minutes I got a whiff of his scent on the breeze — an earthy sandalwood and fresh soil. It was comforting and made me feel safe, like the smell of apple pie out of the oven, or Quick's pine scented aftershave.

We were seated closer now, almost on top of each other, and I could feel his body heat pressed against me even through the warmth of the pool. I was getting lightheaded and dehydrated. The dull throb of a headache had started behind my eyelids. Still, I didn't want to leave.

After a few minutes of comfortable silence, I couldn't ignore the painful pressure in my head any longer.

"Cam?" I asked, turning my body to face him.

"Yes, sugar?" His eyes were closed, sweat beading along his forehead and along the crest of his high cheekbones.

"Thank you for the welcome distraction. I needed this today."

He raised his large hands and put them on my shoulders, his blue eyes tearing through the layers of my shields and seeing into the depths of my soul.

"I like talking to you, sugar. Thanks for taking some of my pain away."

I didn't think, not for a second, as I leaned in and placed a gentle kiss on his bruises, my mouth just barely an inch from his soft, full lips. He froze, not moving a muscle. Immediately, I pulled away, regretting the poor decision to accost this man when all we had been doing was talking. He squeezed my arms and held me there, his eyes full of indecision. Then he bowed his head and gently pushed me back.

"I'll see you around, sugar." He pulled himself off of the ledge and waded through the dark pool toward the stone staircase leading out to the changing rooms.

I couldn't take my eyes off of him, cursing my stupidity. Was I that lonely and pathetic that I needed a stranger's validation? Apparently, I was.

Cam stopped suddenly and slowly turned his head around to look at me. His blue eyes were filled with regret and my heart shriveled in my chest. I watched him disappear into the mist and then sunk beneath the hot water, drowning my embarrassment and my pain.

I needed to stop ignoring the other men in my life and get my shit together. It was time to face my problems.

CHAPTER 22

DREW

A scream filled the previously deadened winter night air. The piercing sound cut through my dreams and into my reality and I shot out of bed.

I hadn't imagined it. It was Mom or one of the girls; the pitchy sound definitely female.

As I struggled to pull on a pair of pants, I peered out my window into the dark field below. I couldn't see anything, but this room didn't have a view of Mom and Dad's next door. Pulling a jacket on over my bare chest, I slipped my feet into my shoveling boots by the apartment door and rushed outside. An old car was racing away down the driveway at breakneck speed toward the mountain road below, tires screeching as it grappled to stay on the icy gravel.

A feminine wail cut through me once again. I immediately recognized Mom's voice.

Shit.

Something was very wrong. I raced through the crunchy snow footpath to get to the house, guilt flooding the pit of my stomach. I hadn't talked to my parents in over a week and hadn't shown up to any of my shifts at the diner. Mom had knocked on my door several times, pleading with me to come out. I had refused to see her, still furious with their choices and the position it had put us all in.

Christmas had been the hardest. Mom had called me crying that morning; I took the call in Shane's bedroom while his family opened their stockings. She begged me to come home, and I had been the world's most heartless son, only speaking to my siblings to wish them a merry Christmas.

None of them knew what was going on; Tom and Charlie wanted their big brother back. Rosie and Dawn thought I was being a "dickwad asshole" to make Mom feel so shitty on Christmas Day. Dad was quiet, no words to say when they really counted.

Fuck him.

My anger couldn't overpower my fear once I saw the side entrance door leading into the kitchen pulled off of its hinges and hanging on an angle. It had been a break-in. Panic exploded in my chest as I started calling out every name in the Johnson family household.

"Mom? Rosie? Dawn? Tom? Charlie!? DAD!?"

This side of the house was still dark, but I could see kitchen drawers had been torn out of the cabinets. The floor was littered with cutlery and white dish towels glowed in the moonlight. Chairs were overturned in the living room, and the TV screen had been smashed to smithereens, half hanging off the wall.

The light of the bedroom hallway glowed and I rushed into the narrow space, only to stop in my tracks.

Dad lay in a puddle of his own blood. The red goo oozed from a large slice in his side, saturating the blush pink carpet. Mom was sobbing as she cradled his head in her hands, her whole body trembling. Dad had turned an ashy white, like salt-stained asphalt.

I ran to grab the house phone on the living room coffee table just around the corner – I hadn't thought to grab my cell from my bedside table – and dialed 911.

"Where are the kids?" My words broke through my mother's trance.

"Your father got them all into Rosie's room and had them lock the door when he heard them smash the door in. I refused to go in with them."

"911, what's your emergency?" A calm male voice answered the phone. I quickly explained the break-in and the stabbing. We'd need police and medics as soon as possible. Dad would die otherwise.

We were advised not to move him, but to put pressure on the wound. I grabbed clean towels from the main bath and placed a firm palm over the gash, not daring to move an inch and risk hurting him even more. On autopilot, I couldn't think, couldn't breathe, as the world as I knew it tipped even further on its axis. We were practically upside down at this point.

Mom rocked back and forth, humming, as tears streamed down her cheeks. Muffled sobs sounded on the other side of the door down the hall.

"It's going to be okay, guys. Just stay in the room, okay? The ambulance is coming. Rosie, hold Charlie in your arms and hold him tight. Dawn, hold Tom, okay? I'll come to get you as soon as I can. Do not open that door."

My voice was as steady as it could be, but I couldn't say it was reassuring. Still, I hoped it was some comfort. They would never be the same if they saw their father – our father – in this condition. It was one thing to suspect, or to hear it happen, but another thing entirely to have the image burned into your brain. I hoped to spare them all from that.

The ambulance arrived moments later. Three paramedics stormed through the kitchen and took over the morbid scene. I pulled Mom in my arms as they bandaged what they could of my father's wounds and placed him on a stretcher.

"Go with him, Mom. I'll send the kids to Charlene's, and I'll be there as soon as I can." I kissed her cheek and pushed her toward the still open door. She climbed into the back of the ambulance.

Once they were well down the driveway, I took in the state of the house with sharper eyes. I didn't want my siblings to deal with the mess, and I wasn't going to be able to do it myself. I'd call Shane on the way to the hospital.

After throwing a blanket over the glaring red stain in the middle of the hallway floor, I gently knocked on the bedroom door. I no longer heard any sounds behind the hollow wood.

"Hey," I murmured softly. "You can come out now." A click came of the lock disengaging and my little brother peeked his head around the door.

"Hey buddy." I opened my arms and he ran into my hug, burying his face into my shoulder. Tom came next, followed by the two girls. I reached to wrap my arms around them all, and we stood in somber silence, now bonded by blood and trauma.

"We're going to be okay," I mumbled into the tops of their heads. "It's all going to be okay."

Releasing the hug, I took in their red-rimmed eyes and stricken faces. "I'm going to get Aunt Charlene to come pick you up. Go pack a bag. Rosie, can you pack Charlie's for him? I have a few calls I need to make. Pack enough for the week."

The police would be here soon and I didn't want the kids anywhere near the crime scene.

How did our family home become a crime scene?

I called Charlene, being as vague as possible. Given the late hour, she seemed to understand this was an emergency. She arrived twenty minutes later, still wearing her pink slippers and purple fuzzy bathrobe. Quickly, she wrangled the kids into the car while shooting fearful glances at me. The police sirens came closer. I wanted – needed – them out of here. No need to add more trauma this evening.

"I'll keep you updated as I know more," I said softly. I kissed her cheek and closed her car door.

She slowly made her way down the icy driveway and disappeared down the mountainside. I allowed myself a solitary minute to collapse. Lowering to the step, I shivered in the cold. I didn't want to be anywhere near the destruction. Taking deep breaths, I tried to recall my first aid training from the ski hill. I was desperately trying not to go into shock.

What was taking the police so long?

An uneasy feeling unfurled in my gut as I considered the scenario. This hadn't been a simple home invasion. Georgio's men had done this. The delay with the police had to be Georgio's doing. Hell, we were lucky the ambulance arrived as quickly as it did.

Exhaustion, fear, and futility outweighed my anger for the moment. I just needed Dad to live. The rest could come later.

The police arrived. The sirens and flashing lights assaulted my senses in the dark night. Two officers stepped out; a tall, silver-haired man who looked to be in his fifties, and a younger woman with her blonde hair pulled back into a high ponytail.

I gave my statement in a monotone, anxious to get to the hospital. I was chastised for sending the kids away before they could speak to them, but I didn't care. I was sinking into an underwater grave, their questions garbled and distorted. Finally, they let me leave as they processed the scene. I'd have to call Shane for helping cleaning up later. No one would be allowed in until they were done.

I went back to my apartment and packed an overnight bag, my body and mind on complete autopilot. I drove to the hospital and held Mom in the waiting room as we sat in the gut-wrenching fear of the unknown.

Dad had been admitted for emergency surgery, but the surgeon wasn't confident of the outcome. Mom couldn't speak and I continued moving through the motions in a fugue state, hoping the numbness could protect me from losing it. My family needed me. I could not lose my shit.

Four hours later, I awoke with a start as the doctor shook my shoulder. Wiping the sleep from my eyes and the small crust of drool from the corner of my mouth, I listened as she explained the procedure, my heart racing.

Dad had suffered a hemorrhage and lost too much blood; he'd had a transfusion and a surgery to try and repair his liver, which had been severely damaged in the stabbing. They had him in a medically induced coma to try and increase his chances of survival. He was alive, but barely. I fought down the panic creeping up my throat and held Mom tighter as she sobbed into my arms.

We'd be permitted to see him in a few hours. They advised us to go home and get some rest. I headed to Charlene's to do just that; Mom sat silent by my side in the car. I was working hard to keep my thoughts from spiraling. I focused on the positive. Dad was still on this side of a grave, and I took comfort in the fact that everyone else in my family was safe, a consideration I'd never had to make until now.

I needed a shower, I needed a drink, and I needed to figure out our next steps. I'd fall apart tomorrow.

Two days later, I climbed out of bed to the sound of my door being beat down. I had been running off of my feet, trying to take care of the family while Dad remained unconscious.

I had no choice but to take over the diner's business affairs. Mom was too busy with the kids and dealing with the police investigation, and I couldn't let my spite destroy everything my parents had built, even if it was from poor choices and criminal ties.

I'd called Shane to have him on standby for when the police finally let us access the house again. He insisted on coming over, but I kept pushing him off. I had too many things to do.

I shut down the diner for a few days; we would have closed down early on New Year' Eve and closed New Year's Day anyway. Word was out Dad had been attacked. I wasn't interested in dealing with reporters showing up, putting any of the staff on the spot. Violent crime was rarely reported on in Cascade Falls, and the Johnson family were about to become a circus show at the zoo.

It was New Year's Eve – it had been hard to keep track of time – and my brain was struggling to keep up as I made my way through my living room to the door. My apartment was a mess, dirty clothes and takeout boxes everywhere. I grimaced at the sour smell in my kitchen. I had left the milk out on the counter during my snack-stupor at two a.m. when I had finally made it home.

"Drew?" a muffled male voice called from behind the door. "Open up, man."

Bleary-eyed, I opened the door to streaming sunlight to Shane and Winter's concerned faces.

"Oh, thank God." Winter wrapped her arms around me into a tight hug.

Shane pulled us both in to his chest, his long arms holding us close. My brain wasn't working yet. What time was it? Why were they here? Had I invited them over?

"Guys?" My voice was muffled as I spoke into Winter's auburn hair. "Can I have my body back?"

They released me almost instantly, and I beckoned them into my dark and dirty apartment. At least it was warm.

We stood in awkward silence for a minute before Winter reached for my hand and squeezed.

"We've been worried sick about you, Drew. When I heard the news..." Her voice thickened and she swallowed hard, tears forming in her blue eyes.

"I am so, so sorry." She shuffled over into my body again, wrapping her arms around me, a little gentler this time, and buried her head into my chest. "What can we do?"

Shane entered my kitchen and rummaged, taking a tin of coffee and filters out of the cupboard. He busied himself with the task while I continued to hold Winter, enjoying the comfort of her body heat and fierce grip. I had been too busy taking care of everyone else; I hadn't realized how much I needed a hug.

I breathed in her lavender scent and my body immediately relaxed. I held her for what could have been seconds or hours. Time stood still in that moment. Eventually, I let go reluctantly.

"I could use some help cleaning up the house," I admitted, not wanting Mom or the kids to have to come back and face the disaster zone along with everything else. "But let's just have some coffee first, okay? I'm not ready to face reality yet."

The three of us settled into the living room, drinking crappy coffee without cream – thanks to my lack of groceries – and stuck to lighter topics.

It took all day, but they helped me put the entire home back in order. We ripped up the soaked carpet and put down a small rug. Then we carried all of the broken furniture to the garage, out of sight and mind. For now.

Shane invited me to his place for New Year's Eve; he and Winter were going to have a low-key movie night, but I turned down the offer. I was heading back to Charlene's for some semblance of a New Year's celebration with my family. No one wanted to do much, but I also didn't want everyone wallowing the night away while Dad was still in a coma. I'd do my best to keep up their spirits, without drowning myself in rum, even if that was the most enticing plan I'd had all day.

I'd have to make some tough decisions in the next few days. The longer Joe Johnson was out of commission, the more I would have to step in. Our family was in danger. Georgio's 'message' had been received loud and clear. I knew I wasn't alone; Shane and Winter would help me through this, and that made me feel a little stronger, a little more capable.

I just wished I knew what the fuck to do.

CHAPTER 23

CAMERON

"**H**ave you considered throwing in the towel on this?" Douglas Fraser's brittle voice from years of smoking too many cigarettes was grating on my nerves. "I don't want to talk myself out of a job, but —"

"We're not quittin'. She was last seen here, and I'm not leaving this alone until we find her alive or in a box."

Doug continued, undeterred, having made this argument before to the same response. "At this point, we've checked all archives and leads in Cascade Falls, Sheldonville, and Kensington. Hell, even my sources in Carlisle can't catch a whiff of her. We can expand our search to all of Sequoia County, but that's going to take time and a hell of a lot more money, kid."

"I'll pay it, then. We're gonna find her, Doug. I can't leave until we do."

There was a brief silence, and I could picture the balding, skinny man with yellow teeth and black beady eyes stubbing out his cigarette, only to light another. What he lacked in appearance he made up for in thoroughness, and many people said he was the best in the business. So far, the best in the business wasn't doing a hell of a lot for me, but I couldn't lose hope.

If I lost my hope, I'd have nothing left at all.

"Alright. It's your cash to burn. I'll expand my search. Give me a few weeks."

He hung up, leaving me alone with my thoughts. I had never known my biological mom, so it was hard to feel any real feelings toward her other than this compulsion to find her, to know I wasn't completely alone in the world. Today was my first New Year's Eve without Momma and Pop, and it wasn't going to be an easy 24 hours.

I allowed myself to think about them for a few minutes a day, refusing to drown in the barrel of grief. I just took a warm sponge bath in it, letting the water cleanse my resolve, just enough to push me forward. Fitting really, since they died in a submerged vehicle at the bottom of the river.

They say true drowning is peaceful, but I don't know how they — whoever they were — would know that, given those who actually drowned were deader than dead. For Momma's sake, I hoped it had been. Pop would have stayed stoic til the end, I'd bet, holding Momma and telling her they'd be okay wherever they ended up.

I'd never seen anything shake that man to his core, and he'd loved Momma more than life itself; one of those beautiful, Oscar-winning movie kind of loves that stood the test of time and heartbreak. If I could ever get out of my mess of a life, I was going to find me a love like that.

I stretched out on the bed, still between the sheets when I took Doug's call. It had been a late night at Bourbon & Blues; the crowd had been particularly rowdy over the holiday season. Many folks showed up to celebrate New Years on Cascade Falls slopes, and the bar had been full of haughty hot heads from the city who couldn't hold their liquor or their tongues. I had been busy.

My muscles ached. I'd taken a few punches from drunken frat boys, after the training I had put my body through the morning before. I yearned for the burn on my body that took the ache away from my heart.

Nine months. I had been in Sheldonville for nine months, with nothing to show for it. When I had decided to pack up what was left of my meager life and head to this part of the country, I had thought it would be a quick trip. I'd hire someone to help me track my birth mom down, we'd find her, we'd get some answers to fill in the blanks of my past and genetics; maybe I'd come to understand why I was just so damn mad all the time, and then I could – well, if I were to quit lying to myself, I would admit I hadn't thought very far past the 'answers' part.

Maybe she'd love me and be so thankful I found her. Maybe she wouldn't, and she'd left because she never wanted a son in the first place. Hell, if I knew. I figured I'd figure out the rest of my life once I had gotten that bit of closure. I never thought about her most of my growin' up years; Momma and Pop were so good to me, I never had much reason to. But now, now I needed something, or someone, to fill that hole in my heart.

Daisy Knight. That was her name. It was the only real thing I knew about her. That and her age, if she was still alive. 42. She had me when she was seventeen, and her parents had kicked her out for becoming pregnant. That's the story Momma told me the first time I had found out I was adopted.

I was ten when we covered a genetics unit at school, looking at our parents' photos and point out the traits we got from each side of the family that we could see. My light brown skin didn't match my parents' dark chocolate complexion, and I hadn't thought to question it until that moment.

I had cried for hours that night, confused as all hell about where I had come from and where I might belong now that I knew I had been someone else's before I became Cameron Chase. Then I got over it. Never gave it much thought until I never had anybody left. My parents were only children. I was an only child. No grandparents still living. Just me. Only me.

So, after I had packed up the last of their belongings and sold as much as I could to cover the mountain of debt left in their wake, I stuffed everything I owned into Pop's sky-blue Chevy Chevelle and left everything I knew on a hope and a prayer that Daisy Knight was still living in Sequoia County and might find a place in her heart for her long-lost son.

I had hated my job and it was a blessing to have a reason to quit. It was early spring when I finally set foot on Sheldonville soil, so I took some work with the closest construction company I could find. It was an easy way to get a job; construction companies were always looking for people who could hold a hammer and hit a nail.

Pop had been a carpenter, and I'd worked with him every summer until college, learning his craft to make enough money to help pay for school. I preferred to work with my head than with my hands, but it was mindless. At the end of the day, I could say, "I did that." There was satisfaction in seeing results somewhere in my life.

I needed the money too. I had made it through college with only a small student loan, only to take on the motherload of all debts when my parents died. Pop's gambling hobby took all of the equity out of their small bungalow, and they owed more than the home was worth in a bad economy. I lost my parents and gained creditors. Fate was playing a cruel joke on the Chase family.

A series of rumbles shook me out of my walk down memory lane. Steam started to billow through the air vents on my floor, and I leapt out of bed before the moisture choked me out. My apartment was the top level over an old laundromat and no doubt illegal. Still, it was all I could afford, so I put up with the Florida-like heat and humidity. It was the most like home I would find in a place like Sequoia County.

I looked at my clock; three in the afternoon. I had to get ready for tonight, anyway. I wished my New Year's Eve plans were anything but what I had gotten myself into this evening.

I rubbed a palm over my face and dropped to the floor to do my usual hundred push-ups. Might as well get my warm-up in early. I was going to need it.

"Mother-fucking cock-eating bastard!"

I looked over my shoulder to see the blond, wiry beanpole of a fella, cursing his wraps up and down as he struggled to tighten one across his wrist.

"Simmer down, Zimmerman," I drawled, focusing on my own gear for the night's fight. "We both know who gets to win tonight, and it ain't you."

I wrapped my own neon blue wraps around my swollen knuckles, taking extra care to secure my thumbs. I had broken my thumbs too many times to count in the early days, and I didn't want any more damage to deal with tonight than absolutely necessary.

Zimmerman grunted, anger flashing across his ugly mug and dark eyes. "I don't know why it's always you these days. My reputation's takin' a hit here."

I scoffed, humorlessly. "He's settin' me up to take a nice fall. He'll make some real money off me then." I continued to wrap my left wrist, my weak point, and made sure it was as tight as possible without impeding its mobility. "Drake will too, so you'll get your cut eventually."

"I don't know when we signed up to be Georgio's whores." His disgust was evident, as if being a 'whore' was the world's worst fate. My late momma would have hit him over the head with a frying pan if she had heard those words.

"I'm nobody's whore," I stated blandly, not interested in getting into it with Zimmerman. He was volatile, a trait I supposed I could claim too on my worst days, but he was also an addict. I had no idea how he could fight with the drugs in his system, but given the number of track marks on his body, he had been doing this a long time.

I'd bet good money Georgio only kept him around because he was useful at drawing a good crowd. He had once been pro before the drugs got to him, which is probably how he had gotten involved with Georgio in the first place. We all had our reasons, but every last one of us was an ant under Big G's thumb, waiting for him to decide to crush us dead.

I blew out a long breath and stood, my large frame taking up too much space in the small locker room.

"Look," I said flatly, eyeing him stoically. "There are over 200 people here tonight. I peeked at the crowd earlier.

Really rich people by the looks of it. Let's just do what we agreed to do and get this over with."

Zimmerman grunted in response and started jumping on the balls of his feet to stretch out. I began to do the same. With any luck, we could be out of here before midnight. Although Georgio made it very clear we should draw out the last round as long as possible.

That shouldn't be a problem; Zimmerman was usually wiped by the third round anyways, whereas I always held back, until the last set of punches when it really counted. I didn't know how much money was on the line tonight, but I could bet it was more than I had made in my entire lifetime. It made me sick what he made off me, all because of one stupid mistake.

A knock on the door took me out of my pre-fight routine, and Travis poked his pretty head in from behind the door.

"Hey man, just checking in. How you feeling?"

I looked at my friend who looked miserable. More than miserable; miserable people looked happy in comparison. It was his first fight night and, while I knew he could blend into any crowd with his smile and wit, he didn't show any of it to me. His breakup with Winter was eating him alive and his mom's health had taken another turn. He and I were no different; we were all trapped in our own lives and lies.

I tried to smile reassuringly at him, my jaw still bruised and sore from a misplaced bare-knuckled punch during the last fight night. I managed to get a kidney shot in to dodge most of the blow, but the damage was enough. I almost lost my teeth.

"All good, man. It's not *my* first rodeo. How're you holding up?"

He grimaced, digging his hands in his pockets. "I'll make great tips tonight, so there's that. Just another way he can keep me here, though. It's fucking sickening."

He took a pack of gum out of his pocket and popped a stick in his mouth, offering one to me. I took it for later; I didn't want the taste of Wintergreen sticking to my mouth guard.

"I keep getting groped by drunk housewives drenched in Chanel. I think they think I'm for sale too." He rolled his eyes in disgust. "Maybe that's the direction I'm headed. I've already sold my soul to the devil. Will selling my body be any worse?"

It was dramatic and rhetorical, I knew, but I gave him a little shove in response. "You're not a whore either."

He blinked at me, confused, and Zimmerman piped up behind me. "Sure, he ain't."

"Shut up, Zimmerman." I growled and nudged Travis out of the room, following him into the dank hallway of the club's basement. I put a hand on his shoulder. "Seriously, you okay?"

He wiped his hands down his face and attempted a smile. "It's not the way I had pictured spending my New Year's Eve, you know? Just ... stay safe, man. I don't like the look of that guy."

I let out a throaty laugh. Travis' concern was sweet; the man had sugar for a heart. "I've fought Zimmer more times than I can count. He ain't gonna hurt me tonight. I promise you that."

I gave his shoulder a brief squeeze and then pushed him lightly down the hallway. "Now get gone before Big G has your ass, or you might end up a whore after all."

He snorted and a rare grin flitted across his face. Then he turned, heading back to the big ballroom where the fighting ring was set up.

I walked back into the tiny locker room to continue getting ready, amped with the adrenaline anticipation of a good tussle. Tonight, I fought to win.

The rage in me was a rising tide as I pummeled into my now unconscious opponent. The referee and the announcer struggled to pull me off of him. I had no control over myself in this state, just muscle and madness, and raw, brutal strength.

My chest heaved when I was finally ripped away and pushed into a corner. I took in deep gulps of air, muttering my practiced mantra over and over until I could regain control of my senses and shake off the demons that possessed me in a boxing ring.

The red haze of violence clouding my eyes lifted and I watched the crowd disperse, moving on to other celebrations for the new year. Georgio's men were everywhere, distributing drugs and party hats, like the people hadn't just been thirsting for another man's blood to drown in. This quiet town was just as twisted and debauched as any big city I'd seen.

I toweled off and snuck out the side set of stairs leading up to the back alley for a smoke. I needed the nicotine to settle my nerves and even me out. Disgusting, but it was effective.

I was only in my shorts in the frigid night air, but the freezing temperature helped ground me too. A guy I didn't recognize was already standing there smoking in a parka and big snow boots. This was a staff-only spot, so he had to be one of Georgio's guys.

"Great fight tonight, man." The guy nodded to me and I gave him a gruff "thanks" in return. I hadn't wanted company with my cool down.

"Hey!" Looking down the steel steps, I saw Travis walking up. He too, was dressed for the weather. "That was some fight, Cam! You're a machine!"

Travis I could handle. I didn't make friends easily, but this man had a way of getting under your skin. Not like a tick bite, where you didn't want to even think about the kind of diseases they're sure to give you, but like a medical implant you know will keep you safe from something just as bad, or worse. Travis was safe.

"Thanks," I murmured, lighting and taking a long drag of the cigarette. The head rush instantly soothed the adrenaline fading throughout my body.

The guy – Brett, Travis called him – started talking about a few people he and Travis knew, and I tuned them out, taking in the cold air and the stars like crystals above our heads. I was lost in the Milky Way and my mind meandered like the lazy parts of the Mississippi to the woman who currently took up more space in my thoughts that she should.

My search for solitude at the spa had been pleasantly shook up by the beauty, and I was surprised by how easy it had been to talk to her. I didn't talk to many people. I didn't *want* to talk to many people. I couldn't help feel a little bit of guilt in my gut. She had kissed me, not the other way around, and it hadn't really been a kiss anyway. But she had been Travis' girl, and that was a code I wouldn't break, not on my life. I needed to tell him. I snuck a look at my best friend in the state — maybe even the whole world at this point — when I noticed Travis had turned a panicked shade of pale.

"Yeah," Brett said, shaking his head emphatically. "You didn't hear? The news said it was just a random break-in, but a lot of the guys here think Georgio called in a hit. The diner guy – John something? Isn't that on your run? Cascade Falls, right?"

Travis turned on his heel and raced down the slippery steps. "I'll call you later, Cam."

I shrugged at Brett and stubbed my smoke before heading back into the hidden illegal bar to get dressed and go home. I had made Big G his money, and now it was time to call it a night. The ball could drop with or without me. I just hoped next year wasn't the same shitstorm of a Sunday. A man could dream.

CHAPTER 24

TRAVIS

Winter wasn't taking my calls.

It was its own form of torture, her refusing to speak to me. I had known from the moment I had admitted to myself I was falling for her that the day would come where my circumstances would royally fuck me over; and boy, had they ever.

The last few weeks had been painful. Mom had taken a turn for the worse, Devon was finally admitted into another expensive facility sure to fail and keep me chained to Georgio for the rest of my life. Despite everything, I was juggling to stay on this side of the grass. I couldn't keep my head on straight. Winter invaded my thoughts like a three-star general waging war on my brain.

How had I fallen so hard so quickly? Was I that starved for attention? She had unlocked something in me I hadn't even known was there, and I was being a spineless, helpless sap. I didn't know how I could make her trust me again, but I would do whatever it took.

She wasn't perfect. I was just as hurt as I was desperate to make amends. She had dropped me, literally *dropped* me, like I had no value or meaning in her life, when I *knew* she was starting to feel the same way about me. What had happened to her to make her turn off her feelings so quickly? How could Winter be so cold?

I stared at my phone screen. The spider-vein cracks from too many drops on the floor had warped the wallpaper photo. I needed to change it anyway; it was a selfie of Winter and I in the park, her grinning at the camera and me kissing her rosy cheek. She looked so happy in it. We looked so happy in it. I could puke.

I had puked last night when I heard the news. As soon as Brett had said that Joe Johnson had been stabbed, I looked up the local news on my phone at the back of the bar. Sure enough, the story of a random home invasion popped up in my newsfeed and I had to run to the bathroom to puke up my guts. There was no doubt in my mind that Georgio had ordered a hit on Joe. What if he had ordered something on the diner itself? Winter could have been hurt; she could have been *killed*.

I couldn't say I had liked Joe much – he certainly wasn't very pleasant to me. But given the nature of the circumstances I couldn't say that I blamed him. But no one, *no one* deserved to be taken out in their own home. The man had kids. Fuck, Drew, Winter's friend, was his son. The Johnson family would be a mess. Welcome to the bonanza; I wished they had never been invited to the party.

Once I had finally made it home after the last few hours of my agonizing New Year's Eve 'fight night' shift, full of *Desperate Housewives* wannabes with both men and women thinking I was for sale, I paced the floor for hours, debating the most acceptable time to call her. I settled on 8:00 am, and hadn't gotten a wink of sleep as I watched the clock on my nightstand.

It hadn't mattered anyways because she hadn't taken my call. Or my fifth call, or my ninth. Eight hours later, I was still staring at my phone as I sat in the powder blue vinyl chair next to Mom's hospital bed, willing Winter to call me back. I just wanted to hear her voice. She could tell me to 'fuck off,' for all I cared, I just needed to know she was okay.

The monitors around me beeped their continuous rhythm. They had become somewhat soothing in a way; predictable, at the very least. Mom had been admitted after another bad incident left her on the floor for hours while I had been at work. Her legs had frozen up and she fell, smashing her head on the coffee table.

She had a concussion and her leg had broken in two places. She was foggy and had trouble remembering our conversations. The doctors weren't sure if that was a result of the concussion itself or if the disease was progressing to the late stages. I only left her side to work and sleep, not daring to miss a moment if this was truly her last go at life.

She was sleeping now and I needed to stretch my legs, the weeks of late nights and limited sleep catching up to me. I was restless, a result of living in a constant over-caffeinated and overtired loop. Speaking of, I wanted another cup of terrible hospital coffee sludge. It could burn your insides by the third degree, but it only took two minutes to kick in, and I was here for it.

As I passed the nurse's station, a thought crossed my mind and I cursed myself for having never thought of it before. Joe Johnson was in the hospital. There were only two in the area; could he have been admitted here?

I don't know why I wanted to torture myself even more, but I suddenly felt compelled to see the man in living color. Winter may not be taking my calls, but if I could see Joe breathing with my own two eyes, maybe I could soften this raw feeling in my gut. Maybe.

I called the hospital switch board and asked for Joe Johnson's room number. I was grateful for the years of honing my charms. The operator had been very suspicious of me, but ended up giving me the number within two minutes of chatting her up. I was in luck – probably a terrible way to look at the situation – but he was just one floor above Mom.

I could go see him this very minute.

I poured – a loose description since it had the consistency of gravy – a cup of coffee blacker than my soul from the visitor comfort station and worked up the courage to see the man.

This is not my fault.

I had said these words to myself hundreds of times over the past 24 hours, but they didn't quite land in the zone of believability. I was a man doing my job, due to my own shitty circumstances. Joe had already been laundering for Georgio for years before I came into the picture. I hadn't reported anything to Georgio to make him think there were any issues. Hell, I was just a money mule; I didn't make threats or break bones, or whatever it was that Georgio's muscle had done.

Still, the guilt was there and I couldn't shake it.

In front of his door now, my feet had been working without my brain's involvement. I took a deep breath and peered in; no one was there. I supposed New Year's Day would be a busy one for the Johnson family – the newspaper article had said that they had five kids.

I stepped into the dark room, my eyes adjusting to the man on the nondescript medical bed in front of me. Joe Johnson had lost the spark of life that made him a human being. Laying there instead was a shell of a man tucked underneath the pastel green hospital blanket.

He was as pale as his sheets, his face devoid of all emotion. Multiple monitors and IV lines had been hooked up to his body. He could very well have been dead, save for the shallow breathes that moved his body slightly, and the constant bleep of the heart monitor softly crooning in the corner.

I could puke again. How different was this man from my own mother? They were both tethered to this institution and trapped in their own bodies, no guarantees of making it out alive.

My feet moved before my mind registered, and I left the room, making a beeline for the public bathroom across the hall and emptied my limited stomach contents into the toilet.

When my body finished its digestive exorcism, I decided it was time to leave. I could do nothing for Mom here anyway, and I didn't know how long my body could continue to stand upright in my exhausted condition.

I walked down the corridor leading to the elevator, checking my phone as I went, holding onto some semblance of hope Winter had called me back. She hadn't. I was about to press the button to go down when the doors slid open, revealing a very stressed-looking Drew.

His hazel eyes widened then narrowed into slits. His words bit like ice as he spoke.

"What are you doing here? Come to finish the job?"

My mouth dropped in surprise.

"Are you — what do y–you think I had something to do with this?!" I spluttered. Of all the scenarios I had come up with, this was not one of them.

He shrugged a large shoulder, eyes shooting daggers at me.

"All I know is that you were the one bringing the money. You're the one who works for him." He spat the words like snake venom. "I don't know what you're capable of."

My spine stiffened. That was it for me. I was not a killer; I wasn't a bad guy either, and I was done with people accusing me of being one.

"I don't do threats or attempted murder, Drew. I'm just a guy in a shitty situation like you are." I folded my arms across my chest, daring him to accuse me of something else.

"Oh, your father's lying in a hospital bed, fighting for his life, is he?" His sarcasm was acidic, burning through my resolve.

"It's my mom, actually. Thanks for asking." I shoved passed him and hit the button to go down on the elevator. As the doors started to close, I looked up to find him still staring me down. "For what it's worth, man, I'm really sorry."

I let the doors close shut, and shut my eyes along with them.

Fuck.

I still hadn't heard from Winter and it was driving me crazy. I was becoming a borderline stalker. I didn't want to be "that guy" but I was definitely channeling his spirit.

I picked up my phone for the hundredth time that hour. This called for a desperate last-ditch attempt that didn't involve showing up at her apartment like a true psycho.

Travis Balcom: *Hey. I heard about the attack on Joe. Winter won't answer my calls or my texts. Can you just tell me if she's okay?*

Ten hours later:

Quick Shane Silver: *She's okay.*

Twelve hours later:

Quick Shane Silver: *She misses you.*

Well, hot damn. Maybe something in my life had some hope of turning around after all. I clung onto that glimmer of positivity all the way home.

CHAPTER 25

WINTER

If you're ever interested in taking on additional work for me, please don't hesitate to call.

Georgio's invitation kept intruding my thoughts. It shouldn't be, given Drew's family was currently trying to survive the aftermath of his delivery of the Cascade Falls equivalent of an atomic bomb. I couldn't keep it out of my mind; we needed to do something, damn it.

I don't know why I currently possessed a crusader mentality. I wasn't exactly "leading the masses" material, and really, what could a cohort of random college students do against a man so powerful? Why was I so protective over my high school crush all of a sudden?

Still, my gut screamed to take advantage of the opportunity presented. If Quick and I couldn't help Drew out of this mess, then who would? Ralph Sutton? I'd bet my left kidney the town sheriff was in cahoots with our lovely local criminal underworld, given the lack of response Drew had received for his 911 call. Forty-five minutes to arrive at a home only ten minutes out of town on a clear night at 2:00 am? Give me a break.

I tapped my ragged nail-bitten fingers on Basil's dashboard as I hummed and hawed in the apartment block parking lot. Drew and Quick were waiting for me at Quick's place, and I wasn't ready to go in yet.

We were finally getting together to hash out all of the events over the holidays, to try and decide what to do. Joe still hadn't woken up and if Drew let the diner slip, Eileen wouldn't have an income for her kids. Drew and I would also be completely out of a job, not really something either of us could afford at the moment, even if we had the luxury of bending to our moral code.

I knew what I had to do; I just didn't want to do it. I turned off the car and made my way into the three-story building.

"Hey!" Quick beamed at me as he opened his door, and he didn't waste a second, scooping me up and spinning me around like we always did.

I took a second to hold him extra-tight, breathing in his rich and comforting pine scent. I was so grateful for his presence in my life, and I knew I would be hurting him tonight. I hated the thought, but it was my own fault. I would deserve whatever was coming to me.

I was surprised but equally comforted when Drew wrapped his arms around me just as Quick let me go. I melted into his tight embrace, surrounded by citrus and cinnamon. It was a heady feeling, and my body mourned the loss of his warmth when he stepped back, letting me through into the living room.

Three bowls of snacks had already been set out, and I smiled when I saw my favorite brand of salt and vinegar chips waiting for me. My bestie always took care of me. Three notepads with individual pens set on the coffee table, and Quick had taken out his whiteboard and left it resting on the couch.

"This looks serious," I joked, sinking into said couch and popping a chip into my mouth. "Are we going to start with some small talk and networking foreplay, or are we just going to get right into the pitch?"

"Lots of ground to cover," Quick said succinctly. He took up residence in the seat to my left. Drew settled into the seat on my right, close enough to be thigh to thigh, and I couldn't stop the warm tingles forming in my belly at his closeness.

"Why don't we start off with what we do know?" Drew picked up a notepad and pen.

The boy next door looked deliciously edible in his usual uniform of dark blue jeans and a long sleeve Henley; it was forest green today and it brought out the flecks of deep green in his hazel eyes. His dark blond hair was mussed, like he had been running his hands through it all day, and his beard was slightly longer than usual; a goody-two-shoes in a sinful package.

"Yes!" Quick nodded enthusiastically. "Okay, so we know that Georgio and Camden are involved in something shady with WAQ and Eccles, which means"—His eyes darted to mine and then back to Drew—"that we have to consider our dads might also be involved in something shady too."

I swallowed a lump in my throat at that assertion. He was right, of course. Drew's father wasn't the only one caught up in this cascade of lies. It seemed no one in our lives was innocent.

"But we really have no idea what," Quick continued. "So, I'm going to have to get serious and start digging around. I also don't think we can rule out Logan. He's been heavily involved in these business meetings and there has to be a reason for it."

"Okay, that's a start."

Drew was writing scribbles of notes across the looseleaf pages. The tip of his tongue stuck out to the corner of his full lips. It was adorable, and mildly erotic. All of a sudden, I could feel the ghost of his kisses from months ago on the sensitive part of my neck and I shivered. I guessed a few months apart hadn't completely turned off this crush.

"We know that my parents have been money laundering for Georgio for a decade – almost a million dollars worth in that time. I'll bet that many other businesses in the area are in the same boat. We should look at businesses that are easy to launder cash in Cascade Falls and surrounding towns."

"Okay, wait a minute." I had to step in here before we went down this rabbit hole. "Before we go any further – what exactly are we going to do here, guys? We've got next to no power, and obviously Georgio has his hands in everyone's pockets. What do you think we can actually achieve?"

"Snow," Quick began, his large hands reaching over to grab mine, "every one of us is tangled up in this whether we like it or not. Drew's family is being torn apart right now. Yours and mine could be next. We know Travis is deep in this too, and you can deny it all you want, but Georgio is the reason you're not together. I don't care if we're the wannabe Mystery Incorporated Scooby Doo crew, I can't sit back and watch the people I love suffer. Can you?"

I wanted to mutter something sarcastic about Travis' choices being the reason we weren't together, but my heart wasn't in it, and I got the point. Now was time to let them in on my little secret. I sighed inwardly, mourning the loss of the one piece of the world I had squandered away to be mine and mine alone.

I drew in a breath. "I can't, Quick, and I won't. I'm on board. So, I should just come clean about this now because it will probably help us get some answers."

He and Drew looked at me quizzically.

"For the last two years, I've been performing at Georgio's club, Bourbon & Blues, in Sheldonville. It's a biweekly Thursday night spot, and I sing for a jazz trio called the Mellowtones."

I turned to Quick apologetically and squeezed his hands gently. His eyes were wide in surprise, but he hadn't interrupted me, so I continued.

"I didn't tell you because I didn't want to draw the attention to myself. It was nice having a secret that I didn't have to share with anyone. But the point is that he's at the club often; I think he conducts most of his business out of his office there. It's not a big secret that he runs an illegal underground fighting ring somewhere on the premises. And he once asked me to come work for him, so that could be the 'in' we need."

"What!?" Quick exploded and jumped out of his seat

Wrong thing to say, apparently.

"He propositioned you!? How can you be so casual about that, Winter? And you've been working for him? The fuck?"

Drew just stared at me; his eyes betrayed nothing, but his knee bobbed up and down like that half of his body was having a seizure, so I guessed he was also upset.

I held my hands up in surrender. "I have been working for his legal business, yes. I didn't even know it was Georgio's club until after I agreed to take the gig. And he didn't proposition me, he invited me to be a server, not a stripper. If I were a server there on weekends, I'd bet I could find out a lot more information. Information that we may be able to use."

Drew sighed, leaning over to place his elbows on his knees, his head in his hands. He looked up at me, steepling his hands in front of his face, and turned his gaze on Quick.

"It's a good idea. I can't say I'm happy that you've been singing in his literal criminal den this whole time, but it would be a safe way to keep an ear to the ground."

"That's how you actually met Travis, isn't it!?" My best friend snapped his fingers and pointed accusingly at me. "He works at Bourbon, right? You lied about that too."

"I asked him to keep my secret for me, yes." I said defiantly, peering into the steely gray of his eyes. "It was my secret to tell, not his. We can talk about my secret life as a soul sister later. Yay or nay on the serving idea?"

"Nay," Quick grumbled. "But I see it's two against one, so fuck it. What's next on the list?"

I breathed an internal sigh of relief. My big reveal hadn't gone nearly as badly as I'd predicted, but I also knew the conversation was only tabled, not over. I could wait.

"I'm going to have to call Georgio," Drew admitted sadly. "If I'm taking over for the time being, I know he's going to start his shipments eventually. Why send the message to Dad otherwise?"

Quick rubbed his chin and stared at the popcorn ceiling above our heads. "Travis was the original delivery boy, right? Why don't you tell him that you'll take over, but you'll only deal with Travis? He's someone we know at least. Probably the safer option."

"No!" Drew and I both shouted at the same time.

"He could have been the one who stabbed him!" Drew protested emphatically. "I don't trust him."

"We don't need to bring Travis into this." I spoke over Drew. "I don't trust him."

What Drew had said finally registered. I said, "Travis may be a liar, but I don't believe for a second that he tried to hurt your father, Drew. I don't trust that he's told me everything, but I know he wouldn't do that." I looked him dead in the eye, my tone brokering no arguments.

Drew's eyes turned hard. "Winter, come on. Just because you slept –"

"Alright, that's enough!" Quick held up his arms between the two of us before I had a chance to snap back. He turned to Drew. "Not a good road to travel, man. Quit while you're ahead. And you" – he pointed a finger in my direction – "don't need to kill Drew to prove your point."

"I think we can use Travis. Not necessarily trust him," he continued, making a few notes on his own notepad. "He's the closest person we know working for Georgio, and he's got two ins that we know of – the club and running the money. It would be stupid not to use this connection just because the two of you don't like him. Even if Winter is lying to herself."

I glared at him, showing every ounce of my anger, annoyance, and frustration. "Fine." I gritted out. "But you can be the one to talk to him. I'm not in a forgiving mood." Even to my own ears the protest sounded hollow.

"Okay!" Quick clapped his hands like there wasn't a thundercloud of tension hanging over the room, and grinned at the two of us. He pointed his pen at me.

"Winter – you're going to serve at Bourbon & Blues and try not to die in the process. Drew – you're going to call Georgio and agree to his terms. For now. But insist you only deal with Travis. Since you're the business guy around here, you can make a list of businesses that may be in your situation, or at least give us some direction on this one so we can help you.

"And," he continued, his smile growing wider, "I will befriend Travis and learn everything he knows, while single-handedly sneaking around all of WAQ's classified documents in my father's study to see if there is anything we can find on this elusive bridge tender link."

He beamed at me and I couldn't help but smirk at the asshole's enthusiasm. He was just so damn likable sometimes, even when he was insufferable.

"Is there anything else we can be doing in the meantime?" Drew asked thoughtfully, his tense demeanor vanishing with Quick's goofiness.

"Winter can try and seduce Logan? I bet you he'd talk a lot more with his pants off." Quick winked at me devilishly and I threw a pillow at him.

"Fuck, no. You like cock. *You* seduce him."

"Honey, if that man was a mute, he'd be a helluva lot more attractive."

Drew snorted and I burst into laughter. I snagged the bowl of chips taunting me all evening and grabbed the remote from the table.

Serious talk was over; we had a basic plan, and that would be enough to start. The rest would be up to fate and our Mystery Machine team. God help us.

I had my first set of the year at Bourbon & Blues tonight and I was driving to the club for warm up. Raven had organized an entirely new set to kick off the year and I desperately needed a bit of practice before getting on stage.

I was nervous to see Travis for the first time in person since we broke up, assuming he still worked at B&B and was working his usual shift tonight.

My stomach churned with the thought of seeing him, but it also ached with the possibility of not seeing him. Why did this man affect me so much? How could he have wormed his way under my defenses in such a short time? I had put my walls up for weeks, but I couldn't keep them cemented any longer. The Berlin wall was crumbling, as was my resolve.

I had already called Janet Lindross, Georgio's assistant, and left a message. I had found the shiny gold-lettered card at the bottom of my purse, and saved the number in my phone for future use. Who actually used business cards anymore? What a pretty and pointless piece of paper.

Classes weren't starting up again until next week, so I had hoped to get my new job as a server secured before I dove into textbooks and testing. Would they even still need servers? January was usually a dead time of year for restaurants, though not so much in tourist towns centered on winter activities, so it could go either way.

I had never been to Bourbon & Blues on a weekend, other than the Friday night Travis and I had our first date, so I had no idea how busy those shifts would be. My stomach fluttered at the memories of the two of us cozied up in the corner booth. I missed our chemistry. I missed him. It was time to admit it and face the facts.

I parked Basil in the parking lot and made my way inside the staff entrance, heading for the dressing room The Mellowtones usually occupied before a set. Raven and Brody weren't there yet, so I'd have some time to myself to get ready. I breathed a sigh of relief – I needed the peace.

I was just unloading my costume bag and my makeup when I felt a presence behind me. I looked up to see the achingly beautiful tall drink of water standing in the doorway. Travis' green eyes were as striking as I remembered as he stared through me. His hair was a tad longer on top, and he had switched out his black lip ring for a black pointed stud. His black button-up shirt was rolled up to the elbows, and his tight black pants left nothing to the imagination. I hadn't needed to imagine it, anyway – I had had the whole experience in all its living color.

I chewed my lip nervously, having anticipated some sort of encounter tonight, but I had not expected such close contact. Travis leaned against the doorframe, his arms folded across his toned chest, head cocked to one side, waves of dark hair falling across his eyes.

"Hey, beautiful," he murmured. His eyes raked over my body; not lasciviously, but appreciative, like I was an interesting painting capturing his attention.

I gulped. It was going to be a lot harder to resist him in person than it had been to avoid his texts and calls.

"Hey," I responded, equally softly. I wanted to escape this room and his overpowering presence, but I was captivated by his watchful eyes.

"I've missed you."

Hot tears pricked the corners of my eyes as I finally acknowledged how much I had missed this man too. He had lied to me, he had broken my trust and yet, I couldn't get him out of my head or my heart. I balled my hands into fists to keep from reaching for him.

"I've missed you too," I said, barely audible as I tried not to admit just how much. A tear escaped my eyelid and traced down my cheek. Travis sprang from his perch in the doorway and wrapped his arms around me in a tight hug.

I relaxed into his body, snuggled into his warmth, enveloped in his manly floral scent. My head rested on his chest and I could hear his heartbeat galloping as hard as mine in this moment. He let go, placed his palms on my cheeks, and pressed his forehead to mine.

"I'm so glad you're okay." He placed a soft kiss on my forehead. "I've been worried sick about you."

He pulled me in for the sweetest of kisses; his lips gently pressed against mine, soft and tender; nothing like our previous chemistry, but somehow far more intimate.

I enjoyed the kiss for a moment, and then pulled away. It was too much for me too soon, if ever, and I couldn't let my hormones and heart dictate these next steps.

"We can't," I said simply. I took a step back and looked him in the eyes. "I can't just jump back into being your girlfriend, Travis. You still lied to me. You're still not who I thought you were. Not entirely. This is just – too much."

"Okay." Travis shifted uncomfortably and tucked his hands in his pockets. "Okay, you're right. That wasn't fair of me. I couldn't – you're my kryptonite, beautiful."

He smiled ruefully and shook his head. "Could we try being friends, or at least, friendly? I don't want to have to avoid you when you're here. Seeing you on stage is the best part of my week."

My heart hurt at that admission, but I shook it off. I didn't need to feel guilty about how I felt. I pushed aside the tangled web of Georgio's empire that had caught up everyone I cared about, and tried to focus on the here and now. "Let's try friendly for now. I don't want to avoid you either."

His face broke out into a genuine grin, and if I were less stubborn, I might have changed my mind as I practically swooned at his heartbreaking beauty.

"Friendly it is, then." His faced turned somber. "Winter, you need to know I'm doing everything I can to get out of this"—he waved his arms around the room—"mess. I've been working on it for a while, but I don't want this anymore. I'm not the guy who hurts people, I—"

"Now's not really the time for explanations." I couldn't hear that now. "Let's just try being friendly, okay? Maybe the rest will come, maybe it won't, but I've got a set to get ready for."

Travis winced, but nodded. He turned to leave but then spun around. "May I give you another hug? For luck?"

A real laugh escaped my lips as a tsunami of relief hit me for finally allowing myself to speak to him and let go of some of the anger I had been holding. I grinned and opened my arms to him. "For luck."

He stepped in and wrapped his arms around me, lifting me up and nuzzling my hair.

"For luck," he whispered into the top of my head. "Break a leg."

Then he was gone.

I shut off all of my emotions; I dressed and put on my stage makeup, and then worked through the set list. Raven was putting me through my paces with these song choices. I didn't have the range of the late great Ella Fitzgerald, but she seemed to think I could handle them, so I wasn't about to let her down. It was just the distraction I needed to get me through until show time.

My phone rang five minutes before we were about to go on, and I took the call, recognizing Janet's number.

"Hello?"

"Hello Ms. Wallace, Janet Lindross here. I received your message and I am happy to inform you that we do have a serving position available at Bourbon & Blues starting on Monday. I can send you a hiring package shortly. Will that work for you?"

"Yes!" I said excitedly, relieved this part of our plan had gone much smoother than I had hoped. "That's wonderful, thank you!"

"Please bear in mind, Ms. Wallace, that this position will require some degree of flexibility across Mr. Carlos' other businesses. You will not be required to work any position other than the one you have been hired for, but you may need to work at other locations, depending on the needs of Mr. Carlos' business arrangements. I have spoken with him and we can accommodate your school schedule."

Interesting.

"Yes, that will be fine. Please thank Georg—Mr. Carlos for the opportunity."

I hung up the phone, stomach filled with butterflies for an entirely different reason now. Raven and Brody were making out backstage, and I was grateful they hadn't heard that conversation. I put on the very last dab of lipstick and adjusted my hair and dress until I really couldn't fiddle with them anymore. Finally, I walked out behind the curtain, waiting for my cue.

As I stepped out on stage and looked out into the crowd, my heart leapt into my throat. Not only was Travis leaning against the bar top, his gaze fixated on me in ways that would not be considered appropriate for "friendly" acquaintances; no, that would be something I could deal with on its own.

Drew and Quick, my childhood crush – okay, current real-life crush – and my very best friend, sat at the table directly in front of the stage.

I squeaked in surprise and scrambled to gain my composure. They hadn't told me they were coming and I wouldn't have let them anyway. *Assholes.*

Drew looked at me in wonder, his eyes raking over my navy-blue sequined dress and exposed legs. He couldn't hide his want for me, and my body flushed at the attention. Quick looked incredulous. I'd bet he was still wondering how I had kept this a secret from him for so long. I squirmed under their stares for entirely different reasons.

Oh God, this was going to be my most nerve-racking performance yet.

I took in a breath and turned on my professional, smoky singer voice. "Ladies and gentlemen, welcome to Bourbon &

Blues. We're the Mellowtones, and tonight, like a good bourbon, we're going to mellow you out."

Could someone mellow me the fuck out, please?

I opened my mouth, and sang.

CHAPTER 26

SHANE

"Yes, baby, just like that. Don't stop, fuck, *fuck*!"

Mandy's head bobbed up and down until I didn't have anything left in me to give her. I sank down into the couch cushions as the tension in my body evaporated into pure bliss. She may not be the love of my life, but this woman knew how to get me off in the best way.

She giggled and settled her naked body into mine on the couch for a post-coital cuddle. Her sucking me off was already well into round two, and we had been at my apartment for hours.

We hadn't had a fuck fest like this in ages. I had been wound tight with everything going on with Drew, our families, and the fuckery that was currently our town. Winter's lie had been the icing on the cake. When I wasn't with someone, Mandy was my favorite stress-reliever, and I was glad she was available and ready for the party. I felt more relaxed in that moment than I had felt in months.

I reached for a joint from the coffee table ashtray and lit it, taking a slow, deep inhale before passing it to her. The sweet smoke immediately softened the edges of my thoughts and my body melted back into the couch. Pure fucking bliss.

We lay there for a few minutes, passing the joint back and forth between us, before she turned to look at me, her Betty Cooper blonde hair still perfectly tucked into her ponytail.

"This has to be the last time, Shane. If we keep doing this *like* this, I'm going to catch feelings. We both agreed that wasn't going to work for us."

I sighed, rubbing my large palms down her soft arms. "I know," I said forlornly, looking down into her blue eyes. "Maybe in another life this could have been more than sex. The sex is on fire."

I gently squeezed her ass with the hand that still held her tight to me to emphasize the point. It was, that wasn't an exaggeration. She was the best female fuckbuddy I'd ever had, my first time with a woman notwithstanding.

She smiled softly, a look of understanding in her eyes. "We both knew what this was. Your heart belongs to someone else, anyways. I can't compete with that."

I looked at her, a bit dazed and confused from the THC now coursing through my blood stream. No one else had my heart. I was just a lonely guy having some great casual sex with a friend. I wish someone had my heart. I had a lot of heart to give. The most heart. The *biggest* heart. The –

"I'm going to head out, okay?" Mandy pulled herself up off the couch, grabbing her panties to get dressed in front of me.

I admired her body; petite frame, curvy as hell, a sexy girl-next-door meets Sweet Home Alabama. She was funny, and kind, and uncomplicated. Why I couldn't bring myself to feel more for this woman was beyond me.

I reached out to pull her into me for a big bear hug. She laughed and nuzzled into my neck one last time. "Be good, Shane Quicksilver."

Then she left. Left me to stay laying naked on my couch, puffing the last of the blunt in my ashtray, alone with my thoughts.

SQ: *Still on for tonight?*
Travis the Betrayer: *Yeah, man. 7 at your place?*
SQ: *Yup. Bring beer.*
Travis the Betrayer: **thumbs up emoji**

I put my phone in my pocket and turned back to my computer, trying to sift through some of the copied files from Dad's office I had stolen before I left home from winter break. So far, I was coming up with nothing, so I was also working the other angle on our agreed-upon "to-do" list – Travis.

When Drew and I had gone to Bourbon & Blues to see Winter perform, it had two purposes. One, to see what she had been hiding from me for two fucking years, something I didn't want to think about or consider in that moment, and two, to connect with Travis in person, assuming he would be working at the club that night.

Since Winter had met Travis at Bourbon & Blues and said that was the only night of the week she worked there, I made an educated guess we'd be able to run into him that evening if we showed up. I had been right.

I wanted to meet with him privately to bring him up to speed. Explaining it all over text would be a massive pain in the ass, and I wanted him to be able to offer some input. This guy was our in; we needed him, whether Winter or Drew liked it or not.

"Who are you texting?" Winter looked up from the assignment she was working on from my bed, a cute little smile scrunching up her nose. "Drew again? You and Drew have the cutest bromance I've ever seen. They're going to write a screenplay about you two."

A big booming laugh escaped me as I considered that. Drew was a great guy and he was definitely becoming my second bestie. If our bromance inspired other bromances, so be it. I'd bromance him every day of the week.

"I'm sure he'll be thrilled. Who do you think would play me?" I joked, wiggling my eyebrows suggestively. "Not a lot of hot Native actors to choose from, so maybe I'd just play myself. Drew's lookalikes are a dime a dozen."

Winter threw a pencil at me. "Drew is not a dime a dozen! He's got a certain charm that would be hard to capture. *You*, however, could be played by any big-mouth with a black shoulder-length wig."

I stuck my tongue out at her and grinned. "You think just anyone could take on the role of *the* Shane Quicksilver? I've got a 'je ne se quois' too, you know. All the ladies and gents be lined up for this hunk of man meat." I snorted as another pencil sailed passed my head.

I turned serious, not wanting to keep my plans from her. She wasn't going to love that Travis would be in my apartment a few hours from now, but it had to be done.

"I was texting Travis. He's going to come over tonight and I'm going to walk him through our plan to see where he can be useful."

Her smile turned to stone as she looked up at me. "I still don't see why that's necessary."

"We need his information and he wants to help. Isn't that a good thing? He's trying to right some wrongs, Snow."

"He can't right *all* of his wrongs," she muttered darkly as she folded her arms across her chest and stared at me frostily. I laughed internally at my pun.

"Okay, you're being kind of confusing, since you told me you guys kissed the other night. Don't tell me you're going to turn into a righteous robot again with your feelings for him."

"Excuse me?" Her voice turned glacial and volcanic at the same time.

"You know what I mean." I cocked my head and looked at her, knowingly.

She arched a brow, her jaw ticking in the way it always did when she was feeling defensive.

"No, I don't, *Shane,*" she hissed, aggressively emphasizing my proper name that she never used. "What. Do. You. Mean?"

I inhaled sharply. It was time to just let it all hang out in the air, come what may. My Snowflake was my platonic soulmate, my best friend in all ways, but she couldn't see her faults if they hit her in the face.

"You don't let people get close to you, Snow! Not really. You're warm and sunny and welcoming to everyone you meet, but you hold them at an arm's length. How many girl friends do you have, friends that you've actually made since high school? One? That blue-haired chick? You hide behind our friendship like it's a reason not to get close to anyone else. It's not healthy, Winter. And I know why. I know how hard it is to trust people after —"

"Shut up, Shane! Just because I don't have the same roster as you to draw from, I –"

"Oh, come on," I shot back, "pot calling the kettle black, don't you think? You slept with how many people last year – 20? 30? You have no problem having fun, Winter, and I support that. Of course, I support that. There's no slut shaming in this house. You'll let men into your bed, but you won't let them in!

"Travis lied, he did. That's his to own. But you were *happy* with him, Snow. And from what I know, what he lied to you about had nothing to do with how he felt about you. Maybe you should cut him some slack. You're not going to find the perfect person before you can be willing to go all in. You'll be waiting your whole life."

I paused to catch my breath. I was pissed, really pissed now, and she needed to know it.

"For fuck's sake, I just found out about you moonlighting as a jazz singer. Me! Your very best friend. You've known me my whole life, but you can't even totally open up to me? It made me feel like shit, Winter. Here you are, following a passion of yours and *killing* it, and you left me out of it. I thought we shared our dreams. I thought I was that person for you."

My voice broke off then, not realizing how much this omission had bothered me until that second. It was stupid, something so silly making me feel this raw, but it did. My Snow had kept this secret from me.

When I saw her up on that stage in her gorgeous 1920s getup, complete with sequins and pin curls, something shifted in me. Something I wasn't keen to examine or explore at the moment, but it made my heart... squeeze. I was so damn proud of her; her confidence, her talent, the easy way she captivated her entire audience, me included. I had always felt fiercely protective of her, but it had felt different. I had wanted to whisk her away into a fairytale castle and protect her from everything dark in this world, to keep the beauty of her essence and her voice safe. It was weirdly possessive. And foreign. And I didn't want to think about it.

It also made me feel shitty because other than some sexcapades with Mandy, which really didn't mean anything to me, not like *that*, anyway, I had shared everything with Winter. Yet, she hadn't shared this with me. Why had she felt the need to keep something so special from me of all people? Her Quick?

Had she not held the same space in her heart for me that I held for her?

She drew in a deep breath and pushed her papers aside.

"I'm going to ignore everything you just said, except that last part. We'll come back to the first part when I'm no longer in the mood to clobber you over the head."

She got off the bed and plopped herself down on the couch next to me, gently pushing my computer off of my lap and resting her head on my shoulder.

"I'm sorry, Quick." She stroked the side of my arm as she nestled into the same spot she had a million times before. "I never wanted to keep it from you specifically. You know I haven't had anything that I could keep as just my own, not since —"

She broke off that sentence before we both took a trip down the haunted memory lane.

"When I found my voice again, it was like I could fully be myself again, you know? Like I didn't have to hide, or pretend, or put on a brave face, or meet anyone's expectations. I could just... be. Be whoever and whatever I wanted on that stage, and no one would know the difference. It was – is – empowering. I didn't want anyone to take that away from me. I'm sorry I thought that you would."

Okay, I'd table this conversation for now, but it wasn't over, not by a long shot. To be continued, Winter Wallace.

I wrapped my arms around her and held her tight. "I would never take anything away that makes you happy, Snow. Ever. I love you." I kissed the top of her head, satisfied with her answer.

I should have known where her need for secret-keeping came from. Sometimes it was easy to forget. I knew she never forgot, and that thought brought a zing of pain across my chest.

"Think about what I said about Travis, okay? Don't do anything you're not ready for, but don't hold yourself back from a chance at being happy either. Please?"

I tucked her auburn hair behind her ear and tilted her chin to look into my eyes. They were more green than blue today, her freckles peeking out from under her eyelashes. I was struck by just how beautiful my best friend was. I didn't notice it enough.

"I'm happy with you, you know," she muttered and grabbed my hand, tracing patterns with her fingers along the back of it. "You, me, and Drew can all hole up in the mountains somewhere and I'll stay happy."

I chuckled and squeezed her again before reaching for my laptop with my other hand.

"I'll never be enough for you, Snow. Drew may never be enough for you either. Aim for the world and see where it takes you." I kissed the top of her head and let go of her hands and this conversation. "Come on, we both have to get our work done."

She walked back to my bed and settled into whatever she was doing and I went back to my deeply unsatisfying spreadsheet. Hopefully, Travis would get us farther than I was.

Travis was seated on my couch, beer in hand, and we had spent the last hour going over his sob story. I thought Drew and Winter's family dynamic sucked, but Travis took it to a whole new level with his drug-addict brother, his sick mother, and the hole he kept digging deeper into with Georgio as a result. It just went to show that you never knew what someone else was struggling with. I really felt for the guy, and wondered if Winter actually knew everything Travis had told me. It was hard to imagine her writing him out of her life so easily if she had.

"So right now," he said, "I really don't have a whole lot of new information, other than the fight nights are getting bigger and there are more serious players. I've worked two of them now and they're really intense. It's not just people you would expect to attend either – the governor was at the last one. There's a lot of money at stake, and I know for a fact that Georgio is rigging the matches."

Holy shit. How pissed would people be if they found *that* out? I filed that away for later; a useful card to play when the time was right. And speaking of right, *I* had been right. Travis was a goldmine.

"You know that guy, Logan? He's been at Bourbon & Blues a lot lately. Nothing suspicious that I've seen exactly, but way more frequent than usual. There might be something there too."

Yes! I had been joking about fucking Logan, but I was relieved that kind of subterfuge wasn't going to be necessary to figuring the guy out. If Travis could keep tabs on Logan when he showed up at the club, that could be an in to try and connect him to all of this – whatever *this* was. No one was sure of anything at this point.

"All right, man. I think we've got enough to work with here. Now, here is what I'm thinking…"

I walked him through my thoughts and he agreed that the plan was a good one. We'd just have to wait for the perfect opportunity.

CHAPTER 27

LOGAN

"I don't care if you like it. It's your responsibility and you have a reputation to maintain. You'll be a man and you'll fulfill your duties to this family."

I gritted my teeth before turning to face the miserable fuck. I was not having this conversation again.

"Please, Stan, remind me what those are again? I didn't hear you the first million fucking times."

My father's face turned purple. Good. Maybe the fucker would forget to breathe and pass out and die already.

"It was one indiscretion. It's been buried. If you wanted monogamy included with the deal, maybe you should have modeled it yourself."

I looked at my watch, willing the minutes to speed the fuck up. Any time spent with this man was time I'd rather take a blow torch to my ass cheeks. Satan would have been a better father.

The devil himself came to the surface as he grabbed me by the collar and yanked me hard into him. Stan's true nature shined through now; no putting on airs for the public. Years of beatings and bruises had been hidden behind closed doors and paid-off house staff.

I grabbed his wrists and pulled him off of me. I wasn't a twelve-year-old boy anymore. He couldn't hurt me now, but he still liked to try.

"Nice try, old man. I'm not your puppet, so fuck off." I brushed off the sleeves of my tailored navy suit coat and adjusted my tie. "I took care of it. I don't need you breathing down my neck, and I won't be as gentle if you touch me again."

Stan's watery eyes shot daggers at me as he caught his breath and settled back into his chair. His rage issues were finally going to put him into an early grave, and I was here for it.

We were waiting outside Hillary's lawyers' office in the pretentious private sitting room. Today, we'd finally get to read the inheritance documents, the prophecy that dictated the rest of our lives.

Hillary's grandmother, Rose Marie Lane, had left everything to Hillary when she died. She'd had an axe to grind against her son and wanted to stick it to him, I guessed. Not that Camden needed the money. He was a multimillionaire and wouldn't need to work another day in his life, but the man was a greedy fucker. I couldn't count the number of business deals he tried to take from me, even though I was his betrothed son-in-law. Luckily, I was more of a dick than he was.

Small towns dealt in secrets, and I was better at it than most. I was good at seeing a sure thing, thanks to Stan beating it into me and to my world class education, but the secrets were what kept me in the game. I knew both Camden and Stan's secrets, the deeply buried ones, making me untouchable unless they decided to kill me. I really wouldn't put it past the fuckers, so I was on constant guard around them. They weren't good men, but neither was I.

I had been trying to learn Georgio's secrets too, but I hadn't had much luck. Whatever the fuck was going on with this insider trading crap that M referred to was locked up tighter than a virgin pussy. I wasn't looking forward to that phone call.

"Gentlemen? Please come in."

Frederick Lawson, Hillary's cunt of a lawyer, beckoned us into the office.

Hillary and Camden were already sitting on the leather sofas. I spied a crystal goblet of some amber liquor and walked over to pour two fingers in a glass. Frederick Fucknuts could put it on her bill.

"So?" I quirked an eyebrow as Stan sat down across from Camden. I stayed standing, leaning against the bar cart with as much "fuck you" energy as I could muster. Stan would be pissed I hadn't sat next to Hillary, giving her a kiss like we were madly in love. But I wasn't pretending here. Everyone in this room knew what this marriage was.

Frederick cleared his throat. "As you are all well aware, Miss Rose Marie Lane left a sizable inheritance to Ms. Hillary Lane, to be released in full upon her marriage on or before she turned twenty-five. We were under strict legal requirements to leave her last wishes sealed until three months before the stated wedding date. As that is today, we are now going to open and read her final rights regarding her estate."

"We're aware, Frederick. May you please read it to us already?" Hillary snapped.

"You and Camden haven't heard this yet?" I asked, surprised by this. Why were they here beforehand if they didn't get the first peek?

"No," Frederick stated matter-of-factly. "It was Ms. Rose Marie's express wishes that the document be read in front of both Hillary and her betrothed. Your fathers are here as a courtesy only."

Stan's face flushed at that, and I grinned. "Well, let's hear it, then. What did the old bird want us to know before making Hillary a very rich woman?"

Everyone glared at me, but they could fuck right off. Hillary walked over to me and placed her hand in mine, grabbing the drink in my other hand and downing it in a single gulp.

"Thanks, I needed that."

I smirked and reached over to pour myself another drink while Frederick shuffled his papers. It would take a few drinks to get through this conversation. The high from the hit I had taken on my way here was already gone, and I was itching for a new buzz to take the edge off.

Stan and Camden were salivating right now; all these years of forcing us together and planning our futures had been for this moment. I hoped they choked on it. I could pretend I was better than them, but I wasn't. I needed Hillary's money far more than they did.

"All right, I will read the document in full, and then we can ask our questions, hmmm?"

He cleared his throat.

"In the matters of the estate of Rose Marie Lane, the entirety of her assets shall be put into a secured Trust Fund for her sole granddaughter and named heir, Hillary

Elizabeth Lane. This fund is to set up Ms. Hillary Elizabeth Lane's future business interests and provide her with the means necessary to build the Lane empire as she deems fit."

I shifted in my seat, irritated by the stupid man's droning voice. Get to the good stuff, Fucknuts.

"Nothing is more important in this world than to love and be loved. As such, it is expected that Ms. Hillary Elizabeth Lane will not solely focus on her studies, but also on a suitor. Ms. Hillary Elizabeth Lane will marry her chosen suitor on or before her 25th birthday in order for the aforementioned assets to be released."

I grinned, toasting the old bird with my half-empty whiskey glass and tossing a smirk in Hillary's direction.

"It is essential that Hillary's suitor is marrying her with proper intent. A condition for the fund transfer will be that the suitor sign a prenuptial agreement, forgoing any right to Ms. Hillary Elizabeth Lane's inheritance for current or future use. Legal safeguards have been put in place to ensure that Ms. Hillary Elizabeth Lane cannot be coerced into poor investment practices or bullied into releasing funds for insufficient purposes."

What the fuck? What the actual fuck? This was not the plan. A sick feeling crept into my stomach. I caught a glimpse of Stanley turning purple, and Camden looked just as sick.

"The funds are also deemed non-transferable. Should Ms. Hillary Elizabeth Lane expire prematurely from anything deemed unnatural causes or suspicious death, the entire estate shall be left in managed trust and divided among the following ten charities of Sequoia County."

Frederick Fucknuts' voice wavered as he looked around the room. The tension in the air could choke a man. I squeezed the glass in my hand so hard I felt the crystal crack between my fingers.

"WHAT!?"

Stan-the-man, patron Saint that he is, cracked first.

"This is – that isn't what – this is BULLSHIT!" Spittle flew from his toady lips in pure rage. I would be loving the show if I wasn't about to explode myself.

I was filling with panic. Pure, unadulterated panic. I needed more bourbon.

I filled the goblet still in my hand to the brim and turned toward Hillary beside me, in her own state of shock.

"Did you know about this? Was this all a trick to bag a husband and make off with millions in the meantime?"

"Are you kidding me?" She glowered at me. "Why the fuck would I go through this absolute charade of a wedding if I knew it never mattered in the first place? Do you think I'm marrying you for *love*, of all things?"

Maybe if we hadn't been forced together, we could have become the power couple that bent the world to our will. But she didn't love me, and I had never loved her; now here we were, still fucked.

Numbness spread through me. This wasn't going to work. Legal workarounds wouldn't do a damn thing for this arrangement. Old Rosie must be having a fucking field day in her grave right now, knowing she was able to fuck Camden over one last time. I would relish it, if I wasn't getting screwed with a razor dick too.

"She had a sick fucking sense of humor. You need to be married to get the money, but you can't marry anyone who is expecting to share the money, and she's telling you this three months before your – our – wedding date. Why would we even bother now? Like you said – this was never for love. What's the fucking point?"

Camden broke his silence, but he should have kept his mouth shut.

"This changes nothing. Hillary will simply see how many good investments there are in Sequoia, particularly the ones that we have already discussed *at length.*" He gave her a meaningful look. "And the wedding will go forward as planned."

"The fuck it will!" Stan roared, his fist waving in the air at Camden. "What advantage will Logan get now that he's being locked out of the family fortune? What advantages do the Eccles get at all? Years of planning *wasted!*"

"Fuck off," I snarled to Stan and Camden. They were getting on my last nerve, and I needed to get to my car and bury my nose in some sweet powder before I really went postal on their asses.

Everything I had been counting on to pay off my debts to Georgio was now gone. All of my planned investments would need completely different backing. The financial security that would give me an escape route from M was fucked. I was a millionaire in assets only. With my debts and Georgio's hold on me, I wouldn't have any liquid cash to speak of. I needed a new plan, and fast.

Hillary finally spoke up. "Frederick, if I choose not to marry anyone, do I lose the family fortune?"

The weasel of a man had practically sweated through his suit, his greasy brow wrinkling in terror as the whole family around him prepared to go to war.

"I believe so, yes, Ms. Lane. Miss Rose Marie was very specific that you had to be married on or before your twenty-fifth birthday in order to receive the inheritance funds."

"And nothing about an annulment or divorce? If I were to marry Logan and then divorce him shortly thereafter, would I still have access to my inheritance?"

"Yes, I believe so. There is nothing within the documents to suggest that you and your spouse must remain married in order for you to continue to draw from the fund. But I would not advise marrying anyone without the proper—"

"Yes, thank you," Hillary said, "that will be all of your unsolicited advice." She turned to Camden.

"So, Daddy, it looks like I'm in the power seat here. I will be marrying Logan to get *my* money. Then, when I see fit, we'll get a divorce. *I* will decide which companies I invest in, and *I* will put the money toward the causes I support. And, if you're persuasive with your pitch, some of your companies may be included in my portfolio. In exchange, I'll move forward with your ridiculous expectations for this sham of a wedding, and I'll even kiss the governor's baby to sell it. Capisce?"

It was a shame nothing was real between us, because Hillary had never been as hot to me as she was in that moment, all Barbie power moves and bitch backbone. I wondered if I could really turn on the charm and find a lucrative loophole somehow. A baby? Would our kid get half her money, and then I could take it from the kid? Taking candy from a baby, but millions. So many millions.

I was grasping here. Fuck, I needed to turn myself around with a hit. I was getting irritable and twitchy.

"No, not capisce, NOT CAPISCE!"

Stan really was going to die of a stroke in this office today, and I wondered if I was still included in *his* will. I'd have to check that out when I left. If I was, maybe I could off him for the quick cash I needed. The world would be better off, and I would directly benefit. I shook my head. I wasn't a good man, but I wasn't a killer. Too fucking bad.

"Logan won't be marrying *you*," Stan-the-man spat the word viciously, "if he's – *we're* – not going to benefit. This conversation is over. Camden, you and I will be speaking about this in private."

Fuck Stan. Fuck Stan and his audacity at thinking he still had a say in what I did and did not do. Sure, this wedding had been a farce Hillary and I had been pushed into all of our lives, but now, now he was practically forbidding us to get married because he would no longer get his payout? Fuck him. I'd find another way to get the money I needed, even if that took seducing the fuck out of Hillary for real, but the time for his input was over.

"I'm marrying Hillary, Stan, so fuck off."

He whirled on me, eyes bugging out of his head like a fucking grasshopper on meth. He reached for my collar again, but I grabbed his wrists, forcing him down into the chair before he could try anything stupid.

"Your reign is over, King Eccles. I'm still marrying the Queen."

I threw him a vicious smirk and offered my hand to Hillary. She hesitated, then straightened her shoulders and interlaced her fingers in mine. I pulled her toward the doorway, the delicious call of cocaine calling my name as I grappled with my new reality.

"Frederick, make the arrangements to proceed," Hillary called out to Pencil Dick McGee as we left the office, leaving our fathers to stew in their own resentment and disappointment.

She dropped my hand as soon as we were out of sight. "I'm sorry."

She sighed as we headed toward the elevator.

"I had no idea this was even possible. Neither of us wanted this in the first place, and now ... *fuck*." She punched the elevator button like it had personally offended her family and turned to face me, her eyes filled with real regret.

I was surprised to feel a genuine sense of relief we didn't need to pretend any more. We were just two people who had been royally fucked by our parents, and grandparents, apparently.

"We'll figure it out, Hil. You're not going to lose on this anyways." I shrugged my shoulders. "You're still going to be swimming in money."

She gave me a sad smile and shook her head. "There's a little girl inside of me that wanted to marry the love of her life, Logan. Instead, I'll be marrying you to get a trust fund. How superficial can you get?"

We took the elevator in silence, and when she left, she kissed my cheek. I was buzzing for my next hit too much to notice, and made a beeline to the Audi. Nothing mattered until I could get my head on straight.

Then, I could come up with a plan to save my ass.

"I have a proposal for you."

I was sitting in Georgio's office, about to make my pitch. After 72 hours, it was the best I had come up with, but knowing what I knew about Georgio, it was solid.

"Oh?"

I had to be careful with how I presented the offer. Georgio was Camden's business partner in all of his legal enterprises, but I didn't know how much he knew about our 1800s-style forced marriage-for-money arrangement, and I wasn't interested in creating any more rumors, especially rumors that could hurt my businesses. Avoiding rumors is what had gotten me into this fucking mess in the first place.

"There's going to be a delay in getting access to Hillary's inheritance," I began, shrewdly eyeing the man behind his mob-boss desk. "But you know I always pay my debts. Why don't we play a little game?"

Georgio's ice-blue gaze assessed me. Good, he was interested. That was all the leeway I needed.

"I want in on betting on one of your fight nights." I leaned forward in my chair. "I want in on the action, and I want to bet three to one odds on the newer guy – Cam something? If I win, you take the winnings as yours to cover my debts."

He steepled his fingers. Fucking cliché, but it worked for him. This guy didn't get to where he was without clout and intelligence, and I could see him running the numbers in his mind.

"And if you lose, Logan? If you lose, you'll be in even deeper. How do you propose we make it right, then?"

I was prepared for this question, even though I was confident I would not lose. I had been watching Cam for months and my gut was tingling that he was the next investment "sure thing."

"If I lose, I'll sell you my Front Street property at well under market value price, and we can inflate the contract value to shelter some of your... assets."

That was a delicate way to put it, that's for fucking sure. He had been wanting that property since I snapped it up from Camden two years ago, thanks to my cache of secrets. I knew it would be too enticing to pass up. My future was banking on it.

The room was deadly silent for a few moments. I held my breath as Georgio considered the transaction. Finally, he smiled.

"What a great opportunity you've presented me with today, Logan. You've got yourself a deal."

He stood up and shook my hand, pointing at the door behind me.

"I have some business to take care of, so please, make yourself comfortable at the club. I'll have Tom come by with a little something stronger."

Yes, fuck yes. This week was a disaster of epic fucking proportions, and today was coming up aces for Logan Eccles. Thank fuck.

I walked down the stairwell into the club and made a beeline for the bar. I ordered my usual Old Fashioned from Colin and went to sit in one of the center tables to wait for Tom.

As I sipped my drink, I noticed the familiar curves and auburn hair of my favorite sexy temptress carrying a drink tray and tending tables.

"Cheating on Joe, Winter? The man gets attacked and you jump ship to the dark side?" I winked at her suggestively, enjoying how she bristled in my company.

She wasn't playing hard to get; I knew she couldn't stand me, but that made her even more attractive. Delicious forbidden fucking fruit I would love to get a taste of.

"Can you get anymore callous, Logan? How did you get to be such a fucking dick?" She rolled her eyes and continued to place dirty glasses on her tray from the table beside me.

"Lots of practice," I said with mock-sincerity, throwing her another wink. "Are you singing tonight? I'd love to hear more of that voice on stage. It'll give me something to jerk off to later."

"Fuck off," she growled as she did her best to ignore me, pushing past me to head back to the bar. I took in her lavender scent as her thighs brushed my shirtsleeve and my cock stirred to attention in my pants.

"I'd rather fuck you, princess."

That made her stalk off in the other direction, and the satisfaction it gave me to get under her skin like that was as close to being high as sober could get. I got off on her pink cheeks and the fire in her eyes. What I wouldn't give for her to hate-fuck me.

Tom showed up a few minutes later, and I downed the rest of my drink to get back out to my car for a quick buzz. Georgio had agreed to my terms and, despite a shitty few days, my luck was turning around. That was good enough reason to celebrate.

CHAPTER 28

DREW

R*ing – Ring – Ring*

I waited anxiously for Georgio to pick up the line. Janet, his assistant, had given me his direct number to call when I explained to her there had been a change in management at Johnson's while Dad recovered, and we needed to discuss the new "drop-off arrangement."

The acid in my stomach was eating a hole into my esophagus. I had popped half a bottle of Tums today, eating the fizzy tropical-flavored chalk nuggets like candy as I paced the diner's office and psyched myself up for the call. I had never wanted any part in my parents' agreement with

Georgio; I had been willing to walk away from the diner to never have to deal with this in the first place. Now, now I was literally stuck in the quicksand of petty crime and illegal activity. I wasn't going to have a stomach lining left at this rate.

Ring – Ring – Ring

I was about to hang up when a crisp, authoritative voice answered.

"Yes?" Georgio said. Nervous, I cleared my throat. I forced steel into my backbone and sat taller in my chair. I was not going to be Georgio's bitch here. I could be in control.

"Hello, Georgio," I said in what I hoped was the confident voice of a man and not the squeaky voice of a terrified teenager. "This is Drew Johnson."

"I know who you are, Drew. I know this number. What can I do for you today?"

He was amused. That turned my stomach acid into motivating fire. Fuck this man for his control on my family, playing with us like little puppets and fucking with our lives.

My nerves settled and my practiced business voice took over.

"I'm calling to say that since Joe is out of commission, I will be taking over the diner. As I have no other option, the arrangement you made with my father will continue, but I would prefer that Travis Balcom be the only one from your... organization to make any deliveries here. I take the safety of my people very seriously, and after what happened to Dad, I'm not very trusting these days."

I held my breath. It wasn't the most amicable delivery, but it was getting harder to hold back my anger.

"That can be arranged," Georgio said in a clipped tone. "I'm glad you're not reneging on our contract. That would not be a wise business move on your part."

I didn't miss the threat hanging in his words. I was about to say goodbye when he spoke again.

"Drew, I've recently made an arrangement with another party that may be of interest to you. Are you a gambling man?"

"No," I said flatly. I was the exact opposite of a gambler. I was a play-the-safe-route-until-I-die man, but so far that strategy was doing nothing for me or my loved ones.

Georgio laughed lightly and continued. "There will be an event happening at my private club in two weeks from today. A gentlemen's fight. Why don't you place a bet? If you win, I'll remove Johnson's from my collection of business partners. You'll be free and clear to do what you wish without my... interference."

Sweat beaded on my brow. The offer was not what I was expecting, not by a long shot. Georgio was playing me, I was sure of it.

"And if I lose?" I croaked out, tentatively curious what he could possibly do to my family to cause us any more pain or harm. A lot. He could do a lot.

"Nothing at all," the austere man said casually, as if we weren't discussing highly illegal activities. "Business as usual. But business as usual for the rest of the diner's life, Drew. And there will be consequences should anything happen to it any time soon. I hope I'm being clear."

I gulped. He wanted me to take the bet, that much was obvious. If I couldn't get out from under him as it was, what difference did it make? I wasn't going to pretend I even had a choice here, despite his flimsy attempt to make me feel like I did.

"I'll take the bet. But I'd like to be present to witness the 'event' for myself. Please send me the invitation, so I can attend." I mimicked his professional tone, and determination flooded my resolve. I could take some of my power back, however small.

"I'd place your bet on Cameron Chase. He's our best showman these days."

"I'll take your word for it," I muttered, knowing full well he rigged the fights, thanks to Shane's conversation with Travis. Georgio was setting me up to lose. I had no choice but to go along with it. Winter and Shane could help me sort out what to do with that information later.

The evil puppet master laughed again and hung up the phone. Afterward, I sat in silence for a few moments, pondering my life choices. Before going too deeply down the rabbit hole I had become very accustomed to lately, I buried myself in a busy afternoon of inventory and paperwork, tasks I had been putting off since we had reopened a few weeks ago. It felt good to concentrate on something I knew like the back of my hand; something that didn't cause a crisis of moral conscience every time I looked at it.

A soft knock came at the door hours later.

"Hey." Winter peaked her head into the now darkening room and smiled. "How's it going in here?"

A genuine smile crossed my face. Since Shane's 'peacemaking intervention,' as he called it, Winter and I had been rebuilding our friendship. I couldn't deny my attraction to her any longer; our years-long history from going to school together and working at the diner were culminating into something deeper and, despite my previous reservations about being her boss, I didn't want to squash it anymore.

Could I really claim being into her was an HR faux pas when I was willingly laundering thousands of dollars of cash for the local crime ring each month? My report card of ethics was at a solid D-minus right now. I might as well sail through and make it an impressive F.

I wasn't going to be able to stay away from her, even if I locked myself in handcuffs and barred the door. When she got up on stage at Bourbon & Blues, a moment before she saw us had made me fall even harder for her than back in the chip aisle all those years ago.

She was radiant, uninhibited, with a sense of sensual recklessness and danger, but still with the poise of the 1950s icon I had come to compare her to. Her voice had given me shivers, but her stage presence? I wanted more of that version of Winter Wallace in my life. In my life, and in my bedroom.

"I'm about to finish up," I answered, as I stood and stretched my legs. "What's up?"

She settled into the archaic tweed chair across from the desk, her orange polyester diner shirt covered in the evidence of a long, hard day.

"I wanted to give you an update. I just got my schedule from B&B and it looks like I'm working Georgio's next event night. I even had to sign a non-disclosure agreement."

"What? Is that even legal?" I frowned, not liking this development one bit. It was one thing for her to work for Georgio's legal club, another thing entirely for her to serving drinks to the low-level criminals and thugs in the state. And me. I couldn't forget that I would be attending too. I grimaced at the thought.

"Apparently. I mean, it's a legal enterprise, just illegal activities, although no one is saying that. It's labeled on my schedule as 'Gentlemen's Night'." She laughed caustically.

"I know I originally agreed that this was a good idea, but now I'm having second thoughts. This could be really dangerous, Winter."

"Oh, like dangerous as in accepting weekly payments from the local gang to launder for them? That level of dangerous?" She cocked an eyebrow at me pointedly. "Yup, I can see why you'd be worried."

Getting up from her seat, she came around to stand in front of me. "Besides, it's not your decision to make. Quick's right. I'm not willing to stand by while the people I care about get hurt."

Winter leaned into me, and the soft scent of lavender tickled my senses. She looked up at me with her big, beautiful blue eyes. "I care about you, Drew."

My heart shouldn't have stuttered at those simple words, but it did. Fuck me, this woman had me in a vice grip. My Audrey Hepburn.

I brushed a stray lock of hair behind her ear, then cupped her cheek as she peered up at me.

"I care about you too."

I held her by the chin as my lips brushed hers. As soon as our mouths touched, my body flooded with heat. What was intended to be a gentle gesture turned into a passionate clash of teeth and tongues. I had been right to stay away from her for as long as I did; clearly, I couldn't trust my urges when I was alone with her.

I picked her up by her hips and lifted her onto the desk in front of us, parting her legs and stepping in between her thighs, feeling the heat of her core against my swelling cock.

My whole body shuddered with lust. I wanted to strip her bare, right here, right now, and fuck her raw. Damn the consequences. I had fantasized about this moment too many times since I had tasted her like this last. I groaned into her mouth at the memory.

My body pressed into her harder, hard enough to feel her nipples pebble underneath her shirt and scrape across the fabric covering my chest. My hands squeezed her thighs and traced a line up to her waist, roaming to cup the soft lace covering her breasts. I was inching my fingers underneath the fabric when she broke away from me, her cheeks pink and lips swollen from the intensity of our kiss.

My cock twitched in my jeans, hard as a rock at the sight of her. I loved the effect I had on her body. I wanted to put my mark on her again and feel her warmth around me as I made her come so hard she wouldn't be able to breathe. I desperately hoped the storage room was available.

My excitement dimmed when I saw the hesitation in her eyes.

"I – I have to tell you something."

She bit her lip, indecision written all over her face.

"I really like you, Drew. I want to see where this could go between us and I really want to keep kissing you, but I – I would be stupid if I didn't admit that I still have feelings for Travis. I don't know if they're salvageable, I don't know where they'll go, but they're real, and I don't want to hurt you while I try to figure them out." She looked down at her hands and sighed. "I don't want to let you go, either. It's incredibly selfish of me, I know."

She pulled away from me, putting distance between us. Her eyes were apologetic and she looked like she was preparing herself for a slap in the face.

I cursed internally; if I hadn't pushed her away, she may have never met Travis and this conversation wouldn't be necessary. I wished she had met anyone else; anyone but one of Georgio's lackeys, particularly the lackey who had been the harbinger of doom to the Johnson family.

If it were anyone but Travis, would I be okay with sharing her if it meant she would be in my life?

"Winter," I began hesitantly. How did I word this without coming off as a dick?

I sighed heavily.

"Winter, I'm not going to pretend that I like the guy. I don't. I don't trust him and I really don't like how involved he is with Georgio, even if we are trying to use it to our advantage."

She nodded and swallowed hard. "Okay, I respect your —"

"You didn't let me finish." I grabbed her hands in mine and searching her face for the truth. "Do your feelings for Travis affect the way you feel about me? Am I going to be left in the dust if Travis decides he can't share?" I paused, realizing I had to admit this to myself as much as to her.

"I can't – I can't have my heart broken, okay?"

She craned her neck and kissed me softly, smiling into the kiss.

"I can guarantee you my feelings for Travis do not affect my feelings for you. They are mutually exclusive. And if"– she pulled back from me, looking seriously into my eyes–"I get to this point with Travis again, we will be having the same conversation about you."

The ache in my heart subsided at her sincerity. Travis couldn't be trusted, but I knew Winter and I trusted her. I trusted her with my heart.

I lifted her into my arms and kissed her fiercely, trying to convey everything I was feeling; my relief to be able to have her, my determination to keep her, and the demanding, raw need to taste her. She kissed me hungrily, sucking on my tongue and nipping my bottom lip with her teeth, spurring me on. I was about to spread her wide open on the desk and devour her whole when a knock at the door interrupted my stupor.

I reluctantly pulled away from her lips, leaving a soft trail of kisses down the sensitive flesh of her neck. "Yeah?" I called out in between sucking a moan out of her wicked little mouth.

The door swung open and I froze, turning toward it with equal parts embarrassment and lust-fueled 'I-don't-give-a-fuck.'

Shane took one look at our compromising position and broke out into a lazy grin. Was that – heat – I saw behind his eyes? He slowly walked into the room, his gaze traveling up and down our entwined bodies.

"I've been waiting for this for *ages!*"

He pounced on the two of us like a koala bear, wrapping his arms around us in an awkward hug.

"Who kissed who first? Inquiring minds want to know." He winked at Winter teasingly, and let us go, stepping back to plop into the chair Winter had been sitting in minutes earlier.

"I saw Winter's text about her schedule and thought I'd pop in after my lessons today. What's the scoop?"

Winter pulled away from me and perched herself on the corner of the desk, facing Shane. My body mourned the loss of her soft skin and consuming heat. I wasn't waiting nearly so long to kiss her again.

"I had to sign an NDA to work the next 'Gentlemen's Event' in two weeks, which I'm pretty sure is the legal euphemism for a fight night," Winter said slowly, leaning back as she turned to look at me. "It's not my first choice, but I can bet that Travis will be working it too. We can keep our eyes and ears open together."

"I actually spoke to Georgio this morning." I rubbed the back of my neck in concern. "He practically pushed me into betting on Cam as an attempt to gamble my way out of our 'situation'." I used the air quotes sarcastically. "I'm going to be there too. So you'll have backup at least."

"What? Explain that, please." Shane looked confused, so I outlined the entire conversation.

"So, the theory is that he's banking on you to lose, just to humiliate you and force you to stay in the situation you've already agreed to?" Shane summed up succinctly.

I nodded.

"What a bastard. A manipulative, crafty, bastard. Snow, what if we talked to Travis? Maybe he could talk to Cam and confirm? I don't like the idea of you guys going into this not knowing the rules of the game."

She nodded slowly. Obviously, she didn't want to be the one to have the conversation, but I didn't push it and neither did Shane. They could bicker about who was approaching that subject later, because it definitely wasn't going to be me.

I started to pack up my bag for the night and Winter went to grab her coat from the staff room. Janice was closing and we were done for the day. The three of us walked down the long hallway together and out into the familiar dining room.

It was the end of supper rush on a Saturday. The weather had been shitty the past three days and skiers hadn't been able to get out onto the hill, so the diner had been quieter than usual.

Sheriff Sutton waved me over to his booth, and I nodded to Winter and Shane to go on ahead of me.

"Hi, Drew, how's the family these days?"

I winced at the question, well used to it by now but it still brought up the bitter memories of Dad's attack every time it came into conversation.

"Doing better, thanks for asking. I've been meaning to come into the station, actually. I wanted to file an inquiry about the length of time it took the police to show up the night Dad was attacked."

Ralph froze, the plastic smile on his face waxing cold. "I don't think you want to do that, son. No sense in questioning the intentions of good, hard-working people, is there?"

My smile and my spine became rigid. "I think, as a citizen of this town, its important that we make sure our first responders can protect us in the appropriate amount of time, don't you?"

"Of course," Ralph said smoothly, his well-practiced politician-like cadence taking affect. "I just wouldn't want you getting caught up in the powers of this town, Drew. I think it best you stick to what you know, and leave us to stick to what we know, hmmm? It'll be less messy that way."

I blinked, taken aback by his thinly disguised attempt to threaten me. This town was buried under layers of corruption so deep, it would take an avalanche to slough the shit off and start fresh.

I nodded without speaking; my fury and disgust were only going to get me in more trouble at this point. I walked out of the building that had long been my prison and my home, turning around to inspect for cracks in the paint and chips in the bricks.

When this was all over, I was leaving this town. When Joe woke up and took over his business, when my friends were graduated and heading off to their futures, when I could breathe without worrying if Georgio was going to suffocate me, I was leaving it all behind too.

I would never look back.

CHAPTER 29

CAMERON

"We need to talk."

Georgio's crisp voice filled the empty liquor cellar well below Bourbon & Blues. I was storing kegs alone in the sub-basement of the building, a task he got the bouncers to do instead of the shipping company. I was positive they held drugs and all kinds of other illegal things, but I wasn't brave enough to peek into them to check. That was a surefire quick trip to a shallow grave.

I adopted the casual tone I always took with Georgio, layered with Southern sweetness. It was the tactic I had used for years to appear less physically threatening as a large biracial man living in the South.

"Sure boss, what can I do for you?" I stood up from the keg I had wheeled into the far corner of the concrete room and wiped my fingers on a dirty rag from my pocket.

He stood in the doorway, his tall, lean frame appearing more sinister by being backlit. He was wearing his typical cream-colored suit – so impractical for anyone living in a northern climate, but it went with his vibe, I guessed. Georgio also played the appearance game, downplaying his power through classy outfits and charm. I was no better than anyone around here; I got sucked in too, and I'd pay for it for the rest of my life.

"Saturday's fight," he said, coming into the room and placing his hands in his pockets. "You're not going to be able to make it through the third round."

That was all he said. My stomach dropped, but I had been waiting for this moment. I had been allowed to win the last four fights in a row, and my reign of glory was coming to an end. I wondered how much money he had riding on my win after that kind of track record. Hundreds of thousands if my last win was any indication. I hadn't seen any of the cash, but Travis had heard some mutterings from a few of the guys who worked the numbers.

In fairness, I could have won all of those fights without them being rigged. Drake's guys were decent fighters, but they couldn't compare to the working body of a Southern boy and the pure rage I harbored within.

I rubbed the back of my neck; the beads of hot sweat had now turned cold. "Understood. Any particular way I am to go down?"

He smiled his real, dark, and dangerous smile, not the pretty teeth-showing simper he used when up above. "Be creative."

I nodded again and waited for him to leave the room before turning back to the task at hand. I needed to get these barrels in place and the fuck out of the basement before the contraband they were carrying tainted me too – more than I already was.

I came back upstairs a few hours later, more than forty barrels delivered and put away today. It was a huge shipment, even by Georgio's standards, and I didn't want to think about all of the people who would be hurt from his business revenue streams. The thought put a sour taste in my mouth.

I had another twenty minutes before my bouncing shift was to start, so I headed to the bar to get some water from Travis.

A new band I had never heard of were practicing before their set started in an hour, playing acoustic covers to popular rock songs. They were pretty good, and the music helped clear away the cobwebs of my thoughts as I got into the headspace to be high security at the classiest bar in the county. I could compartmentalize like the best of them, a trait from my momma.

Travis was cleaning glasses and arranging the wide array of liquor bottles on the mirrored shelving behind the counter.

"Hey, man, can I get a water?"

"Sure thing." Travis handed me a cold bottle and went back to the Amaretto bottle he had been filling.

"Listen," he said, his body language casual, but his voice tight and wary. "I need to talk to you about next week's fight. Georgio made a deal with Winter's friend, Drew, and he's made him bet on you to win. I'm guessing that means he asked you to throw the fight, right?"

I froze, not wanting to have this conversation here, but knowing Travis wouldn't bring it up without a good reason. I gave a shallow nod and cracked the cap off the water bottle. Travis had told me he was helping Shane and Winter get some information on Georgio, and I had heavily advised against it. I didn't want anything to do with an uprising against the devil.

"Is there anything you can do?" Travis pleaded with me softly, keeping his shoulders relaxed and his gaze trained on the liquor, as if we weren't discussing anarchy in the owner's own club.

"His dad is already on death's door, and the whole situation is just completely fucked. If you could —"

"You know you can't ask me that." I pushed away from the bar, trying not to let my irritation show. My best friend was in the exact same position as me, but unlike me, he had people he cared about that he was trying to protect. I respected that, but he knew better than anyone that I didn't have a way out, and I resented the fact that he was asking me anyway.

I spun around, walking away from the bar to tamp down my emotions before they got the better of me. A small body hit my front hard. She let out a high-pitched squeak and a deadened thump sounded from the floor when I finally registered what had happened. I had just walked into someone.

All anger washed away from me like a cleansing tide and I bent down, offering a hand out to the pretty dark-haired beauty sitting in a puddle of spilled drinks. I knew she had started working here as a server recently, thanks to Travis, but I hadn't worked a shift with her yet.

Winter was a sight for sore eyes, her black tight-fitting t-shirt, black skirt, and lace tights highlighting all of her beautiful curves, and the pink lipstick she wore matched the tinge in her cheeks. She was the image of a true Southern belle if I ever saw one.

"Hey, sorry there, sugar. I didn't see you there," I said soothingly, pulling her up and rubbing my hands down her arms to check for injuries. "Are you alright?"

An embarrassed smile traced her lips as she brushed off her apron. "I'm okay, thank you. I should have seen you — you're hard to miss."

I grinned, liking the fact that she had noticed me, far more than I should. The memory of her lips brushing my jaw lit up my mind; I tried my best to ignore it.

Travis appeared beside me with a bar towel and a mop to wipe up the spill. I grabbed the towel from him and gently wiped the cherry syrup that spattered the front of her chest. Droplets clung to her skin along the line of collarbone down to just shy of her breasts beneath the fabric of her shirt.

She shivered beneath my touch and I stopped immediately, my cock stirring with interest in my jeans. I should not be affected this way by this woman. Nothing good could come of it.

Travis eyed me quizzically. I shook my head dismissively and handed back the towel before stepping back from the two of them. "I'd better get going. Let me know if anything starts to hurt, okay, sugar? I've got some wraps and Tylenol in my kit bag if you need anything."

I turned on my heel and headed toward the locker room to change into my uniform for the night shift ahead. I could only hope I wouldn't have any more chance encounters this evening.

"Cameron Chase?"

I was getting out of my car in the small parking lot behind the laundromat. The only reserved space was for me, but that didn't stop some asshole college kid from taking it to lug in their laundry at all hours of the day. I was grateful that no one had taken it on me. I was in no mood to trek the half block back to my apartment by parking on the side street nearby.

The voice wasn't familiar and I turned to see a tall, dark-haired man, probably close to my age, dressed in a dark wool dress coat and slacks. He reeked of money and entitlement and I had no idea what he would want with me next to my poorer-than-poor man living situation.

"Yeah?" I finally answered back, wanting my curiosity satisfied but equally wanting to get in from the weather. It wouldn't be the first time I questioned my sanity moving to a place this cold.

"My name is Logan Eccles," the man said plainly, sticking out a leather-gloved hand for a shake. I took it dubiously. Who was this guy and what did he want?

"I have a proposition for you," he continued, eyeing my apartment warily. "Can I come inside?"

"Uh, yeah, I guess." I was taken aback by his brashness. Money could do that to a person; make them think that they deserved the world and owned everyone in it.

I scrutinized his size and determined that I could easily take him if anything were to go down, as long as he didn't carry a gun, and he really didn't look the type. He probably had people to shoot his enemies anyways – wouldn't dirty his hands doing the real work.

I unlocked the door that really didn't need a key to get in, and trudged up the stairs to my humid dungeon, tossing the keys on the small table by the door as I entered. Logan, whoever he was, followed behind me.

I turned to face him, crossing my arms and assessing him. "What do you want?"

"No pleasantries, I like that." He grinned at me, and I realized in that moment who he looked like — that guy on the TV show, Lucifer. He could easily be a Lucifer now that I had a chance to give him a solid once-over. Smooth mannerisms and a charm like Georgio's, but with evil in his eyes. Great. I didn't need any more Georgios in my life.

"I'm betting on you at this week's fight. I wanted to incentivize you a little to make sure you win."

Who was this simpering man from the Billionaire Boys Club? 'Incentivize' me? I cocked an eyebrow and stood wide and tall, adopting the power pose that made lesser men cower. "Oh yeah? And how do you propose you do that?"

He pulled out an envelope from his breast pocket and threw it on the table beside my keys. "That's $12,500. Let's call it a down payment. I'll pay you the other half when you win." He smirked, like $25,000 was enough to own me. The familiar heat of anger simmered within my belly.

"So, you want to buy me, is that it? Pay the poor fighter a little bit of money, so he can make you even richer? Fuck you, and fuck your little game."

I closed the distance between us and grabbed the soft flesh above his elbow, pushing down on the pressure point, hard. "Get the fuck out of my apartment before I put you out myself." I growled.

The man didn't cower like I expected. "$25,000 is a lot of money for anyone, Cameron. Consider it. I'll let you keep that half while you do."

He pulled out of my grip with practiced ease. I had underestimated him. He straightened the collar of his jacket and gave me another calculating grin. "I'll see you Saturday."

When he was gone, I looked at the envelope, sitting innocently on the table, even though it was anything but. I didn't want to touch it, but I'd be outright lying to myself and Jesus if I said I couldn't use it.

Travis had asked me to win the fight. Logan offered to pay me to win the fight. Georgio had made it clear I was going to lose the fight. Without an exit plan, I couldn't go against his demands. I didn't have the answers I had come here for, and I wasn't willing to risk it all to walk away now, even if that was an option.

I sunk into my lump of a couch and turned on the television, hoping a poorly-written sitcom could distract me from my shitty situation. I fell asleep to the laugh track, imagining it was the gods in the clouds making a mockery of my life. Probably was.

CHAPTER 30

WINTER

It was oddly hot down here; the sticky kind of heat that lingers in the air when too many bodies are in too small a space. All this, despite the fact this part of Georgio's club was well air conditioned and three stories below ground.

That was probably an odd thing to be noticing as I made my way through the burgeoning crowd, casually working my first illegal event. Okay, 'casually' was a stretch. I was sweating bullets underneath my black dress shirt and tan pants and drops of sweat clung to the back of my neck, irritating the skin beneath my starched collar. Perhaps it wasn't so hot down here after all; I was just on the borderline of an anxiety attack and about to pass out in the imagined Florida-like climate. Perfect.

The ballroom down here was oddly tasteful for such an occasion. High cocktail tables covered in black linens dotted the perimeter of the room, with misty globe lights set in the center of each table. The lighting was purposefully dim on the outskirts, casting a seductive ambiance, despite the frenzied energy in the room.

The middle of the ballroom featured a large square boxing ring – *why was it called a ring, anyway?* – similar to the wrestling rings Quick and I grew up seeing on cable TV. Four spotlights hung from a large catwalk overhead, one for each corner, and the effect was so bright it was almost blinding. Absolutely no one, no matter if you were in the farthest corner of the football field-sized room could possibly miss who was punching who at any given moment.

Servers like me were everywhere. I had counted seven in total when I had last gone up to the bar to fill my drink orders.

Travis was working tonight and a new guy I had never seen before. Brad? Brett? I had already forgotten. I had figured there would be many new faces down here this evening, both staff and guests, and I hadn't been wrong. I only recognized Travis and Maria as regular Bourbon & Blues staff. The rest I had never seen before in my life, at the club or in town. I wondered if they were part of Georgio's other operations, but then shook my head. Of course, they were. Isn't that why Travis was here too?

Speaking of, the beautiful man was working the bar with ease like he hadn't a care in the world, and I both loathed and envied him for it. He was as handsome as ever; his wry smile and back-lit kiwi-green eyes took in every customer who approached his counter like they were the only person in the world. It was his gift, but it made him even harder to read when I was still trying to decide whether or not I could trust him again. The more I was near him, the more I wanted to. He called me his kryptonite, but I'd be a liar if I said he didn't have the same effect on me. I just couldn't figure out if it was the green kind or the red kind. A bit of each, likely.

I scanned the crowd while I submitted the drink order into the electronic system for Travis to fill. I could see Drew hanging back in the far corner at a cocktail table. With an untouched beer in his hand, he looked incredibly uncomfortable. He and Travis were opposites that way; Travis could fit in anywhere, and Drew – Drew was not making any attempts at trying to fit into this crowd.

Quick, of course, couldn't be here. It was an invite-only fight. Unless you had certain connections with Georgio, for obvious reasons. So unless he convincingly played Drew's wealthy queer partner, he was staying home.

Quick had also pointed out during the planning stages that Georgio did know who he was, even if he didn't know much about him. He had been present at a few above-board construction engineering collaboration meetings with WAQ, so sneaking in, as if that was even a safe and feasible option, wasn't happening.

I could see some pretty high-profile guests here as well. Our state governor, Sheila Phillips, was here – the sassy thing must have had a thirst for blood, or maybe just the money that could come along with it. I saw Sheriff Sutton too, but I averted my eyes and walked quickly away before he could see me. It was a very weird experience, because chances were I was going to see many people I knew tonight, and they would see me, but we'd never be able to talk about it in public or in person without the risk of serious consequences. It was the very literal reenactment of Fight Club.

Logan, of all people, was also here. He had been lingering in the shadows, talking to a younger guy who had his back turned to me for most of the evening. His silhouette looked familiar, but I just couldn't place it. Whoever it was, they were in heavy conversation.

I should have known Logan would be here in some capacity. The man's ego and appetite for risk were just too great. As long as he left me alone, I'd be okay. Well, as okay as I could be in this situation.

The atmosphere was heavy and frenetic, like a rock concert. Everyone around me was high on something; the drugs, the drink, the element of risk and danger. Whatever their vice was, you could almost taste it in the air. I didn't like its cloying flavor on my tongue.

I grabbed the drink tray Travis had filled for me and gave him an appreciative smile. Now closer to him, I could see the shadows of dark circles under his eyes, and the crease of frown line wrinkles around his mouth. He wasn't as put together as I had anticipated, which gave me an odd sense of relief. I didn't want this to be a normal Saturday for him; I wanted our Saturday nights to include popcorn and Netflix and naked snuggling. I blinked and shook my head. Where had that thought come from?

He gave me a wary smile back, gaze briefly searching mine. He must have been satisfied by what he saw, because he dipped his head in a nod and then winked, all trace of his previous concern gone. His charm dialed up to 100 as he took the order of a pretty older woman in a red velvet cocktail dress next to me. She giggled under his attention. I couldn't fault her, as much as I wanted to roll my eyes. I knew what having his full attention felt like, and I had giggled like that too.

Every so often, the hairs on the back of my neck stood to attention, despite the lingering slick of sweat, and my hind brain could feel the undeniable prickle of someone's gaze. I had tried to look around amid the many bodies surrounding me in the crowd, but I couldn't find anybody paying any particular mind to me, so I shook off the feeling. All of my senses were on overdrive; I was grateful I could be a server on autopilot, regardless of where it was. That skill set was serving me tonight.

The microphone in the center of the ring boomed. All at once the deafening chatter in the room came to a halt. This was the moment everyone had been waiting for; pleasantries were over and the true party could begin.

"Ladies and gentlemen," Georgio began, his tailored cream suit and black dress shirt making him look like a Caribbean mafia don. "Welcome to tonight's event. I am thrilled to have you all here in my little club to enjoy the night's festivities. I will not waste anyone's time with introductions. We all know why we are here and who we came to see. Please welcome your tributes this evening; Cameron Chase and Maven Thatcher!"

I had been expecting a cheesy introduction with a short greasy man in a mustache in a purple ill-fitting suit announcing the fighters with the annoying bravado of a sports announcer, but I should have known Georgio would be much classier than that. Don't ask me where that imagery came from; watching too many wrestling matches, maybe.

I paused my drink serving to watch the fighters come through a side door and walk the red carpet onto the boxing mats. Cam wore a loose pair of white shorts, tied tightly around his trim waist, and a familiar warmth stirred low in my belly. This man was fucking gorgeous.

I hadn't seen much of him during our time in the water at Haven's Head, although I had seen glimpses of his body under the water's ripples and through the mist. But nothing like this.

Not only did he had the face of a forbidden angel with his piercing blue eyes, pouty lips and high cheekbones, no; his sculpted arms, molded and rounded shoulders, toned biceps and corded forearms could pick me up any day of the week. His cut abs and defined Adonis belt peeking from under his waistband, the bubble butt shadow beneath his shorts, and the definition in his calves and hamstrings all showed the audience just exactly how strong Cameron Chase was.

I had to keep my mouth shut out of fear of drooling all over my tray. I didn't even look at the other guy, a dark-haired muscle-head in blue shorts. No, Cam required all of my attention in that moment. Fucking *hot.*

"May I have my drink, miss?" An amused voice to my right asked, and I blinked rapidly, shaking my head out of my trance.

"Yes! Sorry." My cheeks flushed as I went back to work, delivering drinks and taking new orders as the fighters got into position.

I made my way over to Drew even though he wasn't in my section. I took a look at the lukewarm beer with two sips taken from it and raised my eyebrows.

"Hey, are you doing okay?" I gently brushed my fingers over his shoulder and squeezed. "We're all playing the game here tonight, Hardy Boy. We'll make it out of here okay."

His hazel eyes flashed at the nickname, and I smiled. He was my Hardy Boy; dependable, strong, protective, insightful. I didn't like the idea of him being here and also in harm's way, but I took comfort that we were here together. Drew made me feel safe and secure most of all.

He fiddled with the label on the bottle and nodded toward the fight ring. "I just wish I could predict the outcome. I know what he's supposed to do. I just can't help but hope he'll change his mind."

I nodded in understanding. Neither of us knew what Georgio had on Cam, but we could guess it was something big for him to be in this situation. Hell, I hardly knew anything about the man at all, other than his favorite treats and books and movies. A small voice in the depths of my heart spoke up. *But you want to.*

"I'll hold onto hope with you." I squeezed his shoulder again and headed back to the bar.

If I thought the room was loud before, it was a cacophony of noise now. Shouts and screams and bells all filled my ears. It was pure civilized chaos, which didn't look so different from anarchy to the untrained eye.

I looked behind me just once and saw Drew had moved from his solitary table at the back, making his way through the crowd toward me. Good. Maybe he could stay at the bar with Travis and just be close to me while the rest of the night played out.

I turned around and assessed the horde of people; I was strategizing a way forward without getting elbowed in the head by a feisty viewer when my heart stuttered in my chest.

There, sitting at one of the tables toward the front of the crowd with a stunning blonde woman, a woman who was not my mother, was Darren Wallace.

He hadn't seen me. At least I don't think he had. I ducked my head and speedwalked back to Travis and the relative safety of the bar. My stomach curdled and my mind raced with all the reasons my father could be here in this crowd. Not one of them was good or legal.

The noise, and the heavy air, and the sickening realization my father wasn't at all the man I had thought, and the true context of where I was and all of the reasons of why I was here in the first place came crashing down on my head. I could feel the first tugs of a true panic attack pulling at my periphery – a feeling I hadn't had in years.

I stumbled to the bar, my skin crawling with heat. The noises of the crowd had dimmed into a familiar underwater gurgle when my body snapped to attention.

The ear-piercing crack of firecrackers took over my senses; the booms of soul-splitting sounds surrounded me and a thick fog filled the large room – was that smoke?

A hand slid into mine as I grappled with this sudden shift in atmosphere. Panicked screams replaced the excited shouts from moments before, and another wave of cracks filled my ears.

No, it wasn't firecrackers. It was gunshots. The room was filling with smoke and gunshots.

All hell broke loose.

CHAPTER 31

TRAVIS

"I'd love another cocktail, handsome."

The overly-made up woman in her mid-forties had stationed herself at the bar at the beginning of the night and hadn't left me alone for more than a few minutes. Her focused and unwanted attention was exhausting.

"Coming right up, Darla."

I flashed her my warmest smile and busied myself at the counter with her Cosmopolitan and the many drink orders that kept coming in. I had never worked a night this busy and the crowd was the largest I had ever seen. There was an eclectic mix of black tie and ballgowns, worn jeans with cowboy boots, and everything in between.

I had taken my directive from Georgio very seriously. Along with slinging watered-down drinks and avoiding sexual assault from the many alcohol- and perfume-soaked women who tried to touch me, I constantly searched the eyes of our patrons, to see if anyone was out of place or being shifty. Almost impossible really. This was a highly illegal event in a secret room deep underground; *everyone* was technically out of place and being shifty.

The only shifty person I had recognized completely was that Carson guy Winter and I had encountered at the grocery store; the man had made Winter turn to ice and send me home. He chatted with Logan most of the night and I was keeping a close eye on him, for Winter's sake. I hoped she hadn't seen him. All of our nerves were fried, and I didn't want the added stress of that asshole on her plate too.

I looked up from my task and smiled to see Winter making her way back through the crowd toward me. Her hair had come out of her bun, framing her face in a very sensual way, like she had just been roughly fucked in the bathroom. My memories of that one time we shared in the staff washroom upstairs ... I swallowed hard. I couldn't allow myself that distraction tonight.

As much as I didn't want her here, I was grateful we were working together so I could keep an eye on her. She was moving gracefully through the throngs of people, scanning the room with her eyes when I noticed her freeze in time.

Something was wrong; she was swaying as she stumbled back toward me, her face whiter than a sheet. I dropped the lemon I was zesting and ran around the bar top to grab for her when the ear-splitting sound of a gunshot echoed through the room.

Fuck.

Panic seized in my chest as the worst-case-scenario of the evening played out. Despite all of Georgio's security checks at the door and the private invite-only to the fight itself, someone had smuggled in a weapon. Or had one of Georgio's men had made the shot?

Another crack echoed through the room, followed by another, and a thick smoke rose from the ground in multiple places across the large space. This wasn't a random guy; this was a coordinated attack.

Winter was right in front of me now, panic and confusion all over her face. I grabbed her hand and tugged her to my chest.

Screams and shouts filled the chamber, and the hiss of the smoke grenades and the occasional shot made it impossible to think straight.

"Come on!" I shouted to her, barely hearing myself over the crowd. "We need to get out of here."

She snapped out of her vacated state and looked around frantically. "We need to get Drew!"

Fuck. This might have been a literal life-or-death situation, and I was leaning toward the latter at this rate. We could barely see anything in the haze of the room and it was getting harder to breath as the smoke got closer.

"We have to *go*, Winter. Now!"

I spun her around in the opposite direction and pulled her hard through the crowd. I felt a hand grab my bicep. I moved wrench it away from me and made out a face through the smoke.

"Can you get us out of here?" Drew asked, sounding surprisingly calm in this fuckery of a situation.

"Yes. Somewhere safe, at least. But we need to move *now*."

Drew grabbed Winter's other hand and we pushed through the writhing mass of people. I was grateful for his solid strength keeping us afloat as we were bobbed through the throng like an ocean buoy; if any one of us fell to the ground, we'd be trampled.

I wasn't able to make out much in front of me, but I had prepared myself for this moment. I had learned every inch of the sub-basement the first time I had gotten access to it. I hadn't trusted Georgio's literal underground operation was as safe as other employees had claimed, and in my travels, I had found a hidden cellar behind a storage room. No doubt it was used for drug running, but last I checked it had been empty, and it was the only place I could think of that could keep us protected.

There was no way we'd make it to the two stairwells and out of the building with this amount of people competing with us for a spot. Luckily, the storage room was the opposite direction to the stairs, so the number of bodies we had to push through got less and less as we pushed forward.

I heard another shot, followed quickly by a woman's scream; I hoped to God no one died here tonight, but I was going to make sure it wouldn't be us.

"Travis!" Cam's familiar deep voice bellowed behind me, and I briefly paused to turn my head in his direction. He closed the distance quickly and nodded. "Tell me what to do."

We had discussed what to do if something went to shit at one of these events. I had told him loosely where the room was, since I hadn't been able to show him outright. I was relieved he had made it over here himself, and was ashamed to admit that in the chaos and trying to get Winter to safety, I had forgotten about my best friend.

"Let's get to the room and figure out a plan after."

I turned on my heel. With Drew and Winter still attached to me, Cam at my back, I led them down a long corridor filled with smoke.

"Cover your face!" I yelled. Untucking my shirt, I brought it up to cover my nose and mouth. I touched the wall and used it as a guide, walking as quickly as I could without stumbling. We came across a body or two but the hallway was mostly deserted.

The cold room was to our right, and I ducked into it, letting go of Winter's hand, and made a beeline to the back wall where the entrance to the secret space was hidden behind a metal storage shelf. It had been empty when I first found the room, but it was now full of heavy metal cans and boxes.

I nodded to Cam and Drew. "Help me move this."

Without needing anymore instruction, they jumped into action and the three of us pushed the shelf along the wall just enough to get the door open. We wouldn't be able to move the shelf back in place to completely hide our location, but there was nowhere else to go. We'd have to hope this would be enough, for now.

I opened the old wooden slab door built into the earth and peered inside. The room was dark, but it had ventilation, so we could breathe through our terror, at least. A muffled crack from somewhere beyond the walls broke our tense silence and I sprang back into action.

"Get inside!" Drew and Winter scurried into the space and Cam followed close behind.

"I'm coming too." Logan Eccles appeared like a demon in the doorway of the cold room, looking worse for wear in a ripped suit jacket, a long trail of blood trickling from his temple.

Fuck. I wasn't going to leave him out here to die, or worse, to leave him to go tell someone where we were, and then we would all die.

"Get in." I motioned to the doorway and he pushed passed me into the small space. I quickly followed behind him and sealed the door shut.

"Is everyone okay?" I asked in the dim room, barely seeing their shadows as the earthen walls absorbed all of the light. None of us had our phones to even turn on the flashlight feature. Guests weren't allowed to bring them in, and staff had to store theirs in the lockers up above in Bourbon & Blues.

No, we weren't okay. We were the farthest thing from okay. We were trapped three stories below ground in an illegal underground bunker that was either raided by the feds or attacked for another reason entirely, possibly gang related.

Whoever it was on the other side of that door, they had guns, a lot of them, and they weren't afraid to use them.

We had no food, no water, to way to contact the outside, and no clue when we would be safe. We didn't know if help would even be coming. Even if it did, we would probably be arrested and jailed.

The boxer, the bartender, the diner boss, the businessman, and my beautiful girl, trapped within a cellar under our own cascade of lies.

We were fucked.

Excited to find out what happens next
in the Cascade of Lies saga?

Nights of Winter, Cascade of Lies Book 2
will be available on February 29th!

About the author

One day, Cora Flynn decided to sit down and write a book – for funzies.

What started as a fun project on maternity leave became an entirely new adventure between the pages of her created worlds; complete with characters who've become her best friends, an abundance of book boyfriends, beautiful bromances, and story plots that keep her up at night.

When she's not writing, Cora attempts to manage the chaos of a two-toddler household with her extremely patient husband, while maintaining a job in the 'real world.' She loves reading as many books as she can fit on her Kindle, her bookshelves, and her nightstand, and doesn't discriminate against any genre, although reverse harem will always be her favorite.

Come on and join the fun on Instagram and TikTok by following @coraflynnauthor.

9 781999 038823